Death's Head

A Novel By

Eric B. Olsen

authorHOUSE®

AuthorHouse™
1663 Liberty Drive
Bloomington, IN 47403
www.authorhouse.com
Phone: 1 (800) 839-8640

Published by AuthorHouse   08/16/2017

ISBN: 978-1-5246-7108-2 (sc)
ISBN: 978-1-5246-7107-5 (e)

for Megan

Introduction

I'll never forget something that I heard one night in Seattle. It was in the summer of 1989 and I was attending a backyard barbeque at the home of the bass player from the band I was playing in. We were out on his back deck with our former drummer, Patrick, my best friend and a would-be author like myself. I had been writing for a few years and completed a few short stories, but the goal for both of us was to become published authors, preferably novelists. Talk soon turned to writing, as it usually did when the two of us were together, and he said something that I've always remembered. "The only difference between us and them," he said, referring to published novelists, "is that they've written one." It was one of the most inspiring things I can remember hearing at the time. If only it had been that simple.

By then I had already been working for a few months at my dream job, as a clerk at the University Bookstore, and had been reading voraciously as part of my self-study as a writer. Recently I had re-read *Coma* by Robin Cook, one of the first true medical-thrillers ever published, as well as some of the author's later works. But in my capacity as a book clerk I was also exposed to many other novels I never would have read had

I simply been a regular member of the book-reading public. I remember specifically being drawn to a new mystery novel written by former Los Angeles medical examiner Thomas Noguchi, *Unnatural Causes* from 1988, and later the sequel, *Physical Evidence* from 1990. Another mystery novel about a medical examiner that came out during the time I was writing this book was *Postmortem* by Patricia Cornwell, which was published in 1990. Though I was certainly influenced by all of these authors, I can't remember now exactly what it was that motivated me to write my own medical thriller, especially since my primary genre of writing at the time was in the horror field. But I'm pretty sure that the idea for the novel came first and the research into neurosurgery came later.

I read every book I could find on neuroscience for general audiences, and there were precious few at the time. The only one that comes to mind now is *Matters Gray and White*, by Russell Martin, which had been published in 1987. In terms of fiction and narrative, there were a lot of other influences that I'm sure had gone into the idea for the book. In addition to the novels of Thomas Noguchi and Robin Cook, I had also done extensive study into Nazi Germany and The Holocaust while an undergraduate at the University of Washington as part of earning my bachelors degree in history. There were also several films that were highly inspirational for me, among them *Marathon Man* and *The Boys from Brazil*, both of which dealt with Nazi doctors after the fall of the Third Reich. I probably had designs on making my own contribution to stories of that kind, with the goal of having my novel mentioned in the same breath as those two films. The one novel I can remember that was certainly influential in writing the second half of my story was *Pursuit* by Robert L. Fish, which was published in 1979 and that I had first read in the mid-eighties. It not only dealt with plastic surgery by a Nazi doctor, but also with ex-Nazis in South America. All of these things had an impact on the kind of story I wanted to tell, but initially the task seemed so monumental that it took a while for me to get up the courage to take it on.

I do remember distinctly how that happened, though. It began one Friday near the close of my shift at the bookstore. I had been reading and writing for several years and burning to do something significant, like writing a novel. All day I tried to imagine what that would entail, how long it would take to write an entire novel. Since I regularly read such works in a day or two, I reasoned that if I were able to write as fast as I read, that I should be able to write one in the same amount of time. So I simply decided I would do it. I would write an entire novel in one weekend. Of course, the thought is laughable now, but it was exactly the kind of motivation I needed, and the very next morning I set out to do just that. On October 21, 1989 I sat down at the desk in my studio apartment and I wrote the first pages of what would eventually become my first novel, *Death's Head*.

Somewhere in the middle of the process of writing the novel I met a woman named Megan who had the same affinity for fiction that I did—though far more literary than my genre preferences—and also happened to be an excellent copy editor, though without a dime to pay her nothing ever came of it at the time. She worked at the bookstore as well, and we began dating and eventually married. But once that happened she began poring over my half-finished manuscript and corrected multiple copies of every new chapter as I tried to create an interesting novel that people would want to read. Thanks in no small part to her, I became a better writer in the process and dedicated the novel to her. Finally, fifteen months later, I had done it. I had become a novelist. Success in that regard, however, is something that I had achieved essentially on my own, with the generous help of my wife at the time. Getting the thing published, however, was going to be an altogether different story, something that would depend on other people sharing my vision and a willingness on their part to shoulder the financial responsibility of printing it, publicizing it, and getting it into bookstores. That's when everything ground to a halt.

Mostly, no one wanted to take a chance on it, and from my perspective today it's easy to see why. Going back and editing the novel for publication it's clear that the first half of the story isn't really that good. I like the historical sections that precede each chapter of the main story, but the current timeline about Steve Raymond and his girlfriend Janet is pretty dull stuff. As the two timelines get closer and begin to intersect, however, the writing gets better. And that makes perfect sense. I was learning a lot during that year and a half and my writing was improving the closer I came to finishing the book. So the last half of the story was bound to be better. On the bright side, no one said they hated it, but it obviously wasn't good enough that they couldn't resist it. The most positive comment that I received came from a literary agent who said that if I'd written the thing ten years earlier he was sure he could have sold it. In the eighties publishers were still willing to take a chance on unknown authors and try to help them build an audience. But by the early nineties all of that was over. Most publishers then were only looking for name recognition in order to guarantee sales. As a result, I was forced to put mystery novels by television personality Steve Allen, tennis star Martina Navratilova, and weatherman Willard Scott on the shelves at the bookstore, while my manuscript languished in a box in my apartment.

Nevertheless I continued to write novels, hoping one day to gain a foothold in the world of genre fiction and from there begin to build an audience for my work. So I tried my hand a mystery novels and even used my protagonist from this book, Steve Raymond, as my amateur sleuth. I made it as far as getting a literary agent who genuinely enjoyed my mysteries, but she didn't have any better luck than I had with *Death's Head*. And so it's not until this publication that my first novel is finally going to be able to be read by an audience. Also included at the end of this volume is the short story "Stella," the only historical short story I ever wrote. The book is the second in a series of my fictional works—all of them unpublished—that I want to give form and substance to by getting them into print. It may not be a great novel, but it is a solid piece of work and has some inventive things in it that I'm still proud of. Hopefully readers of today will be able to discover for themselves some of the immense joy I had in writing it over twenty-five years ago.

Eric B. Olsen
January 21, 2017

It is a rare and special good fortune for a theoretical
scientist to flourish at a time when the prevailing
ideology welcomes it, and its findings immediately
serve the policy of the state.

> Dr. Eugene Fischer
> Kaiser Wilhelm Institute, Berlin, 1943.

Do you fully understand what it is that I have done—
I, the outlaw, the so-called war criminal? Right here in
this godforsaken place, I have created a scientific miracle.
I have turned the whole world into a laboratory.

> Gregory Peck
> *The Boys from Brazil,* 1978.

Poland, 1945

12 January 1945, 4:26 p.m., Oświęcim.

A small naked boy was led into the room by one of the SS guards, a meaty hand around the child's bare upper arm. Two men in white smocks awaited him. The boy, no more than ten years old, ran up to the dark-haired man as soon as he was released.

"*Onkel, Onkel*," he shouted as he tried to throw his arms up around the man, but the man reached out a hand and grasped the boy's neck, preventing him from getting any closer.

The dark-haired man was always very kind to the children, giving them candy and patting them on the head when they gathered around him. They called him Uncle because he was just about the closest thing to family that any of them had left; most of their parents were gone—"up the chimney," to use the camp slang. But at this moment the man did not appear to be feeling very avuncular.

"Hurry up, Zindell," he said to his associate. "I have to leave soon; the car will be here any minute."

Dr. Konrad Zindell was methodically setting out an array of surgical instruments on a tray and answered without looking up. "Yes, *Herr Doktor.*"

After he had finished, Zindell beckoned the boy to him, but instead of coming the boy looked back up at the man he had called *Onkel.* The dark-haired man smiled, revealing the gap between his front teeth, nodded at the boy, and gently pushed him toward Zindell.

The boy's twin brother was waiting in the adjoining operatory where Zindell had examined them both earlier in the day. Zindell was fortunate to have such excellent specimens to work with. The twins that Dr. Mengele used for his eugenics research were perfect.

"We will be under way shortly, *Herr Doktor.*"

Mengele said nothing. There was really no reason for him to be in the room at all. But ever since he had first helped Zindell with his surgical technique, and even after the student had surpassed the teacher, Mengele had insisted on being present every time Zindell operated. He had no genuine interest in Zindell's experiments, though; he seemed only concerned with the surgery, usually leaving the operatory shortly afterward.

Zindell helped the boy lie to down on one of the concrete slabs that Mengele had erected since removing his marble dissecting table. Everything in Mengele's lab that wasn't nailed down had been packed up and shipped out to God knew where. The reason was simple and the echo of artillery fire in Zindell's ears confirmed it: the Russian Army was almost on their doorstep.

Reports, charts and all other evidence of human experimentation had been burned, crematoria had been blown up and patients too infirm to march had been shot. All signs of the work they had done here was to be destroyed. Almost. Mengele had personally seen to the departure of his research on eugenics. Likewise, Zindell had taken great pains to preserve his own research, ultimately more important he felt, than Mengele's, and a specialty of his since college: brain mapping.

He gave the boy a small injection and waited for him to lose consciousness, hoping it wouldn't take too long, as Mengele's patience was obviously wearing thin. When he was satisfied that the boy would not wake up, he drew a line around the crown of his freshly shaved head with a blue pen and, index finger extended over his scalpel, expertly cut along the mark. From the instrument tray he took up what look like a large, flat spoon, actually a surgical instrument of his own design which had been manufactured by prisoners in the metal shop, and deftly separated the cranial muscle beneath the scalp from the boy's skull, allowing the bloody flap of skin to fall to the floor.

To stop the flow of blood, which was now completely covering the operating field and flowing onto the table, Zindell cauterized around the entire incision using a soldering iron, modified to his specifications by camp inmates. Next, he cleaned off the exposed skull, drew another, smaller circle directly on the cranium and picked up his surgical saw. Although the blade was curved and much finer and sharper, it still reminded him of a hack saw. The blade etched deeply into the bone on the first pass and, with the precision of a man who had performed the procedure hundreds of times before, he detached a nine-centimeter section of the boy's skull without so much as damaging a capillary beneath. With the aid of his surgical spoon he removed it and placed it in a bowl of saline solution.

He could feel Mengele behind him now, watching, concentrating on his every move. He could smell him too, a mixture of stale breath and perfumed hair tonic. Zindell began to breathe through his mouth and tried to block the presence behind him out of his mind.

He secretly wished Mengele would leave him to his own devices, but openly acquiesced to his authority for the sake of his research. At this point he could little afford to risk the tenuous relationship he had so painstakingly cultivated.

It had been more than a stroke of luck to become associated with Mengele in the first place. Decidedly that; it had been a miracle. Through a chance meeting with Otmar von Verschuer at the Kaiser-Wilhelm Institute in Berlin, not to mention a healthy bit of cajoling on his part, Zindell had gone from a mere psychology graduate student to Mengele's assistant at Auschwitz, and eventually hoped to become one of the world's leading pioneers in neurosurgery. For some reason it had never occurred to Zindell that the medical community might frown on his lack of medical certification. Zindell's only doctorate was a Ph.D. in psychology.

After opening the skull, Zindell delicately removed the dura, a thin membrane surrounding the pinkish gray convolutions that comprised the cerebral cortex. He had discovered through trial and error that it was easier and less time consuming to simply expose the entire brain, regardless of which hemisphere he was working on.

He caught a whiff of body odor as Mengele moved in even closer.

Two days ago Zindell had run the Gypsy twins through a battery of complete physical and psychological tests, from simple motor reflexes to complex mathematical computations. Any deviation between the two boys had been duly noted on the charts that he kept on every research subject.

The boy's brain bulged slightly now, unconstrained by the skull. It was webbed with tiny capillaries and lay gently pulsating before him. Zindell rechecked his notes for the last time, then leaned in with a smaller surgical spoon and scooped out a portion of the spongy, soft gray matter from the boy's parietal lobe. He quickly turned and slipped it into a numbered and dated bottle of formalin. When the boy regained consciousness he would take him into the adjoining operatory where his brother waited and run the identical battery of tests he had run two days earlier, using the normal twin as the control.

Zindell felt blessed. If there was a God, he had surely been touched by His hand. Work of this kind could never have been carried out anywhere else, or at any other time in history.

Another miracle. He had nearly completed his research on the cerebral cortex and hoped that the Wehrmacht could hang on long enough for him to finish his work on the rest of the human brain.

As Zindell replaced the top of the skull and was fastening it to the boy's head with special clamps, designed again by himself, Mengele turned for the door.

"What do you want me to do with them when I'm finished?" Zindell called after him, referring to the two boys.

He had never known Mengele to have any further use for his twins once they had been handed over, but he always asked just the same. Mengele glanced at his wristwatch before delivering his stock answer.

"Kill them."

Chapter One

1. Monday, October 15, 1990, 7:42 a.m., Seattle.

"Doctor Raymond, Doctor Raymond," a woman's voice announced calmly over the hospital public address system, "code red in ICU, code red in ICU."

Moments later, from the elevator on the fourth floor where the intensive care unit was located, Dr. Paul Raymond burst into the hall and ran toward the nurse's station. His scrub nurse, Demetria Komboukos, was already waiting for him there and as soon as they made eye contact she turned and ran, leading the way to the patient.

"What happened?"

"He had another seizure and then coded." She stopped at the doorway and Raymond ran past her into the room.

"Clear!" yelled a first-year resident to the critical care team that surrounded the bed as he was about to place defibrillation paddles on the patient's chest.

"Stop!" ordered Raymond. He ran over to the bed and looked closely at the EKG monitor for a few seconds. The line was almost flat, but not quite. The tiny visible jags were almost certainly the result of a faint heartbeat, imperceptible to the touch.

"Continue artificial respiration," he directed the nurse who had been breathing for the patient. She immediately placed the Ambu-bag back over the patient's face and resumed ventilation. The resident, who was still holding the paddles in his hand, dropped them to the floor to begin CPR. "Get away from him!" Raymond shouted, and the resident stood back, watching the nurse as she pumped air into the man's lungs.

"I'm not getting much air into him," the nurse said. "I can barely even squeeze the bag."

"Okay," said Raymond. "Let's go ahead and intubate."

The nurse stopped and began the procedure to insert an endotracheal tube, while Raymond used the time for a quick examination. The patient had no pulse, he was sweating all over, and his face was taking on a blue tinge from lack of oxygen. His abdomen was also slightly swollen, indicating that some of the air intended for his lungs was going to his stomach.

The intubation process involved placing a tube down the patient's windpipe. A doughnut-shaped balloon at the end of the tube would then be inflated so that pure oxygen could be pumped directly into his lungs.

"I can't get it," the nurse yelled. "His throat's too constricted."

"Okay, get me some Anectine."

Demetria was already unwrapping an ampule of the drug as he spoke. She drew it into a hypodermic and handed it to Raymond. "Move the EKG screen," he said as he tapped the shaft of the syringe with his middle finger to expel any air bubbles along with the excess drug.

Demetria had adjusted the electrocardiograph monitor above the patient's head to where Raymond could see it by the time he was ready to inject the clear fluid. He placed his left hand on the man's shoulder to steady himself. "Okay, get ready to resume," he said, holding up the syringe in his right. The nurse stood ready, in position to insert the endotracheal tube. The resident froze in place.

Raymond inserted the needle into the IV feed and slowly injected the liquid. Almost instantly the drug paralyzed every skeletal muscle in the man's body. Raymond paid close attention to the man's reaction, then stopped suddenly and extracted the needle. As the man's throat muscle relaxed, the nurse inserted the tube and began pumping pure oxygen into his lungs. Raymond then fixed his gaze on the EKG screen above the bed. The one muscle still functioning was the heart, and the faint heartbeat was still there.

"Epinephrine," he ordered, and almost instantly Demetria was handing him another syringe. Once again the dose was delivered via the IV line and when Raymond was finished everyone in the room stood silently. The only sound was the nurse squeezing oxygen into the patient's lungs and the flat whine of the EKG monitor.

After two full minutes of waiting, the extremely weak beat of the patient's heart began to speed up. The whine ceased, replaced by beeps that were coming stronger and faster and the sharp spike, bracketed by two smaller waves, began to take the familiar shape of a normal heartbeat. Demetria, who'd had her fingers continuously around the man's wrist during the wait, suddenly looked up.

"I have a pulse!" she said, and the room erupted in applause.

Raymond breathed a long sigh of relief. He ran his hand through his hair and looked back at his patient. The color was returning to the man's face and his stomach was no longer distended. He picked up the patient's wrist and checked it himself; the pulse was weak, but it was definitely there.

He turned to the nurse who was still breathing for the patient. "Keep it up until the Anectine wears off and he's breathing on his own." Raymond waved another nurse over. "If his heartbeat gets up over 180 a minute I want you to give him some Valium. I also want a new EKG run as soon as he's stable." Then Raymond turned to Demetria. "And I'd like you to prep him for surgery, stat." She nodded.

"You," he said, pointing to the resident, "follow me. Terrific job, people," he added as he reached the door. Raymond stopped at the ICU desk to talk to the duty nurse. "I want you to call down and schedule me in the OR ten minutes from now. I'll want a full staff, and notify nurse Komboukos of all the details; she'll get in touch with me."

"Yes, Doctor."

Raymond wheeled around, pushed through the doors of ICU and turned down the hall with the resident following in his wake. "Get up here," he said, and the resident moved alongside Raymond, walking at a brisk pace to keep up.

"What's your name?"

"Greenwood."

"What do you think you were doing in there, Greenwood? And where the hell was Baker?" Raymond was referring to the scheduled doctor on call.

"Baker needed the morning off, so I told him I'd cover for him."

Raymond turned and straight-armed the door to the doctors' changing room, banging it against the lockers as it opened. He stopped in front of his own locker and began to undress. "You know you almost killed him   "

"He arrested! I got the call—"

"Did you bother to check the goddamn chart?" Greenwood averted his eyes from Raymond's glare and stood silently. "You might have been a hot-shot prodigy in medical school, kid, but here you follow orders just like the rest of us."

"I *did* look at the chart."

"Are you kidding me? Then what the hell am I hauling this around for?" Raymond threw his small pager unit onto the clothes he had laid on the bench. "His chart said specifically that I was to be notified, 24 hours a day, at even the slightest change in his status."

"I thought . . . We thought we had it under control. We thought we could save him."

"*You* thought *you* could save him," said Raymond, his finger pointed at Greenwood for emphasis. "Are we speaking the same language here, or what?"

Greenwood stared back at him, defiant.

"Let me put it another way, kid: as long as he wasn't fibrillating you could have barbequed that guy's heart with those paddles and still wouldn't have been able to get it going again. This is only your first year of residency, Greenwood; don't screw up your career by trying to play Super Doc, okay?"

"Yeah, sure."

"Look, I try to be as helpful to the residents around here as possible, but you don't want to cross me up. Accidents are one thing, but if I ever catch you trying to kill one of my patients again I'm going to see to it personally that you get your Ivy-League ass thrown out of here. And believe me, I've got the clout to do it. Now get out of here and try and do your job right next time."

Greenwood stormed out of the locker room and Raymond let him; there wasn't time for further confrontation. He had finished putting on his scrubs and was just shutting his locker door when Mark White, the chief administrator of the Elliott Bay Medical Center, walked into the room.

"Where do you think *you're* going?"

"I'm due in surgery—"

"Oh, no, you're not."

"Jesus, can't a guy fart around here without you finding out about it?" More to himself he added, "You'd think those nurses could keep their mouths shut."

"They're not paid to keep their mouths shut. The word is you're going to try some experimental brain surgery."

"It's the only thing that'll save him. It's a relatively simple operation—"

"You've never *done* this operation."

"I've done it a hundred times."

"On monkeys! Jesus Christ, Paul, you don't have any kind of authorization whatsoever to experiment like—"

"It's the only chance this guy's got."

"You *still* need authorization."

"No one has to know."

"Don't patronize me, Paul. I found out two minutes after you scheduled the surgery. And what if the guy winds up dying on the table? Do you really think you can keep this quiet?"

Raymond slid the green cap off of his head and threw it into one of the hampers and leaned back on a locker directly facing White. "What the hell's going on around here, Mark? You were a doctor once, too. Don't you remember how it used to be? If I don't try something this guy's going to die, but suddenly we're all afraid of our own shadows. How the hell am I supposed to save people if you won't let me operate on them?"

White took a few steps into the room and sat down on a bench opposite Raymond. "Look, Paul, I realize you've had a lot of success with your vivisections, but you're going to have to ease back on the human experimentation."

"Ease back, my ass! You have no intention of implementing my program. The only reason I'm here is so you can keep your research money coming in. Why don't you just admit it? Insurance companies have guys like you by the balls."

This remark prompted White to his feet, his face beginning to redden. "Listen, friend, without guys like me, *your* balls would be in a sling and your ass would be out on the street, or worse yet, in jail. At this point you're lucky to still be experimenting on animals." White was nearly shouting, his index finger in Raymond's chest.

Raymond pushed his way past White and began to remove the rest of his scrubs. "I don't know why I even stay here."

"I'll tell you why. Because Bay Med's the best research hospital in the country, and because no other hospital administrator would let you get away with the shit *I* let you get away with."

"Oh, so just because we graduated from medical school together and you decided you have to watch out for me, I'm supposed to get on my knees and kiss your ass?"

"No, you're supposed to recognize that I'm your friend, and that I'm just trying to do my job. I'm on your side, Paul. And if it means anything, I think you're right. But if I get kicked out of here you've got to know that you're going to be following me right out the door. As it is I have to do a goddamn song and dance for the hospital board every month. If it wasn't for your success with the Smart Probe both of us would have been gone a long time ago."

"That's bullshit and you know it. You haven't let me even get close to the OR with that thing. Christ, Mark, it's performed brilliantly in the lab, but I can't seem to get it anywhere near a real patient. I'm on the verge of a major surgical breakthrough here, but I can't do anything until you get off my back."

The hurt was evident in White's eyes. Raymond ran his hand through his hair and sighed. Neither man said anything for a few moments. "I'm sorry, Mark. It's just that I get so goddamn frustrated. I remember how things used to be and I just . . . I don't know . . ." Raymond sat down. White walked over and sat next to him.

"What the hell do you think it's like for me Paul? You think I don't get frustrated? I didn't go to medical school so I could sit behind a desk pushing papers all day long. But I'm still just as much of a doctor as you are. And if guys like me didn't do our jobs, guy like you wouldn't have any place to do research at all." White put his hand on Raymond's shoulder. "Please understand, Paul, I have to do this."

Raymond was about to continue the debate but then exhaled audibly and extended his hand. "Oh, hell. I'm sorry, Mark."

"So am I, Paul. So am I." The two shook hands and White stood up and walked over to the door. He turned back as if to say something but Raymond was leaning forward, his head in his hands. White pulled open the door and walked out.

2. 8:15 a.m.

Raymond didn't have time to go back to his office and sulk, though he thought he might like to. In dividing his time between research, teaching, surgery, examinations and administrative duties, there was precious little left to waste brooding about Mark White. Necessity winning out over indulgence, he waded into the rest of his workday.

Raymond bypassed the lab and went straight to his office. Rita Heinz had the phone to her ear but waved him over as soon as he appeared. She was only the third secretary he'd had since arriving in Seattle in 1976, and he hoped she'd be the last. She was damn good.

His office was located smack in the middle of the neurosurgical clinic, which was now housed in the new neurology wing of the ever-expanding Medical Center complex. And though Raymond could have had his office situated anywhere else, he chose to be on the front lines. Before the move he had felt he was spending half his time running between his office and the examination rooms and the OR.

Now his office opened up right behind the big horseshoe-shaped reception desk that Rita shared with the half-dozen nurses who worked in the clinic. But while the examination and operating rooms were more accessible to him, the downside was he was also more accessible to his house officers, residents and medical students. What he sacrificed in privacy, however, was more than made up for in efficiency.

"Sorry about your surgery," Rita said, hanging up the handset.

"Jesus, did someone announce it over the loudspeaker?"

"That was Demi."

"Oh."

"She says Houston's vitals are stable; his fluid count's up to sixty cc's an hour, urine output's dropping, and pain response in minimal."

"Damn."

"Do you still want the EEG?"

"Yeah."

"She'll check in with you after rounds."

"Thanks."

The patient Raymond had just brought back to life was Nick Houston, temporarily anyway. Houston had arrived in the emergency room yesterday, coming straight from his job in the mailroom of the *Seattle P.I.* after being knocked unconscious by a blow to the back of his head when he fell trying to fix a piece of machinery. Raymond had been called down to the ER and through a mixture of experience, expertise, and a hell of a lot of luck, they had managed to keep Houston from dying.

A CT scan showed bleeding in the frontal cerebellum and an angiogram located an aneurysm in his left internal carotid artery. Conventional wisdom held that Houston's condition was inoperable. Raymond didn't think so. But beyond any guesswork, one fact remained indisputable: without some kind of intervention, experimental or not, the man would soon die.

And that's where things became sticky. The personnel department at the newspaper confirmed that Houston had no next of kin and therefore no one to sign a consent form. Without it, any program of treatment had to be channeled through and approved by the powers that be, namely Mark White.

Raymond had no program of treatment to submit because no one had ever tried this procedure before. The Smart Probe that he wanted to use had been developed with the help of the engineering department at the university. Using the latest in fiber-optics and microsurgical technology, Raymond was confident he could stop the bleeding inside Houston's brain without expensive damage to the surrounding tissue. But conventional wisdom also stated that experimentation was not a professional approach to neurosurgery.

Catch-22. He couldn't operate because of the risk that the patient might die on the operating table, but without the surgery the patient was definitely going to die. They were so scared that a relative would come out of the woodwork to sue them that they refused to let Raymond try to save the man's life. It wasn't the first time a situation like this had brought him head to head with Mark White, and it was unlikely to be the last.

Rita handed him a pile of messages and deciphered each one as he leafed through them. Then she ran down his schedule for the rest of the day: exams until nine followed by a visit to Central Imaging to consult on an angiogram, rounds at ten, surgery at ten-thirty, lunch, another surgery at two and another at five.

"Something wrong?" Rita asked.

Raymond had been unconsciously frowning. "Nothing that killing Mark White wouldn't cure."

"I see. Well, let me know if you need anything," she said, "aspirin, booze, a Saturday night special . . ."

Raymond smiled—he couldn't help himself—and shook his head. "No, thanks. I think it'll be enough if Doctor White and I just agree to disagree."

"Suit yourself," she said, allowing a grin to turn up the corners of her mouth. The phone rang and she picked it up. "Dr. Raymond's office . . ."

Raymond glanced through his messages again as he walked into his office. He shut the door and sat down heavily behind his desk, trying to think of what else he could do for Houston. The phone startled him and he flipped the speaker switch.

"You're ready in number one."

"Thanks. Be right there."

The six charts representing his patients for the day were stacked neatly on the sea of paper that flooded his desk. Nearly all of Raymond's patients were referrals from the neurology department, other hospitals, or private physicians. Most of them had seen several doctors before they arrived in Raymond's office, and along with each doctor came a complete set of tests, the results duly noted in their charts. Once they reached him they were tested yet again.

When it was finally Raymond's turn to talk with them they had survived virtually every relevant test known to man, and his examinations had evolved into perfunctory five-minute consultations. Having studied the test results, Raymond would simply offer his opinion of what surgery could do for them, and ninety-nine percent of the time the only question they responded with was, "When can you do it?"

He picked the top chart off of the pile and looked through it on the way to the examining room. His first patient today was Cham Tuong, a sixty-five-year-old Vietnamese male who was suffering from severe headaches.

When he entered the room there were two people waiting there. The slight, bespectacled man sitting on the cushioned examining table was Tuong and the young, raven-haired woman who stood beside him was his daughter, Mai. He had read in the chart that Tuong spoke little English and that his daughter translated for him.

They exchanged greetings and Raymond went to the sink to wash his hands. "Tell me about your father's condition," he said to Mai, and she sat down in a molded plastic chair.

"About a year ago," she said, "my father woke up in the middle of the night with a terrible headache. It only lasted a few minutes and he was able to get back to sleep. After that, it didn't happen again for a few months."

Raymond moved to sit on a stool, listening attentively and allowing her to tell what he had already learned from the chart. Tuong sat very composed and dignified as he listened to his daughter speak.

"Once they started again they began to happen more and more often until he was having them two or three times a night. The pain would go away when he got out of bed, but then came back after he laid back down. It got so bad that he could only sleep sitting up. He was afraid to lie down. Mom and I begged him to go to the doctor but he refused. Finally, two weeks ago, he went out to the kitchen to get something to drink and twenty minutes later Mom found him standing in front of the refrigerator with the door open. He didn't know how long he had been standing there and couldn't even remember opening it. When we brought him to the hospital they told us he had a tumor."

Raymond stood and walked over to Tuong, who smiled and nodded. "Where does your head usually hurt?"

It was clear Tuong had heard this question many times. He made a motion with his hand over the right side of his head even before his daughter could translate.

Although the examination was a routine courtesy, it served an important purpose. Raymond wanted his patients to feel comfortable with him and the idea of surgery. He wanted to alleviate their fear as much as realistically possible. And he felt fortunate that he usually could.

His patients were the lucky ones. Every day neurologists were faced with diseases like Alzheimer's and ALS, which they could do little for as their patients progressively degenerated and died. But if a defect in the brain could be surgically removed or corrected, those patients would have a chance at recovering from illness and reclaiming their former lives.

He wheeled the stool over so that he could face both of them as he talked. "I realize you've heard most of this before but I want to run it down for you again." They both listened solemnly.

"The CT scan we did when your father was admitted turned up a tumor on the right side of his brain. The swelling around the tumor when your father was sleeping is what caused the headaches. When he stood up, gravity pulled the blood away from his tumor and that's why the headaches went away. Once it grew big enough, though, it began to put pressure on the surrounding tissue and that's what caused his memory loss.

"Now, the position of the tumor is going to make it relatively easy to get at; that's the good news. The bad news is that the outline of the tumor on the scan is somewhat irregular and the angiogram wasn't very conclusive, which means the tumor could be malignant.

"If that's the case, it's most likely at an early stage. We'll go in and remove as much of the tumor as possible; then he'll have to be put on chemotherapy to try and keep the parts we couldn't get from spreading. That's just a possibility that I have to prepare you for.

"In my opinion it's benign, in which case we'll simply remove the whole thing and that will be the end of it. I'm just sorry I can't tell you anything more definite now, but either way he'll have to have it removed. It's my recommendation that he have surgery as soon as possible."

Raymond sat and listened while Mai rattled off a steady stream of Vietnamese to her father. When she was finished Tuong looked directly at Raymond and said, "When?"

He told them that they only needed to stop at the reception desk and they could schedule the surgery in as soon as a week. They said their good-byes and then Raymond left them.

Between appointments he received the results of Houston's latest EEG and they weren't promising; they showed severe degeneration in both hemispheres. Without intervention Raymond didn't expect him to last the day. The cranial pressure would continue to increase until the swollen brain pushed Houston's brain stem through the hole at the base of his skull. By now Raymond had resigned himself to the man's inevitable death.

For the rest of the morning Raymond fared considerably better. His first four patients walked right from the examining table to the reception desk to schedule their operations. The last two exams were follow-ups of previous surgeries, both with positive results, and by the time Raymond was filling his mug with coffee and heading down to Central Imaging, his confrontation with Mark White was all but forgotten.

3. 9:06 a.m.

Central Imaging was a series of yellow-tiled rooms situated on the first floor between the hospital and the neurology wing. More than any other diagnostic tool, neurologists relied on the work that was done here to make decisions about patient treatment. Everything from X-rays to Nuclear Magnetic Resonance scanning was performed at Central Imaging and Marty Russell was the technician who ran it all.

Marty had a great shock of red hair and wore wire-frame glasses in what Raymond thought was an attempt to heighten his reputation as a radical. He could be egotistical at times, but no one complained much because of the great expertise with which he manipulated the millions of dollars' worth of equipment for them. For the most part Raymond found him an intense and dedicated young man.

"Hi, Marty," said Raymond, sticking his head into the angiogram control room. "Is Childress here yet?"

Marty waved his hand in Raymond's direction without lifting his eyes from his work. "On her way. I just sent two orderlies up to get her."

Emily Childress was a sixteen-year-old patient who was here for an angiogram. Raymond had been asked by Dr. Matthews to consult on the case so that, together, they might determine whether surgery was an option.

Raymond stepped all the way inside the dimly lit room and tried to stay out of Marty's way. The overhead fluorescents were off, making the monitors easier to view and cutting the glare on the leaded glass that separated them from the large X-ray machine. But small pools of light trained on various control panels, along with the light coming from the other room, was plenty to see by.

His coffee was cooling and Raymond warmed it up at the coffee maker in the corner. "Hi, Paul," he heard behind him.

After replacing the coffee pot he turned to see a beautiful woman with long, light-brown hair walking toward him.

Dr. Angela Mathews wore her hair tied back and her coat open over a blue silk dress that matched the frames of her glasses. She was thirty-five and unmarried, but at first glance the most striking feature about her was not her beauty, it was her height: four feet ten.

Raymond himself was a good five feet eleven and she only came up to his mid-chest. It was something he noticed every time she walked up to him but then quickly forgot, because while many men tried to make up for a lack of physical stature by being brusque and derisive, Dr. Mathews exuded so much confidence in her abilities, and rightfully so, that her height was simply not a consideration.

"Hi, Angela," Raymond answered.

"She here?"

"Any minute now."

"I brought this for you," she said, handing Raymond an inch-thick sheaf of papers that comprised Emily Childress's chart. "I'm going to see if Marty's ready yet."

Raymond walked over to the counter that ran beneath the banks of viewing lights against the back wall and glanced through the chart as he sipped his coffee.

Emily was the freshman star of her high school tennis team. A month ago she had begun experiencing slight seizures consisting of twitching and numbness that began in the fingers of her right hand and traveled up her arm to her neck and face. Neurology had already run an EEG and a CT scan and determined that she had a deformity of the blood vessels in her brain called an arteriovenous malformation. The angiogram would determine whether or not the AVM was operable. She was currently on Dilantin to control the seizures.

Raymond felt a hand at his elbow and looked up from the chart.

"I want to thank you again for helping me out on this, Paul," said Dr. Matthews.

21

"No problem. I'm just glad I could get away for a few minutes today before rounds."

"Sorry about the Houston case."

Raymond tried not to look as stunned as he felt. "How'd *you* find out?"

"Word travels fast around here." She placed her hand on his arm again and Raymond felt a rush of excitement that he hadn't felt for a very long time. "I hope you know that if I ever wound up like Houston, I'd want you to go for it."

He smiled and was about to tell her that Mark White was the one she should be telling this to when Marty called out to them. "She's here."

Dr. Matthews looked quickly through the glass as the patient was being wheeled into the angiogram room and then turned back to Raymond. "Will you come in and meet her? She's a little scared."

"Sure."

Raymond set down his mug and followed her out of the control room. Though Emily was heavily sedated, Dr. Matthews held her hand and talked to her comfortingly but also with respect. She introduced Raymond and he smiled at Emily and then moved back out of the way.

Dr. Matthews stayed by her patient's side as two technicians strapped her to the moveable table. First, a catheter would be inserted through an artery in Emily's groin and then a dye would be injected into her bloodstream so that they could get a clear picture of the configuration of the blood vessels in her brain, including the AVM.

Dr. Matthews maintained verbal contact with Emily while she cut into the artery and Raymond watched on the monitor as she expertly guided the catheter toward the girl's vein. But during most of the procedure Raymond found himself looking at Dr. Matthews herself. Many times he had thought about asking her to dinner, but somehow he always found an excuse not to. Watching her now, he realized that he would have to make a point of doing so this week.

Most physicians felt that they had to keep a professional distance from their patients in order to make unbiased decisions and to insulate themselves from the patient's suffering. He even did it himself. But Angela Matthews was completely unapologetic about her deep concern for the people she treated and considered her own emotional involvement to be a crucial part of her success. Some of her colleagues kidded her about it but she always laughed along with them, never dignifying their criticism with a defense.

And that, thought Raymond, was undoubtedly her most appealing attribute.

The catheter was now at the base of Emily's brain and Dr. Matthews strapped the patient's head and chin to the table with tape to keep her from moving. Once she had positioned Emily, still reassuring her every step of the way, she was the last to leave the room.

Back inside the control room Marty made some last-minute adjustments when Dr. Matthews instructed him to set the number of images at three hundred, the maximum. Everything was then synchronized with the injector and Raymond walked over to the digital imaging console. An X-ray tube would take three hundred pictures of Emily's blood as it entered the blood vessels in her brain, and store them digitally. Afterward, he and Dr. Matthews would be able to review them at various speeds and select any individual frame to be printed on X-ray film.

"Angela?" Raymond asked. She had remained up by the window and he wasn't sure if she was going to view the images with him as they were recorded.

"Can you watch the screen for me, Paul? I want to keep an eye on her."

He nodded.

Dr. Matthews took the microphone and continued talking Emily through the procedure. "Emily, when I inject the dye it's going to feel hot and it will hurt but I want you to try and hold perfectly still. I'm right here watching you so you don't have to worry about anything." She flicked off the microphone. "Go ahead, Marty."

When Marty began the injection a sob came over the speaker in the control room.

"Don't move, Emily. Please don't move. I'll be through in just a few seconds; I promise."

As Raymond watched Emily's blood filling her arteries, he marveled at how Dr. Matthews took all of the responsibility for her patient upon herself, always the first-person pronoun "I" instead of the more evasive "we."

A few seconds later, as Emily's blood was passing from her arteries to her veins and their webbed structure became more defined, Raymond noticed a concentration of the tiny vessels near the surface of the brain. After a few more images flashed across the screen Raymond was ready to make his diagnosis.

"Beautiful."

"What?" said Dr. Matthews.

"Take a look."

She turned to the monitor closest to her and then looked back at Raymond. "It's not an AVM, is it?"

"I don't think so. It looks more like a capillary angioma. You'll definitely need another CT scan to confirm, but it looks good."

Dr. Matthews walked over next to him as he pointed out the defect on the screen.

"Right here," he said. "It should be fairly easy to remove. We could have her in and out of surgery in a couple of hours. If it goes well, she could go home the next day."

"That's great!"

They were still studying the screen when suddenly Marty yelled. "Something's wrong!"

"Jesus," said Dr. Matthews, already moving toward the door. "She's having a seizure."

Raymond could hear the sobs in the other room escalate to a wail.

"Do we have enough pictures, Paul?"

"We're done here. Shut her down, Marty."

Dr. Matthews bolted from the control room and Raymond watched as she burst into the other room, tailed by technicians. He would have liked to talk with her again before he left, but a glance at his watch told him that if he didn't leave right now he would be late for rounds. Marty was engrossed in resetting his machines so Raymond gathered up his coffee mug and headed for the neurosurgical ward.

4. 1:56 p.m.

Raymond stood silently at the scrub sink prior to his second surgery of the day. His earlier meningioma resection had gone well and he'd even had time to look in on a microvascular decompression that Dr. Utley was performing in the next room. After eating a quick lunch and trying to make a dent in his ever-present paperwork, which was the only drawback to his position as Chief of Neurosurgery, he was back at it again.

Raymond washed his hands methodically. His arms were lathered with soap up to the elbows in a procedure that had begun to take on the form of a ritual over the years. As he scrubbed, he visualized the surgery he was about to perform. Ten minutes later, he rinsed off thoroughly and switched the valve below the sink with his knee to shut off the water.

As he turned he was given a sterile towel and dried his hands, then slipped into a sterile gown that was held out in front of him. One nurse tied off the back while another held open a pair of rubber gloves for him, which snapped loudly around his wrists as he thrust his hands into them one at a time. The mask around his neck was brought up over his face and tied behind the sterile cap on his head until all that showed of him were his eyes. Finally, Raymond entered the operating room.

The patient was a thirty-seven year old female with a tumor behind her right frontal lobe. The rush of adrenaline Raymond always felt upon entering the OR was greater than usual because he wasn't a hundred percent sure of the exact location of the tumor. The only evidence on the CT scan was a slight shift in the midline, the point at which the two hemispheres of the brain meet. It wasn't much to go on, but with his experience it would be enough.

At least there were no bureaucratic roadblocks on this case. The patient had been considerate enough not to be in a coma and had signed the appropriate consent forms.

The anesthesiologist was just putting the patient under when Raymond walked over to confer with the two neurosurgical residents who would be assisting him. "You two figure out where we're going in?"

"It looks like it's going to be right about here," said Foster Endicott, another Ivy Leaguer who had no doubt had his pick of medical schools after graduation. He was pointing to a spot on the CT scan.

Raymond nodded. "Close. I want it moved back a couple of centimeters, though; I think it's going to be a little deeper. Which one of you is doing the craniotomy?"

The other resident, Tomi Orita, raised his hand.

"Shall we?" Raymond said with a motion of his hand, and the three of them walked over to the operating theatre.

Demetria was adjusting some of the instruments on the raised table above the patient and Raymond winked hello at her. She winked back at him and he noticed her mask puff out as she sighed.

The patient, whose head had been shaved and then sterilized with Betadine, an orange-colored disinfectant, was positioned supine on the table. The two residents locked her head into place with a head holder, a vice-like instrument with three metal pins that punctured the scalp and imbedded into the skull to keep it from moving during surgery. Then sterile sheets and towels were draped over her naked body and stitched to her scalp so that the only visible part of the patient was the small area of her head they would be working on.

"You're up, Dr. Orita." Raymond outlined the place he wanted to enter the brain and Orita moved in with the scalpel and traced out a large flap of skin which he then scraped gently off of the skull. The scalp was stitched to the drapes to keep it out of the way and Raymond watched closely as Orita stopped the bleeding with an electric cautery, exposing the yellow-white skull. Now the bone work could begin.

Orita picked up a stainless-steel drill bit, positioned it on the skull and pulled the trigger. The bit turned slowly, shaving off pieces of bone that looked like wood whittles and depositing them on the drapes and on the floor. A special lock on the drill stopped it when it was through the bone. The hole was about the diameter of a dime, and a burr was used to enlarge it to the size of a quarter. Orita went on to make three more holes in a diamond pattern, and then used a bone-cutting attachment to connect them. The piece of skull that he lifted out was wrapped up and placed in an antibiotic solution to be replaced after the surgery.

"Nice work, Doctor," said Raymond.

"Thank you," said Orita.

"Dr. Endicott, go ahead and open now."

Endicott was in the middle of his residency and had already graduated from drilling into skulls, a task that was usually delegated to first-year residents like Orita. Raymond kept his arms folded in front of him as he observed, his hands under his armpits so that he wouldn't accidentally touch something unsterile.

Endicott was very good. With easy and assured motions he carefully cut through the dura mater and stitched it back. Now the brain was exposed. Next, Endicott gently removed the thin arachnoid membrane and moved back from the surgical field. An hour and a half into the operation and it was Raymond's turn to take the helm.

They were working at a spot just above the patient's forehead on the right side and the deviation in the midline was not clearly evident from that angle. I know you're in there, he said silently to the tumor. And I'm coming after you.

There was no natural fissure that Raymond could pry apart to look for the tumor. The only way in was to remove precious cerebral tissue and hope he was heading in the right direction. Using a suction device that he controlled with his foot, Raymond began sucking out tiny pieces of the woman's brain.

It was slow going. Along with the pink bits of brain tissue, quite a few blood vessels were broken. Each had to be cauterized and then the area had to be irrigated, to keep the brain moist, and the excess liquid suctioned out so that Raymond could begin again. He let Endicott do all of the hemostasis and was quite pleased with his work. After an hour he had bored a deep cylinder in the gray matter, a little over a centimeter in diameter. Finally, when he had gone as deep as he dared, and still hadn't uncovered the tumor, he straightened up from the table.

Raymond set down the suction device and closed his eyes. He could feel a slight throbbing on the muscles of his arms, and a tightness in his lower back. His neck seemed to creak as he rotated his head backward.

The operation was well into its third hour now. His next patient would remain prepped for another hour and if Raymond wasn't done by then, the surgery would be postponed until the next morning. When he opened his eyes again he was ready to continue.

"Dr. Orita, I want some frozen sections examined before I go on." Raymond removed four samples, numbered them, and Orita relayed them to a nurse who would take them to neuropathology. He should have thee results in a few minutes. During that time Raymond wanted to take a good hard look at this thing.

"Bring me the microscope."

It took two people to move the huge microscope from the other side of the room, and while he waited Raymond had a moment to notice Demetria. It was a credit to her abilities that he hadn't thought about her thus far into the operation. In a job like hers, where she must have the instrument the doctor wants at the exact instant he calls for it, the only time she would be noticed was if she made a mistake.

Demetria was talking to the nurse whose job it was to pick up the gauze strips that had been used to soak up blood and make sure that the amount that came out of the surgical site was the same that had gone into it. The nurse was busily sorting through the bloody clumps of material that she had retrieved from the floor and arrayed on a towel there.

"We're missing one," said Demetria.

"No way," shot back Endicott.

Even with only her eyes exposed. It wasn't difficult to discern the glare that Demetria sent in Endicott's direction.

"Are you sure?" Raymond interjected before things escalated.

"She counted them three times."

The microscope arrived and Raymond moved so that it could be placed over the patient.

"Well, keep looking. There's not enough room in the site have left it inside."

The microscope itself was sterile and Raymond adjusted the controls until the field came into focus. He was looking for anything to indicate the tumor close by. If he made the wrong decision as to where to continue looking for the tumor, he might wind up sucking out a hole in the woman's brain the size of a baseball without running into it. The tissue looked perfectly healthy, but he continued to study it, buying time, thinking through his next move.

"How's she doing, Dr. Powers?"

"Real good," said Kris Powers, the anesthesiologist.

A few minutes later Raymond tired of stalling and decided to head out in a direction that Endicott had suggested for the entry. The damn thing was in there somewhere and he was intent on finding it. He started the suction device again and had begun removing more tissue when Orita spoke up.

"Lab results are in." Raymond stopped, sucker still running, and cocked an ear. "Number one and two, normal. Number three four, mild anaplasia."

"Son of a bitch," Raymond muttered. The areas he had removed samples three and four from indicated that he had been heading in the right direction all along. If it was true, the tumor was even deeper then he had first suspected. That might also account for the lack of confirmation on the CT scan. With extreme care, Raymond plunged deeper into the patient's brain.

When the tumor didn't surface he stopped again, took two more samples and a break from the action. It had been four hours since the start of the operation. Raymond moved away from the table and walked around to where the sheets of CT scan film were displayed on the x-ray lights against the wall. He looked at them disinterestedly and then turned back around, arms crossed, and waited.

The second hand on the wall clock had made eight sweeps when Demetria yelled out. "I found it," she said, bringing forth a wad of gauze from the folds of the drape. It was the missing one. The other nurse counted again and happily announced that they were now all accounted for.

When the results from the latest samples finally arrived, Raymond moved back into position.

"Samples five and six," said Orita, "low grade astrocytoma."

Raymond smiled under his mask. That was it. And sure enough, with only the smallest amount of probing with the sucker, the multi-fingered malignancy appeared. As Raymond debulked the tumor as best he could, he realized that there was no way he could get all of it. But with drugs and radiation therapy, this woman could live many more years. Without the operation, she surely would have died.

5. 6:37 p.m.

The intensive care unit was fairly quiet at this time in the evening. The night shift had come on duty at five and many of the visitors were having dinner. Raymond walked up to the nurse's station still wearing his scrubs. He asked for Houston's file and received it. Looking it over, he could see that things were getting worse. The EEG he had ordered was flat: no brain activity.

He shut the file and pushed it across the counter before walking off toward Houston's room. On the way he yawned. He rubbed the stubble on his chin and then ran his hand through his hair. He hoped he could get home early tonight; his five o'clock surgery had been rescheduled for seven o'clock the next morning.

When Raymond reached the doorway he stopped for a moment and leaned against the jam. The room was dark except for a lamp over Houston's head. Houston had been breathing fine when he was admitted last night. They had pumped him full of Mannitol to stop the swelling in his brain and it had worked. When the bleeding had started again this morning all hell had broken loose. Now he was fully intubated and the respirator beside the bed was breathing for him, allowing his heart to pump blood to a brain that was no longer viable. But with the intense pressure inside Houston's skull, Raymond doubted whether any of the blood was getting to his brain at all.

Raymond walked to the foot of the bed. IV lines snaked out from under the sheet to fluid-filled bags above Houston's head. His eyes were open, staring sightlessly into space. Raymond flipped back the sheet and exposed Houston's feet. Taking a big toe between his thumb and forefinger, Raymond squeezed hard using his thumbnail until Houston's toenail was white with pressure. No response.

Then he walked to the side of the bed and repeated the procedure on Houston's thumb. Still no response. A functioning brain would have caused him to react to the pain; he would have grimaced or tried to pull away from Raymond's hand. He checked Houston's eyes: this morning they had been sluggish; now they were fixed and dilated.

Along with the flat-line, all of Raymond's observations confirmed that Houston was clinically dead. Most of the physical functions in Houston's body were still being carried out, but whatever it was that made Nick Houston Nick Houston was gone.

Raymond yawned again. In the corner was a padded chair and he walked over and sat in it. It was surprisingly comfortable. Either that, or he was extremely tired. Another yawn came over him and he rubbed his eyes and leaned his head back.

Raymond was roused from his doze by the steady whine of the cardiac monitor. He looked around, startled, but no one else was in the room. He didn't know how long ago Houston had coded, but someone should have been here by now. He ran out into the hall and saw two nurses walking slowly his way. They were laughing and Raymond was indignant.

"What the hell are you doing?" The words rushed out of him almost of their own volition. "There's a code down here."

Both the nurses stopped abruptly and looked at Raymond as if he were an escaped lunatic. "I know," said one with a stern expression on her face. "We were just coming down to take care of it."

"Where's the crash cart?"

"There's a no-code order for that patient, Doctor."

Raymond had awakened with his life-saving instincts at the helm and he was now hit with the reality of the situation. He didn't respond and the nurses continued past him, albeit a little faster, into the room. Houston would be allowed to die.

"Who gave the order?" he said, but he already knew the answer.

"Dr. White."

Of course. Raymond rubbed his face and yawned into his hand. "What about organ donations?"

"His driver's license wasn't endorsed."

Raymond watched for a minute while the nurses detached Houston's dead body from the machines and then he turned and left.

Paul Raymond didn't pull out of the hospital parking lot until after eight. A shower and a shave had momentarily energized him, but for the rest of the evening he had found himself mired in reports for tomorrow afternoon's mortality conference. Still, eight o'clock was early for Raymond: he didn't like to think about all the nights he had come dragging home at midnight.

He was tired and didn't notice the car coming up on his left as he nosed out onto Magnolia Boulevard. He slammed on his brakes just in time to avoid being hit, and in the process was almost rear-ended by the van that was following him out of the lot. This time he looked both ways, signaled, and then drove out into the wet Northwest weather.

The pavement was shiny from the rain, and the light from the street lamps glistened off of the drops that fell from the windshield of his Porsche. It was an older model, a 928 from the early eighties, and was costing him a fortune to keep running, but it was the first real car he had purchased for himself and he had a certain sentimental attachment to it. Rush hour was over and traffic was light as he headed across the Evergreen Point Floating Bridge toward his home in Medina, just across Lake Washington from Seattle.

Raymond was a widower. His wife Lynn had died six years ago from cancer and it had been the lowest and most painful period of his life. Since that time he had buried himself in his work, becoming Chief of Neurosurgery at the hospital and winning several federal grants for research. It seemed strange to him that he had attained most of his success after her death. Before, he had been content just to do his job and spend as much time with his family as possible.

He and Lynn had three children. The oldest, Kristy, was living with her boyfriend in Olympia. They had just bought a house and were engaged to be married, even though they hadn't set a date yet. The younger daughter, Tina, was married and lived in Tacoma. She and her husband already had two children, both boys. Only Raymond's youngest, a son named Steve, was still living at home. Steve was in his first year of medical school, following in his father's footsteps.

Raymond had turned off the 520 Highway and was driving down 84th toward home when he noticed a black van in his rearview mirror. He thought he recognized it as the one that had followed him out of the hospital parking lot but he wasn't sure. He wound the Porsche around the expensive residential area and stopped short of the driveway in front of his home to check the mailbox: a couple of bills, the rest just junk mail which he threw onto the passenger seat.

After pulling into the carport he shut off the engine. Bringing the mail and his briefcase with him, Raymond stepped out of the car and went to the door, fumbling through his keys to unlock it. The house was dark; all the lights were off and the smell of last night's chicken greeted him as he stepped inside. He hit the switch by the door but nothing happened so he walked inside and tried the lamp by the kitchen table: still nothing.

"Shit," he muttered as he set down his briefcase.

Raymond went to look for a flashlight, listening to his footsteps as he walked, the brush of his shoes against carpet changing to a dull echo as they hit the vinyl floor of the laundry room. He was fishing blindly in a drawer when someone grabbed him from behind. An arm came around his throat while another grabbed his left arm, forcing him to the floor. His head banged against the washing machine on the way down and he felt the weight of his assailant land on top of him. He flailed wildly with his free hand but someone else pinned it down. Then he felt the needle enter his right semitendinosus at the back of his leg. He tensed up at first and then relaxed for a moment, wondering what type of drug he had been injected with.

The next thing he knew they had released him.

His first thought was to escape. Raymond staggered to his feet and thrust his hands into his coat pocket in search of his car keys, but they were gone. If he'd dropped them, he couldn't see where they were in the pitch-blackness. He shook his head; the drug was already beginning to take effect. Disoriented, he thought he was heading for the door but he found himself in the pantry. Now his head was spinning. He was rapidly losing sensation in his legs and reached out to brace himself on the door-jam, but he missed and would have fallen to the floor if someone hadn't caught him.

A rush of cold air revived him briefly. He was being carried outside. His vision was blurred, but he could make out a large black vehicle looming in the foreground. Next, he heard the side door of the van open up to swallow him, and then he blacked out.

Portugal, 1947

16 April 1947, 4:18 a.m., Lisbon.

When he heard the front door, Konrad Zindell's eyes opened but he lay still. A gentle spring breeze wafted in through the open window and for a few moments he watched the billowing of the sheer curtains in the darkness.

Zindell switched on the lamp beside his bed and it cast a yellow glow over the furniture in the room where he had spent the last three months of his life. The most prominent piece was a large roll top desk, which regrettably, he had never had occasion to use. Opposite the desk stood an antique armoire and next to the bed were a washbasin and a pitcher.

He automatically reached out and touched the handle of the suitcase lying next to him. The voices in the other room, speaking in German, were barely audible. After hearing a soft knock he sat up and walked over to the door in his pajamas. He opened it a few inches to see a small bronze skinned woman with straight black hair that fell loosely over her shoulders. Her dark brown eyes looked back at him seriously.

"You go this morning, Konrad," the woman said.

"How long before I leave?"

"Five minutes."

Zindell went back to the bed and sat down. He brought the suitcase onto his lap, and like the dozens of times a day since he had come to Lisbon, he opened it to check its contents: two million Swiss francs.

When it was clear that the war had been lost, Zindell had fled Auschwitz and gone directly to Württemberg in Germany. Friends and relatives had prepared a little hiding place, at his request, in his hometown of Singen on the Swiss border. The U.S. Army had come through not long after he had arrived, and he was forced to stay hidden in a furnished cellar for nearly a year.

He received newspapers daily and followed closely the war crimes trials in Nürnberg, reacting to them with a mixture of fear and loathing. In October of 1946, when the executions took place, Zindell decided he would have to leave Germany. His relatives made inquiries on his behalf and located a German dentist named Gerhardt Meissner, living in Lisbon. Meissner mailed his passport to Zindell who, with the help of some friends, disguised himself to look like the passport photo and hopped on a plane for Lisbon.

That had been in January and it had taken this long to arrange safe passage to Brazil. Zindell regretted having to leave Meissner and his Portuguese wife Tereza. They had been very congenial hosts and they had also done a tremendous amount of work on his behalf. Every night since his arrival, one or both of them had gone down to the docks to see if they could get him onboard one of the cargo ships bound for South America. And every night Zindell would go to sleep anticipating the knock on his door that would tell him they had finally succeeded.

He washed and dressed quickly, packing a couple of shirts and an extra pair of trousers in his suitcase. When he heard another soft knock, he pulled two bundles of francs from his case, five thousand each, and placed them on the bureau. He knew the Meissners would never accept the money were he to offer it to them directly. Then he snapped the locks shut, swung the case to his side and opened the door.

Tereza Meissner took his free arm and led him down the stairs to the front door.

"We're going to be sorry to see you leave, Konrad."

He smiled. "I'm going to miss you both very much. You have been so nice to me. I am eternally in your debt."

She stood on her toes and kissed Zindell on the cheek. "Gerhardt's waiting for you in the car. He'll take you to the shipyard." She opened the door form him, taking his hand and squeezing it as he passed through.

"Good luck."

"Thank you."

Meissner's black Mercedes convertible idled in the darkness and Zindell climbed in. He kept the suitcase on his lap and rested his arms on it while Meissner pulled out. The air was warm and the traffic light as they made their way though the sleeping city. Both men were silent.

The drive through early-morning Lisbon was extremely quiet until they approached the *Santo Amaro* dock. Ships' bells and whistles accompanied the noisy auction of fishermen selling to local wholesalers. Good cover, thought Zindell, but the smell is awful.

"Do you still have my passport?" Meissner asked.

"Yes," said Zindell, putting a hand to his breast pocket. "I will send it back to you as soon as I arrive. I don't know how to thank you enough, Gerhardt."

"You can thank me by not getting caught."

Meissner pulled to a stop and both men stepped out of the car, Zindell clutching his suitcase.

"The captain ran guns for Franco and helped locate targets for our U-Boats during the war. He agreed to take payment in Swiss francs. That's the ship over there," Meissner said, pointing to a battle-gray merchant ship. "It's called the *Espírito da Água*. Here's the letter that will get you onboard."

He handed Zindell a letter from the ship's captain, which Zindell pocketed. After the two men shook hands Zindell headed for the ship. He presented his letter to the sailor at the bottom of the gangway and after several minutes he was allowed on deck where another sailor escorted him to the captain's quarters. The sailor knocked on the door and left Zindell.

The man who answered the door was big and bearded. He had a barrel chest and black, pinpoint eyes. For a moment Zindell didn't know whether he had the right man or not, until a smile lit up the man's face.

"Come in," the captain said in German, and Zindell was instantly put at ease.

Two furry paws engulfed Zindell's right hand and pumped his arm and then he was offered a seat. Money was exchanged, drink offered and refused and then Zindell was shown to his private chambers, personally, by the captain himself.

"We will be leaving at dawn, *Herr Doktor*. If you need anything at all, don't hesitate to ask one of my crew."

Zindell nodded and entered his tiny room, containing a single bed with a night table beside it, both bolted to the floor. After he walked over to the table and switched on the lamp, Zindell turned and closed the door. Then he sat down on the bed, pulled the suitcase onto his lap, and began to count his remaining money.

Chapter Two

1. Monday, October 15, 1990, 10:33 p.m., Seattle.

The high A-note screamed into the microphone from the horn, soaring over the loose vamping of the band. That was followed by a deft chromatic run as the sax player drifted effortlessly into the next chord change, and after a few more flourishes, he settled into a riff along with the rest of the group as the singer belted out the next verse of "Further On Up the Road."

Janet Newell was sitting at a scarred wooden table in the Owl Café in Ballard. Monday night was Blues Nite, open mic. After an opening set played by a host band, anyone who wanted to could jump up onstage and jam. She eyed the sax player as he blew a rhythm line behind an embarrassing guitar solo, and smiled. His hair was long and dark, pulled back in a ponytail. He wore blue jeans, tight in all the right places, and a black jacket, sleeves rolled up to his elbows, matching the black tie that hung down in front of his red shirt.

But the face—that was the real draw. He had dark eyebrows that met above his nose, brown eyes that made her want to tear his clothes off every time he looked at her, and large, full lips that, when he kissed her, made her want to rip off her own clothes as well. He stood with his legs slightly apart, moving the saxophone back and forth between them as he played, and she imagined herself as the horn, being articulated with is long slender fingers, a virtuoso performance with her as his instrument.

When the last song of the set was finally over she caught the waitress's eye and by the time Steve Raymond had packed up his horn and arrived at her table, she had a cold Heineken waiting for him and a Ballard bitter in her own hand.

"What did you think?" he said, wiping the sweat off his forehead with his bare forearm.

"I thought the lead guitarist was weak."

"No, I mean about me."

She laughed and the leaned over to him, feeling the heat of his exertion as they kissed. "You were wonderful, as always."

"You really think so?"

"Of course."

"You're not just saying that because I take you places no woman has ever gone before."

Janet barely managed to keep from laughing and then kissed him again. He leaned back in his chair and took a long pull of Heineken, and she watched a bead of sweat run down his cheek, barely resisting the urge to reach over and wipe it off.

The Owl was one of the oldest bars in Seattle and the room was long and narrow, full of smoke and loud talk, not to mention B.B. King blaring from the stereo between sets.

"How was school today?" she asked.

"A real bitch. I swear to God, Houseman's class is gonna kill me."

"Which one is that?"

"Biochemistry." He titled his head back, sliding off the elastic band that held his hair and shaking it out. Then he took another drink of his beer. "I'm exhausted," he said through a yawn.

"Me, too. We should get home. You have school tomorrow and I have work."

Steve turned to her, serious. "You're still coming over tonight, aren't you?"

"Of course," she said, and he relaxed and finished off the bottle. Janet had only taken a couple of sips from hers, but she was through. The only thing she wanted tonight was Steve.

They both stood up and Steve slung his black leather saxophone case over his shoulder, putting his arm around Janet as they walked back to the entrance. She pulled him tight to her body and felt familiar surge of excitement. His dad better not be home tonight, she thought.

Before they reached the door Steve stopped to talk with the drummer for a minute and then they left. He was happy and smiling as they made their way down the block; he was always *up* after he played.

He let out a long sigh and she reached up beneath his hair to massage the back of his neck. He moaned and pulled her closer to him, and when she turned to look at him he was smiling.

"Thanks for coming tonight," he said. "I always seem to play better when you're watching."

"You know I always love watching you," she said, and he giggled in a way that made her laugh in spite of herself. When they reached the truck, he unlocked the doors and they headed for Steve's house.

Steve was a regular at the Owl's Monday-night jam session, and that was where Janet had first met him. Her previous boyfriend—one of the associates at the law firm in Bellevue where she worked—had been a blues nut and taken her around every hot spot in Seattle. One Monday they happened to be in the Owl while Steve was sitting with the host band and she made very definite eye contact with him all night. Nothing had happened then, but the very next Monday she found herself down at the Owl . . . alone.

That second Monday she made a pleasant discovery about something she had in common with Steve Raymond. Each of them seemed to have an intense physical attraction for the other. It wasn't long before they were very much a couple. That had been three years ago.

She had been blown away to find out he was majoring in premed, and that his father was a big doctor in town. She had just moved over from Missoula after graduating from Montana State, and was working as a paralegal, toying with the idea of going to law school.

Steve slid his hand between Janet's legs and squeezed her thigh. She liked his truck because it didn't have bucket seats and she could sit next to him. She put her hand on his, leaned her head on his shoulder and yawned herself.

They had been driving through town in silence when Steve said, "I wish we could live together."

"I do, too. But I barely have enough money for rent without another mouth to feed." She smiled at him apologetically and he shook his head. It was an old discussion, and as much as it pained her there was just no way around it.

"I know," he said, resigned. "And there's no way I can ask my dad to help us out when I can stay home for free while I'm going to school."

Janet lifted her face and kissed him on the cheek. "I'm sorry. I love you, though."

Steve pulled his hand out, putting his arm across her shoulder and hugging her tightly. "I love you, too."

As he held the wheel in his left hand and Janet in his right, they pulled onto the freeway and then drove across the 520 floating bridge in silence to Medina.

Steve nosed the pickup around Janet's car and into the carport alongside the empty space where his father usually parked. Excellent, he thought. Even when his father was home they could still go into Steve's room and shut the door, but it wasn't quite the same as having the place to themselves. And Janet's Bellevue apartment? It seemed as if her roommate was *always* there. When Steve thought about it, he couldn't remember ever being over there when she wasn't.

"Where's your dad tonight?" Janet asked as Steve unlocked the door.

"Who knows?"

He flipped on the lights and they walked in. After setting his saxophone on the couch, Steve walked over to the table.

"What's that?" Janet said.

He turned to her. "Just the mail. Looks like Dad's come and gone already."

"The mail can wait," she said, taking his free hand and hauling him toward the stairs. He had just enough time to flip the envelopes onto the kitchen counter before they ran together up the stairs toward his bedroom. Just as they reached his doorway, he picked her up and threw her onto his double bed with familiar abandon.

Janet made herself comfortable while Steve put on a Charlie Parker CD, *Bird with Strings*. The only passion that even approached what he felt for Janet was jazz, and for Steve it was a bitter irony, because if someone had put a gun to his head and told him to play some jazz on his sax, they'd just have to go right ahead and shoot him. He couldn't play a lick.

Oh, he was fine at blues and there were lots of people who were impressed with his playing. But inside, he knew that if the song had more than four or five chords, he was in trouble. For a while Janet had tried to get him to go into music full-time. He knew that it would never happen, though. He lacked the talent and the inclination, and besides, he was really enjoying medical school.

The slow strains of "April in Paris" came drifting out of the speakers as Steve pulled off his jacket and tie and began to unbutton his shirt. Janet had shoulder-length brown hair—though his was longer, he thought with some amusement—smooth white skin, her face beautifully void of makeup, and blue eyes. But they weren't just any blue eyes; they were so blue as to border on luminescence. They caught his attention from any room he was playing, no matter how dark or crowded it was.

He was toeing off his shoes when she suddenly sat up on the bed. She walked over to him on her knees, and when she put her arms around him, he allowed her to bring him down beside her.

Slowly, they undressed each other. Steve ran his hand through her hair and kissed her face. When he couldn't stand it anymore he pulled back the covers and they climbed inside together. Their bodies responded to each other, overriding the fatigue of the late hour.

As they made love, Steve pushed himself up so he could look at Janet in the soft glow of the night-table lamp, his hair hanging down and framing her face. She smiled at him and ran her hands over his chest. Then their breathing began to quicken along with their movements until both of them had been satiated.

Steve lay heavily next to Janet for a minute or so, feeling the elevated beating of his heart against her side. Then he rolled off of her arm onto his back and sang along with Charlie Parker as he played an intricate passage in "If I Should Lose You." Janet brought her leg up over his stomach and lay her head on his shoulder as they rested, occasionally running her hand across his chest.

When the song was over she laid in his arms for the next hour, and he drifted off to sleep on occasion until the CD ended and she pushed herself up on her elbow to kiss him. "I have to go," she said, though the reluctance was evident in her voice.

"Can't you stay the night? Dad probably won't be home until after we're gone in the morning."

"I'd love to, Steve, but I have to get some sleep. It's already after twelve and, well . . ." Janet looked into his eyes and hugged him. "We both need to get some sleep, and I just don't think we would if I stayed."

Steve yawned and nodded in disappointment. "Yeah, I know you're right. I just can't help myself."

Janet slipped out of bed and went to the bathroom while Steve shrugged on his robe. When she was finished dressing they walked downstairs, each with an arm around the other.

"I'll see you tomorrow," she said when they reached the door.

Steve nodded and slid his hands down her back, pressing her body against his. For a long time they kissed each other good-bye and then Steve watched Janet get into her car and pull out of the driveway. He waited until she was out of sight before he shut the door, and walked back upstairs.

When he reached the top landing he stopped, then turned and went into his parents' room and stood at the foot of their bed. There were times, especially right after Janet had left, when he would think about his mother. Suddenly he felt empty. His sense of being alone was always more acute when his father was on call at night, too. But tonight it seemed stronger than ever.

He stood still, letting the emptiness seep into him. A minute, two, maybe more. And then he was suddenly aware of being very tired. He turned and trudged back down the hallway, climbed into the empty bed where he had just made love to Janet, and fell asleep sooner than he would have expected.

2. Tuesday, 6:40 a.m.

On his way out the next morning Steve looked in his father's room and confirmed that he hadn't been home the night before. He picked up the mail off the kitchen floor and leafed through it over a glass of orange juice and then left for school.

Steve Raymond cut a distinctive figure as he strode through the long corridor that connected Maynard Medical School with the Bay Med Hospital. His standard uniform—white tennis shoes, Levi's, flannel shirt, and ankle length black canvas jacket—was topped off by the ponytail and a small earring. The first year was just classwork anyway; he wouldn't have to don the white jacket and become one of the homogenate until the clinical work during his second year.

The Elliott Bay Medical Center was a sprawling conglomerate of buildings located in Seattle's Magnolia district, overlooking Discovery Park, the Port of Seattle, and Puget Sound. The Maynard School of Medicine, a private facility named after one of Seattle's founders, was only one of the center's many adjuncts.

Later in the day, after Steve had finished lunch, he decided to stop by the clinic and talk to his dad before heading over to the medical school library. The Maynard library wasn't as extensive as the one at the University of Washington, but it was sure better than the collection of out-of-date tomes his dad kept around the house.

Steve would actually have preferred to attend the UW medical school, but one of the perks that came with Paul Raymond's position at Bay Med was a free ride through Maynard for any of his kids. The financial savings were too good for even a doctor to pass up, and so Maynard was where Steve and his father had decided he should enroll.

When he reached the neurosurgery clinic, Rita was away from her desk, and he walked into the office unannounced. His dad wasn't there, so Steve jotted down a note and left it in the middle of the desk.

As he opened the door to leave, however, not only had Rita returned but Demi, decked out in her scrubs, was there as well. The looks on their faces almost made him laugh. "Steve!" they yelled in unison.

"What's the matter with you two? You look like you've seen a ghost."

The phone rang and Rita picked it up, still looking wide-eyed at Steve, while Demi rushed over to him.

Demi had sloe-black eyes that were large and round, an olive complexion, and dark hair. Over the past several years she and her husband had become good friends with Steve's family and he liked her a lot.

"Where is your father?" she asked.

"I don't know—why?"

"I called the house when he didn't show up for his seven o'clock but there was no answer, I thought he might have forgotten. He's never missed an operation before."

"Are you serious? He didn't come home last night. I just figured he was on call or had a late case. What about Rita—does she know anything?"

Demi shook her head. "No, apparently he left here last night about eight o' clock and nobody's heard from him since."

Steve felt a swell of fear rising in him. "That's weird, but he's gotta be somewhere."

Rita interrupted. "They need you back in the OR, Demi."

"Okay," she said, waving. "I gotta go now. But when you see him will you tell him that I have to talk to him right away?"

"Sure," he said distractedly.

"Thanks, Steve," said Demi, turning and heading for the OR.

Steve talked to Rita for the next few minutes and she gave him the same story Demi had. Afterward, he walked slowly back toward school wondering where his father could be. He had been home last night—the mail on the table confirmed it—so he must have left shortly after. But if he wasn't coming back to the hospital, why hadn't he left a message?

Steve checked his watch. He was going to be late for his afternoon class, but he couldn't afford to miss it. As he ran back down the hall toward the medical school, his coat trailing behind him like a cape, he couldn't shake the feeling that something had happened to his father.

After class, Steve was sitting in the library trying to study but he found it difficult to concentrate. Finally he left and went back up to his dad's office. It wasn't big—there was just enough room for a desk and his computer—but every wall was lined with shelves. Medical and other textbooks, papers, trophies, plaques, pictures of Steve and his sisters, mementos, and twenty years' worth of medical research were piled to the ceiling.

It felt good to be there. The big leather chair squeaked when he rocked back to survey the oak table that his dad used for a desk. It, too, was piled with papers and books, reminders, notes, old x-rays, and piles of fanfold computer printouts. It was fascinating for him to observe his father's life in this way.

Steve picked up the phone and dialed the number of the mobile phone in the Porsche and when there was no answer tried the pager, but without success. On a whim he called the house but there was no answer there either. Finally, he called Janet.

They met that night in the cafeteria at about 6:30.

"He didn't come home last night at all?"

"No," said Steve. "And I've got this weird feeling that maybe something's happened to him. I just can't figure out why no one knows where he is."

"Did he say anything about going out of town?"

"No. Besides, Rita makes all his travel arrangements. She says he has a convention next month, around Thanksgiving, but that's it."

When Janet took his hands in hers, he realized how preoccupied he'd been. He'd only given her a peck when he'd first seen her. Now he kissed her full on the lips. "He'll be back," she said.

"Yeah, I know. But the thing is, if something is wrong and I find out I waited too long to do anything about it, I'll never forgive myself."

"Sure, but what can you do?"

"The only thing I can think of is going to the police. Maybe they can watch for his car or something, or put out an APB."

"Steve, the police can't do anything until he's been gone for forty-eight hours."

"I don't care. I can't just sit around and wait."

"I know, but they won't start looking around until he's been missing for two days."

"This is different. I'll just explain it to them."

"But they can't—"

"They'd better. It's their fucking job!" Steve pulled his hands away from Janet's and stared down at the table. She was probably right—Janet knew more about the law than he did—but that wasn't the point. Didn't she realize that he needed to do this? Even if the police rebuffed him he would feel better for having tried. When Steve had lost his mom, part of himself had gone with her. He couldn't bear to lose his dad, too.

Janet reached over and took his hand and he looked up into her eyes. "Steve?"

"What?" he said, his anger completely gone.

"Let's go talk to the police."

They drove to the Magnolia precinct together in Steve's truck. After they had explained things to the desk sergeant he took them into the squad room and had them wait. A few minutes later a man in a baggy brown suit and scuffed shoes walked over and introduced himself.

"I'm Detective Lasky. Will you please follow me?"

Lasky led them through a maze of cluttered desks and talking people. When he finally stopped he pulled out a chair behind one of the desks and sat down, motioning for them to take the seats next to his desk.

"The sergeant tells me that you think your father is missing. Is that right?"

"Yes."

"When was the last time you saw him?"

Steve looked over at Janet, who was holding his hand. She gave him a squeeze and he turned back to the detective. "I haven't seen him since yesterday morning, but he was last seen about eight o'clock last night."

Lasky leaned back in his chair and rubbed the shadow on his chin. "You realize that it hasn't even been twenty-four hours yet, don't you?"

Steve nodded.

"I can't file a missing persons report until at leas forty-eight hours after he was last seen. What makes you think he's missing?"

"He's a neurosurgeon," Steve said, trying to keep his composure. "He's missed all of his surgeries today, and he would never do that. People depend on him."

Lasky nodded. "Anything else?"

"Little things, mostly . . ." and Steve began to relate to the detective all of the incidents that had bothered him: the mail, the unsuccessful phone calls and his talks with Rita and Demi.

Lasky was silent for a moment, as if digesting the information. For a while his head bobbed slightly and he began to rub his chin again. Steve looked over at Janet and she shrugged. At last the detective sat up in his chair, ready to speak, leaning forward with both forearms resting against the edge of his desk.

"There are a lot of reasons why we have to wait a couple of days before we file the report, and for the most part they're valid reasons. But that doesn't help you any and I realize that. Now, while I can't officially open up an investigation until the forty-eight hours have passed, I'll tell you what I *can* do. Why don't we go ahead and take your statement; that way if you don't hear from him by tomorrow night you can give me a call and I can start the ball rolling. Okay?"

"Yes. Thank you very much. That would be great."

3. Friday, 9:50 a.m.

Over the next two days Steve found himself in his father's office more often than not. Most of the time he would just sit in the big leather chair hoping that his dad would walk into the room and put an end to his worry. By now the police had begun to investigate. They had questioned Demi and Rita and some of the other hospital staff, but it really looked as if his father had simply disappeared.

Meanwhile Steve just sat. Sometimes he would dial the phone, and often felt like throwing it against the wall because there was never an answer. The rest of the time he spent sifting through his father's papers. He didn't really know what he was looking for, only that he hoped to find some kind of clue that would tell him where in the hell his dad had gone.

It was on this latest occasion that he came across the letter. He had missed it before because it had been crumpled up in a ball in the wastepaper basket beneath the desk and he hadn't been desperate enough to go looking through it until today. Steve smoothed it out and read it.

Dear Paul,

Hey, it's been a long time. How've you been? Well, so much for small talk. Listen, let me just get right to the point. I'm in a bit of a sticky situation (but what else is new?) and I really need your help. I know you don't have any reason to help me after what happened, but I'm desperate. You're the only one I can turn to.

The truth is I'm sick, Paul, and without someone I can trust to operate on me, I'm going to die. Now before you toss this letter in the garbage and say it serves me right, please hear me out. I'm doing some good work up here. I'm trying to make things right and if I succeed I'll have the cash to do it. But right now it's going to depend a lot on you.

Please don't let me die, Paul. You're a better man than that. You've proven it already. I know you don't respect me, but I've lost any use I had for respect and now I'm begging you. Please call me at the number above. If I don't hear from you in a week I'll assume that the answer is no, but in the meantime I'll pray to God it's yes. Please help me, Paul. You're my only hope now.

        –Howard

Who was Howard? The name didn't mean anything to Steve, but it was evident from the familiar tone that the writer knew his father. Apparently the guy was a Canadian, because the letterhead was from a place called the Columbia Institute for Neurological Research in British Columbia. This Howard might even be a doctor.

Steve wracked his brain for a moment to see if he could scare up a reference to the name somewhere in his subconscious. Nothing. He looked around the room for some kind of directory of doctors that could tell him who this Howard might be. He came upon a huge book about three inches thick that said National Physician's Listing on the spine. He opened it eagerly but was disappointed to find that it was only a listing of specialists, and then just for the state of Washington. Dejectedly, he slid the volume back into place wondering if there was such a listing for British Columbia. But without a last name, even that wouldn't do him any good.

Steve folded the letter up and put it in his coat pocket. He had a seminar to attend today and he didn't want to be late. Coincidently enough, the seminar was on neurology, his father's specialty.

It was near capacity in the 200-seat lecture hall and Steve had to work his way to a seat in the middle of the row. The doctor began with a couple of humorous anecdotes before launching into his lecture. Steve had trouble concentrating and finally put away his notes, not wanting to continue the charade of paying attention any longer.

Down at the lectern the doctor had settled into a comfortable monotone and was rattling off a long list of drugs used to treat brain disorders, commenting occasionally on the people who had developed them. Basic stuff; it was all in textbooks.

". . . used extensively even now. In the past decade several promising drugs have been proven to be totally ineffective in treating various disorders. One of them, a chemical known as uradrine, was even proven to be deadly. It was developed by a Dr. H.L. Phillips two years ago for use as . . ."

Now *that* was a name Steve remembered. His dad had had worked with Dr. Phillips back east, but he moved the whole family to Seattle in 1976 just as Phillips was beginning his work on an antipsychotic drug called uradrine. As far as Steve was concerned, it was the smartest move his dad had ever made.

Unlike similar drugs that could bring about movement disorders, uradrine had no apparent side effects during the testing phase, and there was talk of Philips winning a Nobel Prize. But just as it was about to be approved by the food and Drug Administration, one of his test subjects died, and the FDA temporarily suspended the testing of the drug. Phillips was outraged. He argued that the drug couldn't have been the cause of death, but in his push to overturn the suspension he alienated a few too many people.

The results of the autopsy determined that the uradrine had accumulated in the brainstem and had ultimately been the cause of death. Phillips lost his research grants and was summarily fired from John Hopkins. Lawsuits were filed in rapid succession but by that time Phillips had dropped out of sight, and over the next two years every patient who had been treated with uradrine died.

". . . similar to the way chlorpromazine mimics dopamine in occupying special receptors . . ."

Steve was bored; his mind was still churning over the letter. He took it out of his pocket and read it again, this time paying close attention to every word. When he reached the end his head had suddenly jerked up. "That's it," he breathed and bolted out of his seat. He waded through a sea of legs and when he reached the aisle he ran for the door, disregarding the stares of everyone in the lecture hall.

Steve ran almost the entire way to his father's office and then had to wait for a few minutes until Rita finished talking with one of the other nurses. Finally she came over to him.

"Hi, Steve."

"Rita, is there any way to look up the name of a doctor?"

"Sure, what's the name?"

"Phillips."

She wrote it down. "First name?"

"That's what I'm trying to find out."

She raised her eyebrows at this. "Do you realize how many—"

"I've got first initials. H. L."

Rita wrote them down and then walked back toward his father's office. "Come on," she said. "We'll have to use your dad's PC. The terminals out here are only hooked up to the mainframe." They walked into the office together and she sat down at the desk and turned on the computer. "Any word yet?"

Steve shook his head while Rita dialed the phone and placed the receiver into the modem.

"Who are you calling?" he asked.

"The National Physician's Association has a date base with all their members listed on it. You can access information by geographical region, specialty, or name, like we're doing. If he or she is—"

"He."

"—practicing in the United States, he should be listed." The screen came to life and Rita began typing in commands.

"I don't think he's going to be a current member, though."

"How long ago are we looking at?"

"Couple of years, maybe."

"Okay, good. They have an inactive file that goes back a few years. I'll try that first." Rita went through three menus before finding what she was looking for. She typed in Phillips and then waited.

A minute later, *Phillips, Aaron*, appeared at the top of the screen, followed by a list of other doctors with the same surname. Rita scrolled down the list until she saw the initials H.L. She pulled in the membership number listed after his name and the full name appeared in green, glowing letters: *Howard Lathrop Phillips*.

"Yes!" he shouted. This must be the Howard in the letter, he thought. It had to be. The reclusive Howard Phillips, developer of the killer drug uradrine, was working in Canada and had contacted his dad less than two weeks ago. Steve was looking at the screen, but his mind was racing.

"I take it that's what you're looking for?"

"Perfect," Steve gushed. "Thanks Rita. You're amazing."

"No problem. They don't call me the master hacker for nothing."

Steve laughed and thanked Rita again as she left, then shut the door behind her. As soon as he had exited the NPA's database, he lifted the phone off the modem and dialed the number for the Columbian Institute that was printed on the letterhead of the stationary. He asked to speak with Dr. Phillips.

"I'm sorry but Dr. Phillips is unavailable," said the receptionist.

There was a pause and Steve realized that she was not going to give him any further information.

"Uh . . . could you tell me when he *will* be available?"

"I'm sorry but Dr. Phillips is very busy. Will there be anything else?"

Steve leaned back in the chair, running his hand through his hair and thinking. Getting mad now wouldn't accomplish anything.

"Well, could you at least give him a message?"

"Visiting hours are from noon to four every other Wednesday. If you wish to make an appointment you may see Dr. Phillips at that time."

"Look, I just need to talk to him for a few minutes. I'm calling long distance from Seattle. I'm sure that when he finds out who I am he—"

"I'm sorry but Dr. Phillips has left instructions not to be disturbed under any circumstances. Now, will there be anything else?"

"Yes, please tell him that Steve Raymond called. He knows my father, Dr. Paul Raymond. They worked together and I'd like to talk to him as soon as possible. My home number is 206-555-3821."

After another brief pause, during which Steve hoped that the woman was writing down the information, she spoke again.

"Will there be anything else?"

"No, thank—"

Steve heard the phone click on the other end. "Damn it," he said, slamming down the receiver.

Steve leaned back in the chair and perused the letter again. His father had been gone for three days now and it didn't look like he was coming back. His patients were already being referred to other doctors on the staff. Last night Steve had received phone calls from the other department heads, each expressing their concern. Mark White, the hospital's chief administrator, had even stopped by the house.

He leaned forward and picked up the phone again, this time calling the police department to find out how the investigation was coming. But Lasky told him that he would simply have to wait. Unless someone sighted his father, or the Porsche, there was little they could do. Lasky said he would be sure to call if there were any developments.

But the letter was still nagging at him, even after he had hung up the phone. He hadn't told Lasky about his suspicions because they seemed silly. It was inconceivable that his father would go off to British Columbia without telling anyone, especially leaving his patients unattended. And still . . . No, there had to be some other explanation.

Maybe Phillips didn't want anyone to know that he was in Canada and had asked his father not to tell anyone where he was going. But that didn't fit either; Dad would have had told somebody about the trip. Still, if Steve could just talk to Phillips, at least it would rule out that possibility.

Steve didn't have any afternoon classes Friday and decided to head on home. He picked up his backpack from the floor and slung it over his shoulder. On the way out he stopped in the doorway to look back into his father's office, his finger resting for a moment on the light switch. Numbly he let his hand fall, turning off the lights, and closed the door behind him.

4. 3:19 p.m.

After an hour of sitting at the dining room table and staring off into space, it was clear to Steve that he was not going to get any studying done. By now he had virtually memorized the contents of the letter. He had half-considered going up to the Columbia Institute in person if it was the only way he could talk to Phillips, but strangely, the letterhead contained the phone number but no address. He would have called information, but didn't know how to go about getting a Canadian operator. Finally he decided to call the Institute again.

The same woman answered the phone and Steve gave his name.

"How may I help you, Mr. Raymond?"

"I called earlier today, about talking to Dr. Phillips—"

"I'm sorry but Dr. Phillips is unavailable." Again the statement was followed by silence.

"Yes, I realize that, but I would like to set up an appointment to see him."

"Visiting hours are from noon to four every other Wednesday."

"Yes, I'm aware of that," said Steve, no longer hiding his exasperation. "But I really need to see him as soon as possible. Could I schedule an appointment with him this weekend?"

"Dr. Phillips doesn't make individual appointments. You may see him during visiting hours next Wednesday. Will there be anything else?"

"Yes," Steve almost yelled into the receiver, barely able to restrain himself. "How do I get to the Institute?"

"Just south of Telsen on Highway 86. Will there be anything else?"

"I don't think—" Once again the phone clicked at the other end, but Steve finished the sentence anyway: "—so."

Without hanging up the phone he dialed Janet.

"I don't know, Steve. If you're asking me whether I think something has happened to your father, I say yes. And that's exactly the reason I don't think he went up to that place in Canada. He would have told you. It just seems too far-fetched."

Janet had come over as soon as Steve called, and he had told her everything about the letter and Phillips. During the past few days he had felt as if things were coming unglued; his schoolwork was suffering and he couldn't seem to concentrate on anything. But talking to Janet had helped him keep it together.

The whole situation seemed unreal in a way, but there were some important decisions he had to make. Nothing had been released to the media, but Steve knew he was running out of time. He still hadn't told either of his sisters yet; he didn't want to jump the gun and send them into a panic. But now he realized that if his father didn't come home by Monday he would have to tell them.

"I'm just sick of sitting here doing nothing," he said. "I hate this. I hate just waiting."

"Do you really think we can find out anything in Canada?"

"The thing is I still don't know if he's up there or not," Steve explained. "But he could be. That's the point. I told you I wasn't able to talk to Phillips, and that receptionist . . ." Steve's stomach knotted up at the thought of her. "If Phillips has been in contact with Dad since he sent him the letter I'd like to know."

"But what if he comes back while you're gone?"

"You mean while *we're* gone." Steve paused. "I was hoping you'd come with me."

Janet smiled. "When would we go?"

"Tomorrow. It's only a few hours away. We should be back Sunday night at the latest."

"That sounds fine, but you still didn't answer me about your father."

"I'll leave a note for him in case he comes back, and I can say where we're going on the answering machine in case he calls."

"Do you think we should tell the police what we're doing?"

"No, I don't think so. I just talked to Lasky before you came over and I can call again as soon as we get back."

Janet got up from the couch and walked over to where Steve was standing. He took a step toward her and they embraced. "I love you, Steve. I want to help you find your dad."

Steve looked into her eyes. "I don't think I can do it without you."

"All right," she said. "Let's get packing."

The next morning, a few minutes after 8:30, Steve and Janet left for British Columbia. It was Saturday and traffic was relatively light. Driving north in Steve's pickup along I-5 they made good time, and reached the Canadian border at Blaine around eleven.

Brazil, 1955

21 October 1955, 12:18 p.m., Santa Catarina.

The rain came down in sheets but Konrad Zindell didn't notice. He had been trudging along in the rainforest for nearly an hour, the dense foliage breaking the wind and deflecting the sheets of rain into a uniform shower on the jungle floor. The brim of his white fedora was limp from the water running off it, and every time he looked at his watch the reservoir that had accumulated in the crown of his hat dumped down in front of him.

Just ahead of Zindell walked a native with a machete. He was clearing a path for them; the distinctive ping of the blade as it sheared through branches, fronds and vines joined in with the chorus of the jungle as it creaked and groaned under the strain of the wind and water. The native did his work silently, oblivious to the rain. Behind Zindell walked another native carrying two guns, one slung over his shoulder like a baseball bat and the other pointed at Zindell's back. Finally, mercifully, the man in front stopped. Zindell did likewise.

The man with the guns passed him and gave one of the rifles to his partner. Then they left Zindell and stepped into a small clearing. From his vantage point on the trail he spied a small wooden hut but did not move from his position. It was not because they trusted him that they had left him alone. There was no trust involved. They knew as well as Zindell that he could never find his way out of the jungle by himself. A few minutes later a gun barrel motioned to him through the brush and he followed.

The hut was only about eight feet square. Rain battered against the corrugated metal roof, the runoff cascading in a myriad of individual streams and splatting into the standing water that surrounded the aging wooden structure like a moat. Once inside Zindell unbuttoned the top of his shirt. He was soaked to the skin. The heat in the hut was oppressive and the air felt viscous and smelled of mold. He pulled out a wet handkerchief and wiped the mixture of sweat and rain from his face.

In the middle of the sagging floor stood a rickety table, a man in a white linen suit behind it. He was Brazilian, small and bald, with a dark face ravaged by pockmarks.

"Do you have the money, *Senhor*?" the little man said, smiling.

From the breast pocket of his jacket Zindell took out a huge roll of bills bound with a rubber band and tossed it onto the table.

"*Obrigado, Senhor. Muito obrigado,*" he said, still smiling.

He picked up the money and slipped it into his pants pocket without so much as looking at it.

"Where are the papers you promised?" Zindell asked.

"Patience, *Senhor.*"

From a small leather satchel strapped across his chest the man produced an Argentinian passport, birth certificate and driver's license. Zindell snatched them from his hand and carefully scrutinized each document before glaring back up at the man.

"What kind of shit is this?" Zindell said angrily, throwing the papers onto the table. "I pay you good money and this is the best you can do?"

The man looked unflinchingly into Zindell's eyes and his smile widened. "Ironic, eh, *Senhor*? I think so too."

Zindell looked again at the name on the documents that stared back at him: German Infante.

"This better not be your idea of a joke or I'll—"

"The papers are perfectly legal. I'm afraid you have no choice in the matter of names. Not only was he born at approximately the same time as you but, as you can see, this gentleman was also a physician. I believe that is what you requested."

"I don't want them," Zindell shouted. He turned and began to pace about the small hut. "I want you to find some other papers."

The little man remained calm while Zindell vented his anger, then said, "I don't know how long you have been looking for papers, *Senhor*, but it took me six months to find these. It could take much longer the next time. And of course the price will be higher accordingly."

"I said I didn't want these!"

Instantly, all traces of the smile vanished from the little man's face. "I don't give refunds, *Senhor*. I'm afraid there is nothing further I can do for you today. If you wish to engage my services again you know how I can be contacted."

He walked around the table and was heading out into the rain when Zindell grabbed him by the lapels of his immaculate jacket. Their eyes locked. But Zindell had heard the sound of rifle bolts being pulled back, so he took a breath and let go. "I don't think you realize who you're dealing with," he said through clenched teeth.

The little man recovered quickly and straightened his lapels.

"No, *Senhor*, I do not know who I am dealing with and I like to keep it that way. The only thing I am interested in is your money. You ask for papers and I provide them."

He took a step closer to Zindell.

"No, *Senhor*, I think you should understand who *you* are dealing with.

These men who brought you out here, they work for me, no? If I tell them to kill you now, they kill you. If I tell them to leave you, they leave you. Do you think you could find your way back on your own? How long do you think you would last out here in the jungle?"

Zindell pursed his lips but didn't answer.

"My best guess, and this is only a guess, *Senhor*, is that you would be dead by nightfall." The smile reappeared. "Now, would you like my men to escort you out of the jungle or would you prefer to find your own way?"

Zindell balled up his fists as tight as they would go, then relaxed and turned around. Taking a plastic bag from his pocket, he gathered up the papers from the table, placed them in the bag and put it into his coat pocket. Then he watched as the little man stepped into the rain and disappeared into the jungle. A few minutes later, walking between his armed guides, Zindell headed back to civilization, to Argentina, and to a new life as Dr. German Infante.

Chapter Three

**1. Saturday, October 20, 1990, 7:42 a.m.,
Blaine, Washington.**

Steve looked impatiently at the Peace Arch as he and Janet
sat in line at customs. The unguarded border symbolized the
friendship and trust between the United States and Canada,
but each country still had border stations to check for drugs
and monitor travel.

They were lucky that day. While other motorists were
giving guided tours of their trunks and glove compartments
to the customs officials, Steve and Janet had only to answer
a few questions: why they were going into Canada; how long
they were staying; what, if anything, they were bringing back
with them. Though he didn't say it, Steve hoped the answer to
the last question would be his father.

It was a beautiful day. The sun had broken through the
clouds and when the cab of the truck began to get warm Steve
rolled down his window. They were traveling north up Highway
99 toward Vancouver. He and Janet didn't talk much along the

way; a Ray Brown Trio tape was playing, and they were content to listen and watch the scenery roll by.

They stopped for lunch in Vancouver and had a terrific meal at a little restaurant called Nam. It was there that Steve encountered a major oversight on his part: he had forgotten to get any Canadian currency. The woman who waited on them was very nice; she made the exchange for Steve's U.S. currency and he and Janet continued on their way.

They drove into Telsen at dusk, having been unable to find the Institute on the way there. Steve pulled the truck into an Esso station and while he was pumping gas an old man, who had to be at least eighty-five, came over wiping oil from his hands. His hair was a dingy gray but Steve couldn't tell if it was his natural color or if it was dirty from working beneath cars all day. He guessed the latter. The man was wearing blue coveralls, oil stained and grease spotted. A dirty white oval patch on the front of the coveralls had "Pete" scrolled on it in red embroidery. Pete glanced at the Washington license plate on Steve's truck before stuffing a corner of the rag in his back pocket, leaving the rest hanging out like a tail.

"Up here visiting, eh?"

Steve nodded, his hand still squeezing the handle of the gas nozzle. "Yeah, I guess you could say that. I wonder if you could help us out. We're looking for a place called the Columbia Institute. It was supposed to be on the freeway coming up here but I guess we missed it."

The old man reached up and scratched the three-day growth of white bristle on his chin and then ran his hand around to rub the back of his neck. "What kind of business you got out there, eh?"

Just then the nozzle in Steve's hand clicked off. He topped off the tank and set the nozzle back on the pump. As he was replacing the gas cap the old man continued.

"You don't look like a doctor."

Steve glanced at Janet who was sitting in the cab but could still hear every word through the open window. She shrugged. He turned back to the old man.

"No, I'm a medical student from Seattle. I thought it would be interesting to take a tour of their research facility."

"Visitin' days are Wednesdays. Watcha doin' here on a weekend?"

Steve reached into his pocket for a ten-dollar bill when he remembered that all he had was U.S. currency. "Do you take credit cards?"

The man nodded.

Steve pulled out his wallet and checked the back of all his gas cards for the one with the tiny Esso sign and handed it to Pete. The old man reached out a bony hand and took it but did not move otherwise, presumably waiting for an answer. He pulled the oily rag from his back pocket and wiped his wrinkled brow, leaving a greasy smudge across his forehead, then replaced it.

"Look," Steve finally said, "I'm just trying to get to the Columbia Institute. Do you know how to get there or don't you?"

"Yeah," the old man blurted out, "I know how to get there." He backed away a few steps and then turned. Waving Steve's gas card in the air he said, "I'll be right back."

Steve climbed back into the cab of the truck as the man walked away.

"What was *that* all about?" asked Janet.

"I don't know. The guy's just old, I guess."

When Pete returned he was with a younger man, perhaps in his mid-thirties. He had long, stringy, shoulder-length hair and was wearing a baseball cap turned backward, a white T-shirt and baggy overalls. He shuffled along and stood behind Pete as he had Steve sign the charge slip; then he spoke.

"So, Pete tells me you two are looking for the Columbia Institute, eh?"

"That's right. Do you know how we can get there?"

"Passed right by it on the way in," the younger man said pointing in the direction that Steve and Janet had just come from.

"I didn't see the sign," said Steve.

"Ain't no sign," said the old man as he tore off the top sheet and handed it back to Steve.

"When I called, the woman at the Institute told me that it was right on the way."

The two men looked at each other and smiled. The younger one looked back at Steve. "That's what the woman told you, eh?"

Steve had had enough and he started the engine. "Back this way?" he asked with a quick motion of his hand.

The smiles left the faces of the two men. The younger one spoke. "Watch your odometer," he said. "It's almost exactly 12 kilometers from the city limits." Steve looked with a frown at his odometer trying to remember the conversion for kilometers to miles. "When you've gone about that far it'll be the only turn-off to your right. No light, no sign, just a cement road." Cement was pronounced sea-ment.

"Thanks," said Steve, and he shifted the truck into gear. The two men stepped back as he sped out of the station heading south down Highway 86.

Steve did some quick calculations in his head and figured that the distance to the Institute must be around seven and a half miles. After they reached seven miles he pulled over to let the cars behind him pass and then slowly, carefully watching to the right, drove the next half-mile. Then they found it.

It was just as the younger gas station attendant had said: a tiny slab of concrete that reached out to touch the highway. Steve turned onto the road. A dense wood on both sides made it so dark that he was forced to turn on the headlights. "This must be it," he said.

"It's getting kind of late, isn't it?" Janet asked with concern.

"It shouldn't take too long," he answered, wondering if Phillips would even be there on a weekend.

They had driven close to two miles down the tiny winding road and Steve was beginning to wonder if the attendant had lied to them, when they finally came upon a clearing. He slowed the truck to a stop. Straight ahead was a huge chain-link fence about twelve feet high, barbed wire strung at forty-five-degree angles and forming a V at the top. The woods ended abruptly ten feet in front of the fence and the meadow continued up to it and over a grassy knoll on the other side.

The pavement widened considerably at what Steve assumed to be an electronically controlled gate. There were two video cameras that he could see, one mounted on each side of the gate above what looked to be two-way speakers. There were no signs indicating where he and Janet were, nor did there appear to be any type of buzzer on the speaker. But Steve pulled up to it anyway, rolled down his window and waited.

Instantly a thin, reedy, female voice squawked from the speaker: "Deliveries are every other Friday." A loud hiss filled the space vacated by the voice, which for a moment had reminded Steve of the woman on the phone.

"Uh . . . is this the Columbia Institute?"

"Yes," barked the voice.

"I'm here to see Dr. Phillips."

"Dr. Phillips is unavailable. Will there be anything else?" Her words eradicated any lingering doubt in Steve's mind about who she was.

"I have an appointment," he lied. "I believe Dr. Phillips will see me at once if he—"

"Visiting days are every other Wednesday."

"No shit," Steve blurted out, unable to control his pent-up frustration. He turned when he felt Janet's hand on his. She squeezed but the anger remained and he didn't look at her.

"Will there be anything else?" said the voice.

Before Steve had a chance to answer he heard a loud click and the hiss was gone.

"Let's go back to town," Janet offered.

Steve turned to her. He remained silent and contemplated her as he held her hand. She was wearing one of his white cotton shirts with a jean jacket over the top, Levi's, and penny-loafers. On the hand he held he could feel the ring he had given her last summer, the only adornment she allowed herself. He had never seen her wear so much as earrings or a bracelet in the four years they had been together. Her wavy, shoulder-length brown hair hung loose around her neck. When her eyes finally met his he leaned over and kissed her. She really was a beautiful woman.

"Listen," he said. "Did you bring any other shoes?"

"A pair of sneakers," she answered, eyebrows wrinkled in puzzlement.

"I want to check this place out. I bet if we walk along the fence a ways we might be able to see something."

"Like what? It's dark out already."

"I don't know. We drove all the way out here; I just wanted to check the place out."

Steve put the truck in reverse and let out the clutch a little too quickly. They lurched backwards and Janet's hands shot out to brace herself against the dashboard.

"Sorry," Steve said.

"Just take it easy, okay?"

Steve nodded. After he had backed up far enough that the cameras wouldn't see him, Steve eased into the brush that abutted the pavement. The driver's side was still three feet out onto the road but he didn't plan on staying here long enough for it to matter.

"What are we doing?"

"Just going to take a quick look, okay? Why don't you put on your tennis shoes?"

Janet was shaking her head. "I don't really want to. Can I stay here?"

"Sure. Just wait in the truck and I'll be right back," he said climbing out. Instinctively he looked both ways and then ran into the brush on the other side of the road.

He knew he must be on the northeast corner of the . . . compound. That was the only way he could think of to describe it. He couldn't even begin to speculate on what kind if research would require this much security. There was always the risk that a drug company might try to steal a formula, but what kind of facility would need barbed wire?

The undergrowth thinned out as he drew closer to the fence. Huge fir and spruce tress, whose branches didn't even begin for a good twenty feet up their trunks, stretched to the sky. He weaved his way back to the compound. When he emerged from the woods he was about a hundred yards south of the road and out of sight of the cameras. The reason he knew the Institute had to be down this direction is because he had seen the northern section of the fence from the gate.

The rise of the knoll in front of him was about eight feet high at this point and he still couldn't see over it, but about fifty yards away it appeared to taper off. Steve ran along the fence and covered the distance in a flash.

He stopped when he could see it all.

The squat structure was roughly the shape of a sideways capital H, two buildings really, joined by a small connecting corridor. A tiny slab of parking lot guarded the front rectangular section, and a modest wooden sign, letters routed out and painted black, identified the place as The Columbia Institute for Neurological Research.

The first section was two stories high with full-length windows and glass doors at street level, no windows along the front of the upper floor. Along the side of the entire complex, though, there were long, slender, vertical windows about five feet by one foot.

The middle section was only one story high, a twenty-foot connector that joined the two buildings. His view improved as Steve continued walking.

The rear rectangular section was the largest, four stories high, with windows all around on every floor. The two main buildings were long, perhaps two hundred feet or more, but very narrow with only enough room, it appeared, for a long hallway and rooms on either side.

Steve squinted at his watch: ten to five. It was almost too dark to read the dial. He still wanted to see a little more, work his way around to the back of the complex and get the layout of the place before he came back tomorrow. But the fence never turned the corner. And the configuration of the buildings, lying at an angle from southeast to northwest, was putting him farther and farther away with every step he took.

He judged the distance from the road to be at least three hundred yards now. His heart was racing as he came up perpendicular to the rear of the building and that was when he saw it. His breathing stopped and he could practically hear his heart beating as he looked on in disbelief. He squinted in the dark but it had to be: his dad's Porsche.

"He's here."

Steve had never seriously considered that his father might be here. The truth was that he had just needed some time away from home. He had figured he would talk to Phillips, Phillips would tell him that his father had never responded to his letter, and then he and Janet would go spend the day at the beach or something. When he came home he would be a little less frazzled, a little more confident; he would call his sisters and maybe, while the investigation into his father's disappearance continued, he would be able to get his mind back on his studies.

But suddenly all of that changed. He should have been happy but something didn't feel right. His dad was here and yet he was afraid. His disappearance was all wrong, for one thing. The letter from Phillips was wrong. Why had it been balled up in the wastebasket? Steve looked up again at the barbed wire and noticed for the first time that there were actually two fences in front of him, one placed six feet inside the other.

Jesus, this whole fucking place is wrong.

He could feel his throat begin to constrict. His face was hot with blood and he was sweating all over.

Night had fallen.

Steve ran for the truck.

2. 5:02 p.m.

The longer Janet sat in the cab of the truck, the more grateful she was that Steve had wanted her to come up here with him, though she had no idea what he thought he was going to find in the woods. But that was just like him; once he got an idea in his head, you couldn't budge him.

She remembered his telling her that after graduating high school he had auditioned for a blues review that was going to Las Vegas. When they hired him, he decided to pull up stakes and move to Nevada, over his father's vehement protests. And then he wound up hating every minute of it. He finished out that summer playing, made enough to buy his truck, and drove back home. Three weeks later Steve was enrolled in premed courses at the University of Washington, and it didn't take Einstein to figure out whose idea *that* had been. But Steve insisted that giving up playing music professionally was his idea.

She had pressed him to start again when they began going out, mostly for selfish reasons, but he wouldn't budge. He said the money took all the fun out of playing. Janet, on the other hand, saw it as a way to get him out of that house, and more importantly, away from Paul. She had begged and pleaded with Steve to ask his dad if she could move in, pay full room and board and any other incidental expenses—whatever it would take for them to be together. But the one time Steve had brought it up, Paul had dismissed it out of hand. Oh, he was nice enough, but he was set in his ways—just didn't want them living together in his house. He couldn't have cared less whether they were married or not; that wasn't the point. He said it would be an irresponsible thing for them to do. They had to learn to take care of themselves and not be dependent on him for everything. Give me a break, she had thought. After a while, though, when she realized that Steve was enjoying school and was excited about becoming a doctor, she let it go.

So that was that. Steve could live at home for free as long as he was going to school, and Paul even gave him an allowance. It was laughable. Even with a roommate there were months when Janet had to borrow money from Steve. The Seattle suburb of Bellevue, while not as posh as Medina, shared a border and was a pricey little yuppy enclave that didn't cater much to the working person. As a paralegal, Janet was little more than a glorified secretary, with a salary to match. They couldn't possibly afford to live together, and it was enough to make her want to cry. No, check that. It *did* make her cry.

Before Steve there had been a few boyfriends, some okay sex, a few one-night stands, your basic college-girl love life. But with Steve . . . everything was different. He supported her in so many ways. She had never felt this solid with anyone before, and when she was with him it seemed as if she could do anything. It certainly hadn't started out that way, though. In the beginning it was just sex.

She had craved his body as much as he had hers, and the love part had to catch up a while later. When it did, though, it came hard. They loved each other fiercely, and even though they spent plenty of nights together, it wasn't enough. It was hard to believe that after this long she still wasn't living with him.

And now it seemed like a cruel joke that Paul—the man whose name she had taken in vain on innumerable occasions— was the reason behind their taking a vacation. And that was exactly what she was trying to make this little jaunt. If they found Steve's dad in the process, so much the better. They had had a really good time today and she thought that Steve had seemed a lot more relaxed. It had been a rough week for him and there had been times when she worried that he wasn't going to make it.

As angry as Janet was with Steve's father, though, she had never disliked him. On the contrary, he was very friendly and outgoing, always treating her like one of the family in his home. And over the past few days she had found the affection she felt for him growing into concern over his disappearance. She would be very glad when this whole thing was over.

It seemed to Janet that she had been sitting in the truck a long time when the glare of headlights suddenly flooded the cab, bouncing in streams off the rearview mirrors. She twisted around to see what was happening. Whatever the vehicle was, it had skidded to a stop behind her, then sat idling, high beams carving a swath into the night.

She lifted her hand up slowly and locked her door, then reached over to lock Steve's. She looked at the steering column: the keys were still there. If she had to leave for some reason, she could.

Janet looked expectantly into the woods where Steve had disappeared, trying to ignore the vehicle behind her. It must be a truck, she thought; the headlights rode higher and were bigger and brighter than a car's, making the darkness pitch black beyond the reach of the beams. She suddenly wished she had gone with Steve. If there was some kind of rule about parking along this road, she didn't want to have to move the truck and have it be gone when he got back.

Janet heard gravel being squelched under the tires as the vehicle rolled forward, and she turned her head slightly to watch its approach in the side mirror. It pulled up slowly beside her, the headlights pushing past the truck. When it stopped she could make out what it was: a black Chevy van.

3. 5:11 p.m.

Steve came bounding out of the woods breathing heavily and started across the road toward the truck. But as soon as his feet touched the cement he froze. The truck was gone.

"Janet?" he managed to croak. His first thought was that he had somehow turned himself around in the woods and was on the wrong road. But after he'd walked a few more yards the gate came into view. Steve stopped, took a few steps back and soon found himself back-pedaling away. He turned and began jogging toward the highway, his speed increasing with every step until he was sprinting as fast as he could go. His breath was coming hard now and he felt a thick sweat break out.

"Janet!" he heard himself yell.

The cool night air was tearing at his throat, and his heart was pounding against his ribs in protest. Steve's legs were burning and he kept them pumping as long as he could but he was unable to continue his frenetic pace for more than a mile and slowed down to a fast jog until he reached the highway.

When he finally stumbled out onto the shoulder his throat was raw and his lungs were on fire. Hunched over he began coughing until his body started to shake. He could feel the panic swelling inside of him, reaching up and grabbing his throat, constricting it until it felt no bigger than a pipe cleaner. He fell to his knees and then to his hands, on all fours, tightening his sphincter to keep from pissing his pants. After a few minutes he began to breathe easier.

A few cars hummed by and the presence of other people, even sheathed in their vehicles, calmed him down. "Goddamn it." The words came out shaky and scared. He pushed himself up on his knees and, with eyes closed, yelled at the top of his lungs: "JANET!" Then the dam broke; he began to weep.

Eventually he stopped crying and stood up. Not knowing what else to do, he headed back toward the Institute. The walk was good for him; it cleared his head. He felt a little embarrassed with himself for breaking down the way he had but he had been under a lot of stress over the past few days. And now with Janet gone it just sort of overwhelmed him. What the hell was happening?

Whatever it was he was going to wait it out. He wasn't going anywhere until Janet came back. Though he couldn't think of a logical explanation for why she had left he supposed there must have been one.

Wait. That was what he had to do now. Steve picked out a tree, close to where the truck had been, and parked himself at its base.

Maddeningly, the minutes inched by. The sound of the wind rustling through the trees above him was his only companion. It was lucky he had worn a down vest instead of his canvas coat. He pulled his arms tightly around himself, and while it didn't really warm him, it helped.

Where was she? Steve didn't know whether to be mad or scared. The only time he had felt lonelier was that damn summer he had spent playing in Las Vegas. His mother had died the year before and he supposed he had been looking for a reason to leave. When the chance had come to go, he had taken it. But since he hadn't been especially fond of whoring around with the rest of the guys, or gambling, or working on his suntan, it had been three very boring months. Most of the time he would stay up until seven in the morning watching reruns, sleep till five, grab a bite to eat at the casino, and then play.

He had never been so glad to come home in all his life. So when his father said he could go to school and stay at home for free he thought, why not? In high school, his only electives had been music, and it surprised him how much he enjoyed science courses in college. Premed seemed like the logical direction to go. Janet had almost convinced him to go back to music, but the bitter taste of Las Vegas would be in his mouth for a long time. Until then, Monday nights at The Owl were just fine.

A gust of wind shook the trees above Steve. It was dark and he was cold. After sitting around for half an hour he had had about all he could stand. He couldn't wait around any longer. Agitated and impatient he ran up to the gate. His heart nearly stopped when a motion detector switched on two powerful arc lamps mounted above the cameras, flooding the gateway with light. But the scare only added to his frustration.

"Hey," he yelled, banging his fist on the speaker, "open up. I have to use the phone. It's an emergency."

He waited but there was no response from the metal box.

"Shit," he said and banged on it again. It refused to respond and Steve walked up to the gate and tried opening it by hand. When it wouldn't budge he took a step back and then kicked it with all the force he could muster. The good-sized indentation he made in the chain link only slightly appeased his anger.

"Somebody open the fucking gate!" he yelled. But nobody did. He gave it one last kick for good measure and then turned back down the road. He reached the point where the truck had been, stood there for a moment and, without knowing why, headed into the woods.

He popped out along the fences about fifty feet from the gate and walked on the grass. The lights at the gate had shut themselves off already. When he reached the end of the embankment he saw that there were quite a few lights on inside the Institute. He kept going until the rear of the building came into view.

The Porsche was gone.

In its place was a black van; or maybe the Porsche was just on the other side. Things around him were changing so fast he began to wonder if he even knew what he thought he had seen earlier. Then he heard footsteps, lots of them. The sound came from the darkness beyond the parking lot. Steve crouched down and watched.

He didn't see them until they entered the aureole of light emitted by the building. Six men dressed in military fatigues filed into the van. The vehicle fired up and backed out of its spot, headlights sweeping out into the darkness. Steve hit the ground to avoid being caught in the beams as it squealed out of the lot.

Once it had passed him Steve jumped up and ran along the fence toward the gate. He was halfway there when the lights came on and, afraid they would see him, veered off toward the woods to hide in the shadow of the trees and watch. The van stopped just outside the gate and the side door opened, disgorging five men, each carrying what looked an awful lot like a submachine gun. The driver suddenly appeared in the headlights and with a wave of his hand yelled, "Spread out."

The men dispersed immediately and to Steve's horror one of them began running along the fence directly toward him. There was no time to think. He ducked into the woods, making his way as quietly as possible toward the highway. It was slow going in the dark and he feared that at any moment he would run into one of the soldiers.

Thirty minutes later he heard the comforting drone of cars and could see flashes of headlights between the trees. He stepped gingerly through the undergrowth and eased out to the edge of the woods. His hands were trembling and he leaned against a tree to relax and regain some of his composure.

I don't understand, he thought; I don't understand any of this. He took a deep breath and exhaled in spasms.

There was really only one thing left to do: hitchhike back to town and go to the police. He took another breath. No spasms this time. Good. He let his eyes slip shut. Relax, he said to himself, relax. Exhaustion was catching up to him and he was on the verge of dozing when he smelled it: cigarette smoke.

Instantly, every nerve in his body was back on full alert but he didn't move. The crunch of boots on gravel roared in his ears. Steve's eyes peered into the darkness until he saw him. One of the soldiers was walking down the shoulder of the highway, back toward the road, shinning a flashlight into the woods. He was no more than three feet away and Steve was ready to panic when the soldier clicked off the light and slipped it into his belt. He stopped, took a long drag on his cigarette and flicked the butt into the woods. It landed inches away from Steve's foot.

The soldier pulled out a pack of cigarettes from the breast pocket of his camouflage jacket and extracted one with his lips before replacing the pack. Then, using his free hand to shield the lighter against the breeze, he lit up and began walking again. He was already several feet past Steve when the flashlight came back on.

Steve waited as long as he dared before making a move. He might not be so lucky next time the soldier made a pass. He ground the glowing butt beneath his shoe and slowly made his way back into the woods, moving only when cars passed, then proceeding parallel to the highway for two or three hundred yards until it took a turn to the right. When he was certain that he couldn't be spotted from the entrance to the Institute he waited for an ebb in the traffic and darted across the two-lane road to a field on the other side.

Steve had no idea how many men might be looking for him so he avoided walking along the shoulder and certainly wouldn't risk hitchhiking. It took him three hours to cover the seven plus miles back to town. His watch now read 9:47. He looked for a place to ask for directions to the police department and spied a McDonald's. His stomach immediately began rumbling, reminding him that he hadn't eaten anything since noon.

4. 9:50 p.m.

Janet sat on the floor in the corner of the dark room, as far away from the door as she could get. She had been crying for several hours and her nose was sore from wiping it on the sleeve of her jacket.

A dim bar of light came through a thin window and lay on the floor at her feet. She stared at it now, almost cataleptic. She was cried out, scared out. He body felt drained, empty, and her longing for Steve was the only emotion that filled her.

She had no idea what time it was or how long she had been here; she had left her watch at home. Finally she peeled off her jacket, the right arm rigid with dried snot, and folded it into a pillow. Then she lay her head down, eyes wide open, waiting for sleep to come.

5. 10:00 p.m.

After the tall, pimply-faced boy behind the counter at McDonald's had called over most of his co-workers, Steve had a pretty good idea where the police station was. He walked the few blocks as fast as he could, hunched against the cold, his eyes fixed on the pavement.

When he reached the nondescript brick building it was dark and looked closed. He walked around to the rear entrance just as he had been told, and saw the backlit sign that said Police. Steve pulled open the door and walked up to a bulletproof-glass enclosure. The young female sergeant was very friendly as Steve explained the situation into a microphone. Through a sliding metal drawer she gave him some forms to fill out and promised that another officer would be with him soon.

Officer Dick Pollock was one of the skinniest men Steve had ever seen. He stood as tall as Steve's six feet but he couldn't have weighed more than 140 pounds. His brown hair looked permanently unkempt and his mousy moustache bordered on the ridiculous. But like the sergeant out front he was very compassionate as he listened to Steve's story at his desk in the squad room.

"So, she came up missing after you got back to the road," said Pollock, twisting his chair around and leaning in toward Steve.

"Yeah."

"Did you two have a motel room or any place that you were going to later?"

"No. We were going to do that when we came back into town. When she wasn't there I waited for a while, but she never showed up."

Pollock reached up to rub his forehead and then sat for a moment contemplating. "I think the first order of business should be to give the Institute a call," he said reaching for the phone, "just to make sure that she didn't get lost in the woods around there."

"The truck was gone, too."

Pollock shrugged. "Can't hurt to call." He looked up the number and dialed. "I can also ask about your father," he added.

Actually, the thought of calling the Institute had occurred to Steve, but the likelihood of getting past the receptionist had seemed so remote that he had dismissed it. Just then Pollock put up his hand as if to keep Steve from responding, but Steve was all ears.

"Hello, this is Officer Pollock of the Telsen Police Department. Would it be possible to speak with . . ." Pollock looked down at Steve's statement: "Dr. Phillips, please." Pollock paused, then said, "Thank you."

Steve was speechless. He looked on as the officer began unconsciously rubbing his forehead, unable to believe that the man might actually speak with Phillips. Then Pollock put his hand up again even though Steve hadn't uttered a word.

"Dr. Phillips? Dr. Phillips, this is Dick Pollock with the Telsen police. I was wondering if a young woman who may have gotten herself lost down around your area had turned up there at the Institute. Uh huh . . . uh huh." Pollock looked up and smiled at Steve. "Well, I have a boyfriend here who'll be mighty glad to hear she's safe."

Steve felt a rush of relief that made him want to whoop out loud.

"Just one more thing, Doctor. Do you have a Dr. Paul Raymond there visiting the Institute?"

Steve had almost forgotten about his father.

"Uh huh . . . yes, his son says you sent him a letter of invitation to the Institute. Yes, he's right here. Uh huh . . . uh huh. Well, he thought he saw his father's car in the parking lot, a Porsche nine two eight."

Suddenly Steve wished he had never said anything about seeing his dad's car. Phillips would know that the only way he could have seen it was from the woods.

"Yeah, that's what I suspected but I thought I'd check it out just to be on the safe side. So could you keep an eye out for Mr. Raymond? I imagine he'll be out there shortly—" Pollock paused. "In the morning? Okay, I'll let him know. Thank you very much, Dr. Phillips. Yes, well, we appreciate that. Thanks again."

Pollock hung up the phone and turned to Steve, his shoulders raised and his hands out as if to say "All it takes is a phone call."

"He says you can come out to the Institute and pick her up in the morning."

"I heard," Steve said unhappily. "Why not tonight?"

"Security reasons."

"I wonder if you would be able to take me out there to get her."

Pollock looked at Steve suspiciously. "Why?"

"I've seen their security firsthand. Are you aware that they have armed guards roaming around the place?"

Pollock visibly relaxed.

"Doesn't that seem a little strange to you?"

"No, not really. It's a security facility, after all."

"Who are they trying to keep out?"

"Not out, in. It's a mental institution, the local nut house. From what I understand it's how they fund most of their research. There are probably a couple of people in this office who have relatives in there," said Pollock, smiling beneath his cheesy mustache.

This kind of surprised Steve. Phillips hadn't mentioned anything about a mental facility in his letter. "Is Janet all right?"

"It seems she got scared when you didn't return and asked at the front gate if she could wait inside the building until you called."

"That's ridiculous!" Steve said, outraged. But Pollock was having none of it.

"Listen to me, Mr. Raymond. I don't know what you were doing out there tonight. That's not important. But the Institute is a private facility, not a public one. They own all the land out to the highway, and technically, you were trespassing. Now there was no talk of pressing charges, but I wouldn't push it if I were you. Your girlfriend's out there now and all you have to do is go out in the morning and pick her up."

Steve could feel his face flush with anger but held it in check. "What about my father?"

"Dr. Phillips says he hasn't had any contact with your father. He didn't get a response to the letter. And as far as the car, he says that one of the other doctors at the Institute drives a Porsche. A nine two eight."

The story was preposterous; it was too neat, and this guy was buying into the whole thing. Besides, there was no way Janet would get scared. Steve stood up, unsatisfied but resigned. All he wanted now was to get Janet and get the hell out of here.

"Thanks." He was barely able to say the word. He held out his hand and Pollock shook it with his own limp, bony hand.

"You're welcome. I just wish all my cases were this easy. Good luck. I hope you find your father."

Steve nodded, leaving Pollock at his desk, and walked out of the squad room. He wanted to feel relieved, but didn't. Christ, he couldn't believe he had to wait until tomorrow morning to get Janet.

Exhaustion and hunger were starting to overtake him and he practically ran back to the McDonald's, where he ordered a couple of Big Macs, a large fries and a chocolate shake.

"You sure you want to do this?" said the kid when Steve handed him a U.S. twenty.

Steve sighed. "It's all I've got."

The kid called his manager over to tell Steve what he already knew. "I'm sorry, but I can't make the exchange," she said and Steve wound up paying just under twice what he would have paid back home. He wolfed down the food and felt a little better. His hunger was gone but his uneasiness remained.

As he stepped outside Steve thought about renting a car, but it was obviously too late for that. Aside from McDonalds, everything in town seemed to be closed. Across the street was a motel: The Flamingo. The vacancy sign glowed in pink neon beneath a bird of the same color. When he reached the office of the motel a sticker on the door, "We accept Visa and Master Card," greeted him as he pushed his way into the tired lobby. Good. He wasn't crazy about spending any more cash until he could get to a bank and exchange what little U.S. currency he had left.

The room that served as the lobby was portioned off, and on the other side was a woman in her forties, hair of indistinguishable color, sitting in a lounge chair watching the tail end of what looked to be *Dirty Dancing* on a portable black and white. Steve rang the bell.

"Hi," said the woman with a smile. She stood and turned the volume up on the TV before walking over to Steve.

"Single?" she yelled above the music.

"I just need something with a double bed."

The woman looked past Steve into the parking lot, presumably trying to see his car. "One person or two?"

"Is there a difference?"

"Ten dollars," she said glancing at the TV. Then she turned back to Steve and smiled again.

"One, I guess." Steve pulled out his wallet and handed her his charge card.

She ran it through the imprinter and handed it back, then pushed the guest register at Steve and had him sign it. Next, she opened a drawer and handed him a key.

"One twenty-one," she said, pointing to a spot beyond the TV set. "Just down the lot on your left. Checkout time is 12:30." She smiled and Steve thanked her.

He had no trouble finding his room. He unlocked the door and was met by the smell of amyl nitrite and pine cleaner. He walked in without really looking, switched on the lamp beside the bed and sat down. The firm mattress felt good and he found himself stretching out before he remembered that he would need a wake-up call.

He belched, tasting an instant replay of dinner, then yawned and let his eyes slip shut. The rhythmic rise and fall of his chest was soothing. Fatigue pinned him to the bed and he let it. He would just relax for a few minutes and then call the woman at the front desk. He yawned again.

Argentina, 1965

14 July 1965, 4:16 p.m., Buenos Aires.

A doctor in a white lab coat strode confidently into the reception area of the Perón Medical Clinic in downtown Buenos Aires. He took a file from the haggard desk nurse and proceeded toward operatory number five. The place was a zoo. Perón was one of the busiest clinics in town because it served the poor. Sick and wounded, the destitute of Argentina's capital city were everywhere. They lined the walls, covered the floors and spilled out onto the street. Dr. German Infante couldn't have asked for more.

The hours at the clinic were long and hard but he relished every minute. Here he had an opportunity to learn firsthand the medical skills it hadn't been necessary to acquire in Germany. And what better subject was there for his medical education then the prolific poor of a Third-World country? The patients wouldn't object to his on-the-job training because they didn't know any better, and his superiors would never find out as long as he kept the patients moving.

He flipped through the file, gleaning a few pertinent details about his next patient, one Victor Quintano. Quintano was a farm worker, supporting a wife and several children as well as his parents with his meager income. He was having trouble sleeping. A standard case. Infante pulled open the door and stepped into the operatory.

The man standing next to the examining table was round-faced and husky, a little shorter than Infante, about five eight or ten.

"Mr. Quintano?"

"Yes."

"I'm Dr. Infante." The doctor motioned for him to sit down on the table, and then turned on the water at the sink and began lathering up his hands. "Now, what seems to be the trouble?"

"My arms have been going numb while I sleep. It's getting so bad that it wakes me up at night. They tingle," he said, "like the circulation's been cut off."

"Could you slip off your shirt for me?" said Infante, drying his hands on a clean towel.

Quintano removed his blue chambray work shirt and Infante set about examining the patient's back and arms.

"Do you do much heavy lifting?"

Quintano exhaled audibly through his nose. "That's all I do."

Infante went over to the counter for a minute and silently made a notation in Quintano's chart. When he glanced back up he noticed that Quintano was still stripped to the waist. "I'm sorry. You can put your shirt back on now."

Infante turned and leaned back against the counter facing Quintano. "How long does the numbness usually last after you wake up?"

"Well, if I lie on my back it will go away after five or ten minutes, but I have trouble sleeping that way."

Infante rubbed his chin. "I don't think this is exactly what you want to hear, but my recommendation is that you stop working for a few days and see if things don't get better."

"I thought that might be the case," Quintano said with concern. "I've read that people with jobs requiring repetitive physical labor can develop symptoms similar to mine. As I understand it, the rearrangement of muscle tissue caused by repetitive movements can pinch nerves and blood vessels."

Infante, who would have normally ushered his patient out by now, stood smiling and nodding in agreement. "That's exactly right. Where did you read about that?"

"When it first began to happen I was a little worried, so I went to the university library and checked out some medical textbooks. They said that the symptoms would disappear after a few days and when they didn't, I came here."

"You seem like an intelligent man, Mr. Quintano."

"Thank you. But I can't afford to stop working, even for a day."

Infante walked back over to Quintano and lifted the man's left arm. Then he had him hold out his other arm and went through the motions of another examination, this time palpating Qunitano's mind as well as his body. "Where did you go to school?"

"I've never been to school."

The intrigue on Infante's face was evident as Quintano continued.

"My father had a small farm near San Fernando and from the time I was five I worked side by side with him. My brothers and sisters and I never had time for school so we taught ourselves. I learned to read and write when I was seven and since then I've read just about anything I could get my hands on."

"I admire you, Sir," said Infante. And he meant it. "So where do you work now?"

"San Fernando. My father's land was taken over by a food conglomerate and part of the deal was we were given jobs with the company."

Infante continued the examination, purposely giving himself more time to think. He had been trying to think of a way to get his research from the basement in Singen where it was hidden, ever since he had begun working at the clinic. But greater than the need for his research was his fear of detection. He could never go back to Germany; someone would have to go in his place.

"How much money do you make? If you don't mind my asking."

Quintano didn't mind and Infante had to fight back a wince when he heard the unbelievably small amount. He finished the exam and paced the floor meditatively, eventually stopping directly in front of Quintano. If this man was as intelligent as he suspected, his next answer would confirm it.

"If you could leave the farm and do anything else, what would it be?"

At first Quintano looked puzzled and Infante though that perhaps he had overestimated his patient, but then a smile slowly spread across Quintano's face. "There *is* something I've been thinking about doing for a long time."

Right answer. Infante pressed him further: "What?"

"When I was growing up on the farm my uncle worked at a newsstand downtown. Every night he'd bring home newspapers and magazines from all over the world. It's really because of him that I learned to read. I think if I had any money I would try and open my own newsstand."

Now it was Infante's turn to smile. He was silent for a few seconds as he prepared for his opening gambit. "How would you like to work for me, Mr. Quintano?"

Quintano regarded Infante for a moment without answering, impressing the doctor even more. "What would I be doing for you?" he finally asked.

"Running my newsstand."

"You own an newsstand?" Quintano asked, a tone of disbelief in his voice.

"I'm going to buy one and I want you to run it."

The money to buy a newsstand would be nothing to Infante. Back in 1945 he had seen the writing on the wall and wisely exchanged all the gold he had acquired during the war for Swiss Francs instead of Reichsmarks. Had he hung on to the gold he would have been filthy rich by now, but the thought of two suitcases full of extracted Jewish fillings sitting in a safety deposit box where he could never get at them was out of the question. So he deposited the money in a private Swiss account, keeping with him a small suitcase containing enough francs to live on for a while. When he finally made his escape from Europe in 1947 it was on a cargo ship bound for Rio de Janeiro, and for a while he lived the life of a fugitive in Brazil. By 1953 he could see that the money he had brought with him was running out and two years later he made his move to Argentina.

Now that he was established he lived off of the interest from his Swiss account, which he had wired to a bank account in Buenos Aires every month. Even if the newsstand went bankrupt it would be a small price to pay for the retrieval of his research. "Why?" asked Quintano. "Why me?"

"You don't think you can do it?"

Quintano was already shaking his head in disagreement. "There must be a reason. Why do you want to hire *me*? I won't break the law." He was perfect, Infante thought.

"You're an intelligent man and I'm going to do you the service of being totally honest with you. After that you can decide whether it's something you'd like to do or not."

Quintano listened silently.

"In the basement of a house in Singen, West Germany, are five boxes containing property which I own. I am unable to travel overseas and I need someone to go in my place, to bring the boxes back to Argentina. That's all. Nothing illegal. For that you'll receive enough money to quit your job and move your family into a larger home."

"What about the newsstand?"

"Do you think you can make it profitable?"

"Absolutely."

"Good, because there may be other occasions when I'll need you to go overseas to complete business of mine. In return for your services I'll put up the money for the newsstand."

"And how much will you pay me?"

"Fifty percent of the profits?"

"Net profits?"

Infante laughed. "Of course. But how much that is will be up to you."

Both men were silent for a long time. Then Quintano pushed himself off of the examining table and walked up to Infante, his hand extended. Though Quintano hid it well, Infante could see the excitement in his eyes.

"Okay?" Infante asked.

Quintano nodded. "I'll do it," he said, and the two shook hands.

Chapter Four

1. Sunday, 7:57 a.m., Telsen, British Columbia.

When Steve awoke he sat bolt upright on the bed.

"Damn it!"

The curtains on the window were open, and hazy light filled the room. Next to the bed, the lamp was still on. He checked his watch and saw that it was almost eight. He had wanted to get up much earlier. Steve swung his legs over the side of the bed and headed for the bathroom.

A minute later he emerged. He went to the night table and pulled out the drawer. The Telsen phone book was more of a pamphlet than a book, and Steve had no luck finding a car rental agency. He turned off the lamp and left the room, locking the door behind him.

When Steve stopped at the front desk to drop off his key, he asked where he could rent a car. The owner was wearing a pink bathrobe this morning. She smiled. On the TV Bob Barker was trying to keep his distance from a housewife who had just won a car.

"No place I know of around here," she said. " But there's a U-Haul place down at the end of Simpson Avenue."

That would have to do.

"Or if they aren't too busy next door," she said thumbing toward the Esso station, "Pete might be able to give you a lift."

"Thanks," he said. But no thanks.

Steve started walking toward town. The sky was overcast, a thick, uniform gray, and a cool breeze ruffled his hair. After three blocks he crossed a bridge that spanned the Telsen River and he was soon downtown. The city of Telsen had looked rather normal last night, but now that Steve could see it in the daylight it seemed depressed. Many of the storefronts along Simpson Avenue were empty and even the people looked a little vacant. They went on about their business oblivious to Steve as he walked ten more blocks to the U-Haul rental.

As he passed the police station he thought about last night. He didn't want to talk to Pollock again, but he still felt uneasy about going out to the Institute alone. He didn't believe Phillips' story; there was no way that Janet would have stopped waiting for him. Yesterday seemed so far away now, and he found himself worrying whether she was still at the Institute, even though he knew she must be. By the time he reached the rental lot he was wishing that he had never brought her up here.

He used his credit card to rent one of the familiar orange and white trucks and was soon on his way back through town. The truck wasn't much bigger than Steve's pickup but had a twelve-foot square box on the back. He had rented it for twenty-four hours, but if there were no delays at the Institute he wouldn't need it for more than a couple.

Steve re-crossed the bridge and was approaching the motel when something he saw at the Esso station made him slam on the breaks. Behind him a horn honked. He couldn't risk being seen and shielded his face to avoid being recognized as he pulled into the Safeway parking lot directly across the street from the station. He backed into a slot near the sidewalk and readjusted his mirror.

Parked on the street side of the self-serve island was a black van. *The* black van. He was sure of it.

Steve watched as two men wearing jeans and leather jackets, their hair severely crew-cut, got out. Pete and his partner dropped what they were doing and walked over to the van, listening intently as the men spoke to them. A minute later Pete began pointing in the direction of the freeway while his partner shuffled off a few steps and walked back, adding a few words to the conversation before doing the same thing. Pete suddenly took a step backwards, waving his hands in front of him and shaking his head as if telling the two men not to do something. Or was he begging them not to so something to *him*?

Steve drove with his foot to the floor all the way out to the Institute. He wanted to believe that Janet was safe; he wanted to believe he was just being paranoid, but something in his gut told him otherwise.

He went beyond the turn-off and parked around the bend. It would be a pain in the ass walking through the woods again but he was damned if he was going to drive up to the gate and let them catch him. He knew the van would be back sooner or later. He would wait for it and try to sneak into the compound behind it. The way he remembered the camera placements, he should be able to get in undetected.

It was much easier to move through the woods in the daylight and he easily spotted the fence from a good distance away. Then he crossed the road in order to make his approach from the north. Steve crouched behind a tree just out of camera range and waited. Forty-five minutes later the van rolled up. The gate labored open along a track parallel to the fence to let it through. When the van was safely inside and out of sight Steve raced to the fence and down to the gate and slipped through just before it closed. He was in.

He jogged confidently southward, the grass embankment protecting him from being seen, and when he reached the end he sat down to rest, viewing the building in the daylight for the first time. The front parking lot was still empty and the place looked just as deserted as it had the night before. He stood up and looked around. Nobody came rushing after him, so he walked, exposed, toward the rear parking lot. When he spied the van he pulled back a little, then made for the building. Crossing the strip of asphalt that connected the two parking lots, he noticed something that he hadn't seen the night before: the road continued on into the woods in the direction the soldiers had come from.

He reached the building and pressed his palms against the cold brick. He felt amazingly relaxed and self-assured almost as though he were invisible. The rooms on the end were dark and Steve peeked around the back. There was a loading dock and a big metal door that—

"Hey!"

Steve's whole body contracted in fright, and for a split second he thought he felt his feet leave the ground. Still trembling inside he turned around.

"What the fuck you think *you're* doin'?"

Steve was confronted by a shaved head, fatigues, and a submachine gun: one of the Institute's soldiers.

"I was just . . . I want to see Dr. Phillips."

The soldier snorted. "You're gonna see the doctor all right. Move."

He waved the barrel of the gun and Steve began to walk, but apparently not fast enough because the soldier shoved him from behind. Steve stumbled and almost fell. They walked in silence to the front entrance and passed through the glass doors.

Directly in front of them was a large circular counter, about four feet high. Behind it sat a woman in her mid-thirties. Looking bored and indifferent, she wore the standard white nurse's uniform complete with starched white hat, and Steve was reminded for a moment of Louise Fletcher in *One Flew Over the Cuckoo's Nest.*

The lobby of the Institute was large but very empty. The counter was the only interruption in the fifty feet between the door and the back wall. Instead of the usual hospital flooring, Steve found himself standing on polished concrete. It was cracked in a few places but overall it looked well tended. To each side of him were bus stop-variety wooden benches and, as hard as he looked, there was not a plant in sight. It was clearly a matter of function over form.

The soldier let his gun slip to his side and walked past Steve to where the nurse was sitting. "Tell the doctor he has a visitor."

"Yes, sir." The expression on her face changed only slightly as she picked up the phone and punched in three numbers. Instantly, Steve knew it was the woman he had talked to on the phone. The soldier turned, walked to the door and stood guard, leaving Steve alone between him and the receptionist. When she had finished her call she simply sat and stared straight ahead. It made Steve nervous.

Steve pointed to the benches. "Okay if I just sit over here?" he asked the soldier.

"Dr. Phillips will be with you in a moment," the receptionist said from behind him, and Steve turned. Her expression was exactly as before. And her voice—it was eerie, like a recording.

The soldier nodded and Steve sat down. A minute later the door behind the reception opened and in walked an old man in a white lab coat. When he had passed the desk Steve stood up.

"Hello, I'm Dr. Phillips," the old man said extending his hand. He looked past Steve. "You can go back to your post now." The soldier nodded and left.

Steve noticed that Phillips' hand was trembling slightly. The skin felt loose around the bones but his grip was firm. Steve had expected Phillips to be as weak and frail as he looked and quickly had to tighten his own grip. That was when a strange feeling came over him.

This man was old!

Steve had naturally assumed that his father and the man he had worked with back in Baltimore were about the same age. But Phillips looked much older, in his seventies at least, or possibly early eighties. His hair was gray and very thin on top, his scalp shiny beneath its wispy covering. He wore half-glasses and the skin above his eyes sagged down over his lids, resting gently on his upper lashes. When Phillips smiled Steve noticed the gold, which told him the old man still had his own teeth.

Steve introduced himself and Phillips guided him back toward the wooden doors behind the reception desk. As they walked Steve noticed that Phillips was slightly stooped. It seemed strange because of who he was, but it didn't seem out of character for a man his age.

They passed through the doors and into a glass hallway, which Steve realized was the connecting passage between the two buildings.

"I am very sorry about all this," said Phillips. "But your girlfriend stumbled into our door last night and as the security alarm is activated at ten p.m. we had no other choice than to make you wait and come out here this morning."

Steve also noticed a slight accent, one he couldn't quite place. Phillips' explanation seemed equally out of place. Was he serious? Why couldn't they shut the damn alarm off? But he decided to play along.

"Well, I'm sorry for any trouble we might have caused," Steve said.

"Why did you go to the police?"

This was getting weird. "I guess I just panicked."

"What did you tell them?"

Steve didn't know how to answer. Half of him wanted to tell the guy to go straight to hell, a friend of his dad's or not.

And that was another thing; why hadn't the guy said anything about knowing his father? He hadn't even mentioned the fact that they had worked together in Baltimore. At least he and Janet would be leaving soon, and right now that was more important than anything.

But when they pushed through the doors into the other building, answering Phillip was the last thing on Steve's mind.

Standing in front of him were the two guys he had seen in the van. Only now they were sporting sub machine guns.

"Take him away," ordered Phillips as he turned to the left. "Put him with the girl."

"Lets go," said the bigger of the two men to Steve and stuck the barrel of his gun in Steve's ribs, turning him to the right.

2. 10:35 a.m.

Walking down the long hallway, Steve found it difficult to concentrate with a gun pointed at his back. He tried to fight it, but he found himself almost paralyzed with fear. It was the same feeling he had when he would see a police car with it's lights flashing in his rearview mirror; even if he wasn't pulled over, he still got the shakes. He was shaking badly now.

At least he knew Janet was here.

The gunman he was following stopped abruptly at one of the many doors along the corridor, fumbled with a set of keys and unlocked it. When he pushed the door open the other gunman shoved Steve inside and slammed it shut.

The room was large, with light coming in through six of the oddly-shaped windows along the wall facing Steve. In between the windows were mounted sets of plain wooden cabinets alternating with closets of the same design. In the center of the room were two dissecting tables, and on the wall to Steve's left, two soapstone sinks. Past the tables, at the far end of the room, was a set of large doors that looked like the entrance to a refrigerated storage room.

Steve stood for a minute in one spot trying to come to grips with what was happening. He had been kidnapped, that was certain, but where was Janet? He was walking over to look out one of the windows when he heard a noise from the opposite corner of the room. Clearing the first dissecting table he saw her sitting in the far corner.

"Steve!" she screamed.

He was about to make a move toward her but she startled him and was on her feet and running to him before he could take a step. When she reached him they embraced. He gripped her tightly and felt her tremble in his arms.

"God, Steve, I was so scared."

"Me, too," he said as he clutched her with one hand, the other pressing her head against his chest. When they pulled back he brushed away the hair from her face where it clung to the warm tears on her cheek. Tears of relief, he thought, as he felt his own welling up. A single drop ran down the side of his nose and Janet quickly hugged him again. Now that they were together he wasn't afraid anymore. Concern had replaced fear.

He spoke first. "Are you all right?"

"Yes."

'Did they hurt you?"

"I'm fine. They locked me in here last night and the door didn't open until you came in."

"What happened last night? How did you get here?"

They walked over to the corner of the room as Janet told him about the black van. "Some guy came up to the window and told me he was a part of the security here. I didn't tell them about you because I didn't want you to get in trouble for walking around in the woods." Steve merely nodded, letting her continue as they sat down on her jacket which she had spread out in the corner.

"I told him I was trying to get in to see a doctor and he said if I showed him some ID he could let me inside."

"Did you open the door?"

"No, I just rolled down the window a little ways and before I could even react he had his arm inside and unlocked the door. Then they threw me into the van and brought me to this room and I spent the night here."

"When I got back the truck was gone," Steve said.

"They took your truck?"

"Yeah. I waited for you where the truck had been but you never came so I walked back to town."

"Did you try to hitchhike?"

Steve didn't really feel like reliving his close call with the guards, so he jumped ahead. "No one picked me up. When I got to town I went right to the police. They called and talked to Phillips and he told them that you'd been worried and had decided to wait for me at the Institute, but that you had to stay the night because they couldn't turn off their alarms."

"Those bastards."

"I stayed in a hotel last night and came here this morning. I snuck in the gate but one of the guards caught me."

"You don't think the police are a part of this, do you?"

Steve nearly smiled; conspiracy had never crossed his mind. "Jesus, I don't know. I didn't really think about it at the time. Anyway, the guard took me to see Phillips—"

"You met Phillips?"

"Yeah. The guy is strange—a lot older than I expected. He tried to pump me for information and then had two of his goons toss me in here."

Steve sighed and then, almost as an afterthought, kissed Janet.

"Did you find out anything about your father?" she asked him.

"Oh, yeah. I almost forgot. I saw Dad's car."

"You saw the Porsche?"

Steve nodded. "Last night. Phillips told the cop it belonged to another doctor, but I know it was Dad's."

Then Steve made a move to get up.

"Where are you going?" Janet asked.

"I'm going to take a look at these windows."

Janet stayed seated in the corner while Steve examined the windows. They were, in fact, only about eight inches wide, probably too small to get through, assuming one could break the glass in the first place, which was unfortunately reinforced with wire mesh. When he looked beyond the windows all that was visible of their surroundings was a sliver of trees between the two buildings at the far left, the connector to the right, and the other building in front of them.

Steve's stomach growled. He hadn't eaten since last night but his thoughts immediately turned to Janet. "Did they feed you anything?"

Janet shook her head. "Do you think we can get out?" she asked.

"No. It doesn't look like it."

"What if they split us up?"

The thought unexpectedly quelled Steve's appetite; it was the cop car all over again, but he recovered quickly. "I don't know," he said. "This is the first time I've ever been kidnapped. What's the standard procedure?"

Janet looked at him incredulously and Steve couldn't help laughing. "I'm sorry; it's just so good to be with you." They hugged and Steve continued. "I don't know what's going to happen, but I don't know what to do, either. In the meantime we'll just have to wait. I only hope they'll tell us for sure whether Dad's here."

3. 4:54 p.m.

Most of the afternoon Steve and Janet spent sitting on the floor, neither saying much but each glad to be with the other. But the waiting was tiring, and soon they were lying down in each other's arms. Steve didn't realize that he had nodded off to sleep until he awoke with a start.

"Listen," Janet whispered.

Steve lifted his head from Janet's shoulder and straightened up. The room was much darker now. Soon, he heard the sounds of keys in the door and stood.

"You," came a voice from the open door as Steve helped Janet up. He turned to see one of the armed men, his gun pointing at him. "Let's go."

Steve's body stiffened, and suddenly he felt Janet at his side. "Go ahead," she said quietly.

"But I—"

She turned and hugged him before he could get the words out. "I love you," she whispered in his ear. "They'll bring you back."

"I love you, too."

"Come on," came the voice from the door. "Move it!"

Walking back down the dark hallway Steve could see that none of the doors had windows. Two sets of footsteps echoed as Steve walked ahead of the other man, the dim glow of bare bulbs the only light in the blackness. He looked at his watch; it was a few minutes past five.

"Left," the man ordered. Steve was now at the doors to the connecting corridor between the two buildings. His anxiety was building but he didn't think he was capable of speech to ask where he was being taken. He pushed open the door and could see through the windows that it was almost dark outside. The grounds were well tended and he tried to get a look at the surroundings, but to his left were simply more trees.

As he pulled open the door and made his way into the reception area he looked for the receptionist. She was still at her station. Steve turned to see if the man was still brandishing his weapon; he looked completely bored.

"Hey, turn around," the man said almost whining. "I'll tell you when to stop."

The receptionist hadn't looked at them yet even though they were beginning to round the desk.

"Left."

Steve turned his head toward the desk as he passed in front of it. He looked in desperation to the woman but she had no reaction to his silent plea. She stared indifferently at him through empty eyes as though a man being held at gunpoint was one of the monotonies of her job, along with answering the phones and typing insurance forms.

"Just keep walking," the man said in response to the astonishment on Steve's face. "She can't help you."

This part of the institute stood in stark contrast to the rest of the building. The hallway was lit by banks of fluorescent lights on the ceiling, the floor carpeted, and the walls painted a pastel blue. All of the doors were open and Steve could see beds in every room. Must be for the paying customers, he thought.

As they approached the end of the hall Phillips emerged from the last room on the right holding an empty syringe.

"Stop," came the command from behind Steve. "Wait here."

Steve stopped and the gunman walked ahead to talk with Phillips. After a few seconds the gunman motioned for Steve to come over to them and he obeyed.

In the intense light of the hallway Steve could get a better look at Phillips. His hair seemed even thinner than before and his skin was wrinkled and leathery. His rheumy eyes looked as if they were floating in their sockets but this did not diminish their intensity. The whites were slightly yellowed and riddled with tiny capillaries, but the cold blue irises punctuated by black pupils seemed to be looking right through Steve.

"Your father has been reluctant to cooperate thus far," said Phillips. "I sincerely hope you will be able to persuade him otherwise."

Now that his father's presence here had been confirmed Steve felt even more relieved than he had expected to. And this knowledge seemed to bolster his flagging fortitude.

"I have one reason and one reason alone for allowing you to see your father, and that is to give him a message. You will tell him that if he does not cooperate with us then we will kill you. Is that understood?" Next to Phillips the gunman shifted his weight from one foot to the other. Steve nodded.

"Good. He will be conscious in a few minutes," said Phillips, holding up the syringe. "You will give him the message and leave, immediately. Nothing more. Is that understood?" Without waiting for an answer Phillips continued: "I need not remind you that we still have the girl."

Once inside the room a thousand retorts would run through Steve's mind but for now it was as if he had been struck dumb by Phillips' icy stare. Steve nodded again and Phillips stepped back from the doorway. The gunman moved in behind Steve, and Phillips motioned toward the door. Steve put his hand to the metal plate and pushed it open.

The light was not as harsh as in the hallway. On a standard hospital bed against the wall Steve's father was beginning to rouse. He looked disheveled and confused. One sleeve of the rumpled suit he was wearing was pushed up past his elbow. Steve had seen his father like this only once before. Back when he was in high school, when his mother was still alive, his parents had thrown a New Year's Eve party and his father had had a little too much to drink. Steve suddenly had to fight off a feeling of embarrassment.

"Steve?"

His father was sitting up on the bed now rubbing his temples, trying to shake off the after-effects of the tranquilizer. He swung his feet over the side of the bed and looked up. He was hunched over and his mouth hung open, his eyes mere slits as he squinted first at Steve and then at the gunman.

"Good God, Steve, what are you doing here?" his father said, finally realizing the significance of his son's presence.

"I'm supposed to give you a message from Dr. Phillips. He says he wants you to cooperate, whatever that means."

"I was kidnapped. He wants me to do some kind of surgery but I told him to go to hell. Where are we, son?"

Steve's father ran is hands through his hair and then sat up straight. His eyes were opening more and he pulled down the sleeve of his jacket. He looked as though he wanted to stand up but was afraid he still wasn't steady enough, so Steve walked over to the bed.

"This place is called the Columbia Inst—"

"Hey!" yelled the gunman, brandishing his weapon. "Cut out the small talk and get to the point."

Steve didn't turn around. "Phillips says he'll kill me if you don't cooperate."

He could see the pained look in his father's eyes. Paul Raymond stood up and hugged his son, and as they embraced Steve whispered into his father's ear: "Please, Dad, don't do it. Whatever you do, don't do the surgery. If you can, stall for time."

His father stepped back and held him at arms length. He nodded slowly and said, "Yes, I guess I'd better. I don't want anything to happen to you, son." And then he smiled.

Steve wanted to make sure his father had understood what he meant but he suddenly felt the barrel of the gun in his back. "Let's go."

Out in the hall Phillips ordered the gunman to take Steve back to the autopsy room. On the way Steve worried about the conversation with his father. He hoped that his father would not give in to Phillips, because if he did, Phillips would have no further use for any of them.

4. 5:25 p.m.

The door opened, spilling a dingy yellow light onto the dusty floor of the autopsy room, then slammed shut, locking Steve inside.

"Janet?" he said softly.

"Over here."

In the dark room he felt blind but is eyes quickly adjusted until he could see the faint outlines of the tables. He made his way around the closest one, feeling the cool stainless steel on his fingers. At the end of the table, instead of turning to Janet, he walked ahead and put his hands on the nearest cabinet. It was chest high with three columns of five drawers each. He pulled on some of the handles but they wouldn't budge.

"Janet," he said even more softly, "Are there lights in this room? I didn't notice before."

"The switches are on the outside."

Damn, he thought; if only I hadn't slept so long we could have combed this place in the daylight.

He felt along the cabinet again for the handle of the first drawer and he pulled. It rattled slightly but didn't budge. The lock was flimsy, though; it wouldn't take much to jimmy it open. Just above the handle Steve could feel the round metal keyhole.

"What are you doing?" Janet asked.

Steve turned and saw she was beside him now.

"I just had an idea. See if any of these drawers are open. Maybe there's something in here we could use."

"For what? Steve," she said, putting her hand on his arm. "Where did they take you? Where did you go?"

He turned around and for the first time was able to identify the smell of formaldehyde that permeated the room. "I saw Dad. He's here."

As he said the words she squeezed his arm.

"So, what do they want?" she asked.

"They want him to perform some kind of surgery."

"And we just stumbled into things?"

"It's worse than that." Now both of her hands were squeezing his arm. "Phillips said he would kill me if Dad keeps refusing to do the operation. But I told Dad not to do it anyway."

"Steve! Why?"

"Look, if Phillips went to all the trouble of kidnapping Dad, he must not be able to do the surgery himself. But once Dad goes ahead with it Phillips won't need any of us. I don't know what he might do then, but I don't plan on finding out. So while we still have time we need to find a way out of here."

"What can we do?" she asked.

"For starters I want you to go over to those drawers and see if any of them are open."

"What am I looking for?" she asked walking away.

'Right now, anything."

Steve tugged on all the drawers in front of him with no success and then looked to Janet.

"They're all locked," she said.

He began trying them all again when Janet spoke up. "Hey, look at this."

He walked over to her. The large door between the cabinets was open. The small amount of light that filtered into the room was just enough so that he and Janet could see each other and make out most of the objects around them, but it was still very dark. He pulled the door back all the way to let in as much illumination as possible but he still couldn't see inside. When he reached in, all he felt were lab coats on wire hangers.

"I think it's just a coat closet," he said.

He reached up. There was a shelf above the jackets but it was empty. Then he knelt down to feel the floor of the closet but it, too, was empty. Steve stood up and shut the door, then headed to the next closet.

"I'm going to check this one. I don't think any of them are locked."

Janet followed. He walked over to the next closet; it pulled open easily. Tentatively, he reached in a hand but there were no lab coats this time. Steve could feel shelves along the entire length of the closet. On the shelves were uniform glass containers.

He pulled one of the jars down. It would hold about a gallon of liquid, he figured as he drifted toward the window, but it was only three-quarters full.

"What's in there?" Janet asked.

"I think it's just lab specimens," Steve said, holding the jar up to the window.

From the convolutions of the material he concluded it to be brain tissue, most likely an entire brain. By the size he thought it likely to be human. He turned the jar slowly in the reflection of light coming off of the front building. A large portion of the anterior forebrain was missing.

"What is it?"

"Are you sure you want to know?"

"Why?"

Steve smiled. "It looks like a human brain."

"Really?"

He walked over and set the jar on one of the dissecting tables and then reached into the closet for another. When he brought it to the window he could see it was another brain, only this time the missing tissue was from the left hemisphere. He went back to the table and placed it near the other jar.

The lids on the jars were made of a hard black plastic and were very large, as the neck didn't narrow at all. Steve carefully unscrewed the first jar and smelled the contents, then repeated the procedure with the second.

"Damn," he said.

"What's wrong?"

"The concentration of formalin is too weak."

"Too weak for what?"

"It doesn't matter."

Steve replaced the lid and walked back over to the corner where he sat down. Janet followed and stood over him.

"So how do we get out of here?" she asked, hands on her hips.

"When I opened the specimen jar, I was hoping the concentration would be strong enough to throw it in the faces of the guards and run out of here."

"Are you sure we could make it?"

"When they brought me back here, none of the doors we passed through were locked until we got to this room."

"How may guards have you seen?" Janet asked.

"There was the one who caught me outside, and then the other two."

"Okay," she said, and walked back to the closet. Steve stood up and went after her as she pulled another jar from the shelf and set it down in front of him.

"What are you doing?"

"How are we going to know if any of these concentrations are strong enough unless you check them all?"

Steve felt Janet's strength surge through him and he stood up. He pulled her close, squeezing tightly. She empowered him, and times like this reaffirmed the fact that he could never be without her. He buried his face in the nape of her neck, breathing in the smell of her skin. It reminded him of making love, and he hugged her tighter.

They went about their work and quickly found what they were looking for: a five-gallon jug of concentrated formalin tucked away neatly in one corner of the closet floor.

"Grab one of those jars," said Steve, a jar in each of his own hands. Janet followed him over to the sinks and they emptied the contents. Then they returned to the autopsy table and filled the three jars halfway with the concentrated solution.

As they were working Steve became a little unsettled. He wasn't sure what to make of it and decided not to mention it to

Janet, but each of the jars, well over fifty he guessed, contained a human brain.

A tiny slit of light squeezed its way underneath the door and guided Steve as he walked over to feel for the hinges.

"Good," he said. "The door opens inward."

He returned to the table and picked up two of the jars they had filled. Janet took the remaining one and followed him as he positioned them along the wall a few feet from the door.

Steve whispered to Janet, "If we wait here when the door opens, we'll be hidden by it. I'd like you to take the first one, though. Do you think you can hit him in the face?"

She nodded.

"After that I want you to pick up the other jar and follow me out into the hall. I don't know what's going to happen, but we might need it. The one advantage we'll have is that it's dark in here; we'll be able to see them before they see us."

"What happens if they don't come until it's light out?"

"It doesn't really matter. We'll still be hidden by the door. The important thing is to hit him square in the face; you have to get the formalin in his eyes."

Janet nodded again, then walked back to the opposite corner of the room and put on her jacket. The room was fairly cool, and they huddled together on the floor and leaned against the wall.

Hours passed.

Steve became hungry for a while and then his appetite left him. A little after midnight Janet fell asleep on his shoulder. He didn't wake her. He tried not to think much; his mind was a jumble of images and emotions. Just after two he had to fight off drowsiness that threatened sleep. Finally he woke up Janet and paced the floor for a while. When he felt alert enough he sat back down and they waited. It was just after five-thirty when they heard footsteps.

He wasn't ready. Steve wanted to tell Janet to stop, that they couldn't get away. His bladder urged him to piss but he held it. His respiration deepened and his pulse rate increased.

Adrenaline was working its magic on his body; his mind would have to do the work on his fear. When he told himself that Janet might be the first to die if they didn't escape, his strength returned. He could do it now.

Each of them picked up a jar and Steve looked down to make sure he knew where the third one was. If Janet missed he would have to back her up and hope they would have time to hit anybody else.

He moved her into place in front of him. "In the face," he reminded her.

"I know."

They heard the sound of keys in the lock and readied themselves. The door opened, forcing Steve to squint at the yellow light.

"Okay, you two, let's go," they heard as the door swung open. The gunman stepped into the room and Steve put his hand gently on Janet's arm telling her to wait. When the man turned and nodded toward the corridor Steve released his hand and Janet threw the formalin. In that same instant a bank of white lights came on and blinded him.

Steve forced his eyes open and they snapped shut immediately. He couldn't see, but a loud guttural scream told him that Janet's toss had been a direct hit. As his eyes adjusted he could barely distinguish the outline of the gunman staggering backwards and slamming into the wall.

"What the hell—" Another figure appeared in the doorway.

Steve stepped into his throw and tossed the contents of his jar, but the expected scream had never come. He had missed. The butt of the gun slammed into his stomach and he doubled over, the empty jar clunking to the ground. The smell of the formalin nearly made him vomit. Then the sound of breaking glass hit his ears. He looked up. With one eye shut, the other half-open, he could see that Janet had smashed her empty jar into the second man's face. Now both men were screaming and Janet pulled Steve out into the hall.

His pupils had contracted enough by this time that he could see out of both eyes and, with one hand on his stomach, he reached for the handle and pulled the door shut. The keys were still hanging from the lock. He bolted the door and thrust them into his pocket. Steve only knew of one way out so he grabbed Janet's hand and they ran down the hall.

The doors to the connecting corridor were ajar and they burst through. The single bulb that lit the entire passage made it impossible to see out through the windows. Steve and Janet's reflections ran alongside them, accompanied by the echo of their footsteps. The second set of doors was also open, and they ran into the dark reception area, past the desk and on to the front doors.

"Shit!" Steve said, almost yelling. They were locked.

He pulled out the keys and began to fumble through them. There were about twenty on the ring, but before he could try one, he heard a voice behind them.

"Dr. Phillips?"

Steve and Janet turned in unison: it was the nurse. Bathed in shadow, she was sedately talking on the phone. "There are two people here who wish to leave. Could you come down and discharge them?"

Steve could feel the panic seeping in. He didn't want to be "discharged" just yet. He put the keys into Janet's hand. "Here, try these in the door. I'm going to see if I can get Dad."

"Hurry," she said, trying the first key in the lock.

Steve began sprinting down the hallway when he heard the alarm go off, stopping him dead in his tracks.

"God *damn* it!" he yelled, then turned and looked back to Janet.

"I got it!" she squealed, her face beaming.

The decision had been made: they had to get out now. In another minute a guard would be at the entrance and they would never escape. "God *damn* it," Steve said again and ran with Janet through the doors.

Once outside he scanned the immediate area.

"Which way?" Janet asked.

Steve knew they would be easy prey along the fence, so he grabbed Janet's hand and they headed for the unknown of the woods on the other side of the building.

Argentina, 1975

1. 3 December 1975, 8:34 a.m., Buenos Aires.

"*Muchas gracias, Señor*," said Victor Quintano. He smiled at the tall, middle-aged man who had just picked up the newspaper that Quintano had laid aside for him on the corner of the newsstand counter.

The cherubic Quintano operated one of the most profitable newsstands in Buenos Aries. It was a very lucrative business, as Buenos Aries could claim host to eighteen major daily newspapers, three of them in German, as well as numerous weeklies, magazines and tabloids. Quintano also stocked many foreign papers including *The New York Times*, *Pravda*, and the *Berliner Zeitung*.

The gray-haired gentleman stopped at Quintano's stand every day to pick up one of the German-language newspapers—always Argentinean, though, never the *Zeitung*—and always without paying a single centavo.

For Dr. Infante's part it was a matter of principle, pure and simple. Even though the newsstand he owned was nearly six blocks out of his way, he always stopped by every morning to get his paper.

Infante glanced briefly at the headlines, turned the paper over to examine the bottom half of the front page and then folded it and wedged it under his arm. It was a warm December morning, the beginning of the South American summer, and the temperature was nearly eighty degrees. The cotton shirt, which he wore open-necked beneath his white cotton suit, was already beginning to cling to the sweat on his back.

As Infante approached the small coffee shop that he also frequented on his lunch break, he reached into the back pocket of his pants, brought forth a white linen handkerchief, and swabbed the perspiration from his forehead. He had folded the handkerchief neatly and was placing it back in his pocket when he saw the man in the doorway of the café.

His heart skipped a beat.

The man looked vaguely familiar, but during the last thirty years anyone who had given Infante more than a passing glance had begun to look familiar. He didn't want to meet the man's gaze, instead turning his face forward, keeping the man in his peripheral vision. But the man didn't take his eyes off Infante for a second.

As the distance between the two men closed Infante could see that the man was smoking the last bit of a cigarette he had pinched between his thumb and forefinger, sunglasses perched on his head. When Infante was just parallel to him, the man threw down the butt, simultaneously grinding it out and lowering his sunglasses as he stepped out onto the sidewalk.

"Dr. Zindell," came a voice from behind Infante.

This time when his heart skipped a beat it decided not to start up again for a while. Two steps later when it kicked back into gear it was doing double time. His forehead had already replenished the sweat he had wiped off it seconds before. Keep walking, he told himself. If he hesitated even slightly it would be an admission of who he was.

"Slow down, Dr. Zindell." Now the voice, speaking German, was right next to him. "Dr. Zindell?" The man was peering around Infante's left shoulder; it would probably look funny if he didn't respond.

"Are you talking to me?" Infante responded in Spanish, and turned to look at him. The man was walking stride for stride next to him. The voice was so familiar. He had a feeling he knew this man from somewhere but the dark sunglasses made it difficult to tell.

"I thought that was you, Dr. Zindell. Why don't we sit and have some coffee? Talk over old times together?" The man had taken a couple of quick steps ahead and was walking backward facing Infante.

"I am afraid you have mistaken me for someone else. My name is Infante. Please excuse me now; I'm late for—"

The man stiff-armed Infante square in the chest like a traffic cop, stopping him dead in his tracks.

"I'm afraid I must insist," he said, pausing for effect, "*Herr Doktor.*"

Infante had little hope of extricating himself cleanly from the situation but he tried one last time. He said, "I don't know who you are, sir," although the churning in his stomach told him he would find out soon enough, "but you have obviously mistaken me for someone else."

"No, there can be no mistake," the man said slowly and deliberately. "You are none other than Dr. Konrad Zindell, the famous German neurosurgeon."

With that the man raised his sunglasses and smiled. Recognition was instant and Zindell simply breathed out the name quickly as his mind could form the word: "Uhland."

"Ah, so you do remember your old friend Heinrich. Come," he said, motioning to the outdoor tables in front of the coffee shop. "We must talk." He put his hand on Zindell's shoulder to turn him around and they both walked back to sit down.

"Over here," Zindell said, pointing to a table in the shade, "out of the sun."

They sat down and Uhland took out a pack of cigarettes. He offered it to Zindell but Zindell waved it away. He watched as Uhland struck a match and cupped his hands around the end of the cigarette to light it. Uhland took a long drag and then leaned back in his chair. "So, what have you been up to, Konrad? It is still Konrad, is it not?"

Zindell sighed wearily. For thirty years he had kept to himself, and he'd just as soon keep it that way. As far as the Israelis and other Nazi hunters were concerned he was small potatoes compared to the likes of Eichmann and Bormann. These names brought forth memories Zindell had long since tried to forget.

Had it been fifteen years already since Eichmann had been captured? He could still remember the day: May 11, 1960. Zindell had been on speaking terms with Ricardo Klement, Eichmann's alias, but they had never socialized. Both felt it would be better to go privately about their own business than risk suspicion by being seen together.

Eichmann had been abducted by the Israelis right here in Buenos Aries, and even though Zindell's name had never appeared on the Nazi most-wanted lists, he had been nervous for a year or so after Eichmann's capture. But after a while things had settled back down to normal and the last fifteen years had been peaceful and serene. Until now.

"I've been minding my own business."

"As well you should, Dr. Zindell."

"Please, my name is Infante."

Uhland finished another drag on his cigarette and blew the smoke out of the corner of his mouth. "Dr. Infante," he said with obvious distain, "we hear you have been doing very well for yourself in Buenos Aries."

"Who is *we*?" asked Zindell, not really wanting to know.

"Oh," said Uhland, looking as though Zindell ought to realize who he was talking about, "the good doctor sends you his warmest wishes."

"So that's what this is all about. What does that *Schweinhund* Mengele want with me?"

"Please, Dr. Zin . . . Infante, is that any way to talk about a comrade?"

"Enough bullshit, Uhland. What the hell does he want?"

Uhland let his cigarette butt fall to the sidewalk and ground it out beneath his heel, ignoring the ashtray on the table. "So, Dr. *Infante* is not interested in small talk, eh? Very well, let's not waste any more time." Uhland leaned forward, arms crossed on the table, and lowered his voice. "Dr. Mengele knows that you have in your possession experimental medical data that was acquired at Auschwitz under his tutelage, and he would like it back."

Zindell roared with laughter, rocking back in his chair. Everyone around them turned to look and Uhland quickly brought down his sunglasses over his eyes. "It's shit, isn't it?" taunted Zindell. "I knew it. His data isn't fit to be used as toilet paper. All that talk about genetics, the Aryan Race, the Master Race, it's all a bunch of blond, blue-eyed bullshit." Zindell laughed again. "And now he wants my data, huh? Well, he can kiss my ass."

"He's not asking you, *Doktor Zindell,* he's ordering you to turn over what is rightfully—"

"His orders don't cut any shit with me, Uhland. So you can tell your SS ass-wipe of a master for me that I always thought his theories were shit, and if he wants to see my data he can read about it in the medical journals along with the rest of the world. Now if there's nothing else, I must be—"

Zindell made a move to stand up but Uhland was out of his chair in an instant. He grabbed Zindell by the arm and with his other hand opened his jacket to give him a peek at the gun holstered to his side and an incidental whiff of body odor. "There are a couple of things I think you will be interested in, *Herr Doktor*, very interested in."

Resigned to at least hearing Uhland out, Zindell sat back down. "I'm listening," he said smugly.

Uhland eased back into his seat, his jacket still open and the shoulder holster clearly visible to Zindell. "You should know that the good doctor has been in touch with your bank in Switzerland. They were extremely curious to learn that one of their account holders might be a Nazi."

"Former Nazi."

"Semantics. They informed him that if this were true, the accounts would have to be frozen pending further investigation."

Zindell's smugness had vanished, replaced by deep anxiety. Four years ago he had set up his own private practice, his patients coming almost exclusively from Buenos Aires' flourishing German population. Although he might be able to get by on the money he made from his practice and the newsstand, his main concern was that the Swiss account might lead to the discovery of his actual identity.

"And just to insure good faith on your part," Uhland continued, "the good doctor has decided to contact the Israelis."

Zindell was still listening but now with resigned animosity.

"At first the Israelis were not sure who you were, but after our *anonymous* caller gave them a little background information it was not long before they became very interested."

Zindell was distraught. "So, I either turn over my research to you, or you turn *me* over to the Israelis."

"Correct," said Uhland, lighting another cigarette.

"But if you turn me over, you still won't have the data."

"You can be sure of one thing, Doctor. Regardless of what happens to you, we will still get the data."

Zindell had one more idea. "What if I leave the country?"

"And go where? Do you really think we would go to all this trouble and then just let you leave the country? I thought you would have just a little more faith in us than that."

Unfortunately for Zindell, he did. Leaning back in his chair he could feel the sweat that was oozing out of his body at the thought of Eichmann's execution. He rubbed the corners of his eyes and then spoke. "When does he want the data?"

"Now that's more like it. The good doctor would like to meet with you first, in his home in Brazil."

"What, so you and your thugs can have time to search my house and my office?"

Ulrich took a long drag again, this time letting the smoke drift into Zindell's face. "You overestimate the good doctor. He has neither the time nor the means to hire *thugs*. And why would he want to, what with your being such good friends during the war? Besides, if you try anything, and I mean *anything*, the Israelis will be the least of your worries because I will track you down and kill you personally. And I am far less likely to be as humane with you as the *Juden* would be. Do we understand each other?"

Zindell nodded. "Okay, when does he want to meet? I assume you're providing transportation?"

Uhland stood up and ground another butt under his shoe. "All in good time, *Herr Doktor*. Everything has been arranged. I will contact you when the time comes, but for now you will wait. The good doctor will want to hear the news personally, and have time to prepare for your . . . reunion. *Auf Wiedersehen, Herr Doktor*."

After Uhland had gone, Zindell noticed he was still clutching his newspaper. He took it out from under the sweat-stained left arm of his jacket and flipped it on the table. A cup of coffee sounded good, but when Zindell looked around for a waiter he realized there were none. It was self-serve; he would have to go inside and get a cup himself. Suddenly coffee didn't sound so good.

The newspaper on the table was fluttering in the breeze. Then, for a single second, while Zindell was glancing down at it, a strong gust held the paper open. The small headline riveted Zindell's eyes: U.S. NEUROLOGIST CLAIMS BREAKTHROUGH IS IMMINENT. Then it was gone.

Zindell snatched up the paper and riffled through it. When he found the article he read it over three times.

It was time to call in Victor Quintano's marker.

2. 5 December 1975, 6:47 a.m., Baltimore, Maryland.

The telephone jangled Howard awake. His hand shot out from under the covers and deftly snatched the receiver before the second ring. It had been several years since his residency, yet the sound of the phone was still enough to wake him instantly, even from the deepest sleep.

"Hello?" he said, still a bit groggy.

"I would like to speak to a Dr. Phillips, please."

The voice on the other end was unfamiliar.

"Yeah, this is Phillips." He was lying back now, his eyes closed and the receiver pressed to his ear.

"Hello, Doctor. I recently read an article in the newspaper about your research in America. I am a doctor myself and have been doing research on new neurosurgical techniques and brain mapping." The voice paused. "I think I could help you."

"Wait a minute. Who is this? Do you know what time it is?" Howard could take a practical joke as well as the next guy, but this was pathetic. The accent sounded so phony he could have laughed, but first thing in the morning he wasn't in the mood.

"My name is Dr. German Infante. I can't tell you where I'm calling from; I'm already putting myself at terrible risk by even talking to you."

Howard had propped himself up on his pillow by now and was smiling with recognition. "Come on, who is this really? Is that you, Dave?"

"Please, Dr. Phillips, I don't have time for games. I am serious, and the danger I speak of is very real. I must know your answer today. Will you let me help you?"

Howard's good humor was gone now. He still thought it was a prank call but he decided to play along and find out who it really was. "What makes you think I need your help?"

Howard's current project was trying to create the perfect chemical neuro-inhibitor. This new chemical, he hoped, would be able to temporarily repress certain brain functions without causing any permanent damage to the brain tissue. It would be a tremendous discovery and Howard felt confident that he was on the verge of a major breakthrough, hence the article.

"I have been doing brain research for thirty years now and have pinpointed nearly every function of the cerebral cortex—"

"Excuse me, but did you say 'pinpointed'?"

"Yes."

"Geographically?"

"Yes, I believe so."

"Jesus, I don't have to listen to this. I don't know what kind of drugs you're on, buddy, but if you'd studied a little harder in neurology you'd know that's impossible."

"Don't be foolish, Doctor. From what I've read about your work, information like mine could be invaluable to you. I don't think you can afford *not* to look at my findings."

Howard was silent because he didn't really know what else to say.

"I'll send someone to your office today with the materials," the voice began again. "Once you've looked them over you can decide for yourself whether they will be of value to you."

"Yeah, sure." Howard was tiring of the whole thing by now and just wanted to get a cup of coffee.

"I must repeat my warning, though. You are the only one who should view the materials. The existence of my work must not be revealed yet or your life will be in danger. Do you understand?"

"Uh huh." Howard swung his legs over the side of the bed and sat up. If this guy didn't hang up pretty soon, *he* was going to.

"Very well. I will contact you tomorrow morning. Good-bye."

Howard replaced the receiver and padded out to the kitchen in his underwear. After a cup of coffee and a cursory look through the paper he showered and dressed, all the while trying to forget that weird phone call.

3. 11:36 a.m.

Dr. Howard Phillips was busy working at his desk when he heard a knock at his office door. He was just going over the results of a recent experiment and didn't bother to look up.

"Yeah, it's open."

The door opened slowly but didn't shut and when Howard's eyes raised from his desk they stayed up. A huge man stood in the doorway. He looked Mexican with greasy black hair, silver at the temples, and a thick black mustache. He was wearing a green sport shirt and gray slacks, and he took a step into the room on black wingtips. He smiled at Howard, revealing a gold central incisor.

"I have a delivery for you, *Señor*," the man said with a heavy Spanish accent. "Would you like the boxes in here?"

"Isn't that stuff supposed to go to the lab? I think you need to go down a few floors."

The man shook his head. "No, *Señor*, these boxes are to be delivered personally to you." With that the man left the office and Howard stood and walked around toward the door. As he grabbed the doorknob he was met by five wooden crates stacked on a hand truck.

"This stuff has to be for the lab," Howard complained, but to no avail. The man wheeled in the boxes, pulled out the hand truck and walked out the door. As he turned to leave he flashed his gold tooth at Howard and waved. "*Adios, Señor.*"

Dr. Paul Raymond, a resident neurosurgeon at Johns Hopkins University Hospital, poked his head in Howard Phillips' office just after 2:00 p.m.

"Paul, come in here," said Howard, waving him inside. "You gotta see this."

"What's up?"

"You won't believe the weird shit that's been goin' down today."

Paul had always hated the way Phillips used the campus slang; everything was "cool" this and "mellow" that. Another thing that annoyed him was Howard's proclivity to dress in the campus uniform: wide-leg jeans, Qiana shirts and Earth shoes. Howard slapped him on the back and directed him toward a pile of boxes lying open on the floor. Rooting through them was a young man wearing roughly the same thing as Howard. He had dark hair, a full beard and wire-frame glasses that rode down toward the end of his nose. Paul wanted to push them back up for him, but there they stayed.

"Oh, Paul, this is Gerry Rosen from the University." Paul shook his hand. "Ger's doing graduate work in Germanics."

"What's all this?" said Paul, pointing to the stacks of files Rosen was poring over.

"Sit down and I'll tell you. It'll blow your mind."

Paul winced at the expression and then sat down as Howard launched into the story of the mysterious phone call and the greasy courier. The animation in Howard's voice was matched only by the look of excitement on his face.

"So what kind of research is it?" asked Paul, as Howard took a dramatic pause in his monologue.

Howard was smiling from ear to ear now as he flipped one of the files in front of Paul. "Brain surgery, Paul. Experimental brain surgery. We think the guy's a Nazi."

Paul's first thought was to throw the file back down on Howard's desk simply on principle, but that seemed a bit juvenile and he let the thought pass. Then he turned to Rosen who was nodding in agreement.

"A Nazi," said Howard more to himself that to anyone else, head bobbing, looking for all the world like he was going to burst out laughing.

Paul looked down again at the file in his hand, noting the sketches of cerebral topography and taking into account the shaded area. He flipped through the rest of the yellowed pages. He had taken a couple years of German in high school but he couldn't make heads or tails of the faded type.

"Have you been able to translate any of it?" he asked.

"Tell him." Howard nodded toward Rosen, who looked back at Paul over the top of his glasses.

"I've only been able to glance through about twenty or thirty of the files but I've taken some from every box and they appear to be fairly similar in content. It's only in the first box, the earliest dates, late 1943, that he describes the surgery. He would cut away the top of the person's skull, remove a specific portion of the person's brain, and then test the person against a control."

Paul listened with disbelief, but his methodical mind was still at work. "What kind of control could he have possibly had?"

"Oh, I forgot to tell you," Howard cut in. "They were twins. All of the patients were identical twins, children mostly, Gypsies and Jews. He tested them both first, operated on one, and then gave them the same tests again. Most of the notes deal with the tests and the variations before and after the surgery."

"What happened to them after the surgery?"

"They were killed," Rosen picked up. "Both of them. The end of each file gives a complete autopsy report on each twin as well as visual comparisons of brain tissue removed from the experimental twin and the same tissue of the other."

Paul just sat for a moment trying his best to absorb what Howard and Rosen had been telling him, but it wasn't making sense. It was all too gruesome. It couldn't be true.

"Pretty wild, huh?" said Howard, snapping Paul out of he meditation.

"What are you going to do with this stuff?"

Howard seemed indignant. "What do you mean?" His voice was rising in pitch. "Gerry here is going to start translating the files into English for me today."

"You can't be serious!" Paul said, and Howard frowned. "This has to be some kind of practical joke. You can't take something like this seriously."

"I talked to him on the phone."

"And you really believe that Josef Mengele just called you up in the middle of the night so he could send you his concentration camp research?"

"It's not Mengele," Howard said, his expression far too serious.

Paul just stared at him, stunned, while Howard continued.

"Mengele's field was genetics, you know, the master race and all that jazz. Well, this stuff has nothing to do with that at all, apart from the use of the twins, and that was only as a control device. The guy was brilliant. Not only did he remove every part of the forebrain, but he also took out smaller sections of parts he'd removed in earlier operations. It looks like he was just getting into multiple sections, one on each hemisphere, when the files stop, right near the end of the war."

"I don't believe this." Paul stood up, hoping that the change of position would clear his mind. "You guys should listen to yourselves. This is probably some kind of elaborate hoax and you're falling for it." Paul chose this moment to liberate himself of the file he still held by throwing it on Howard's desk.

Howard just shook his head and turned to Rosen. "Ger'?"

"An extremely expensive hoax, Dr. Raymond, if that's what it is."

Rosen walked over to Paul, took one of the papers from the sheaf in his hand and held it up to the fluorescent light. "See that water mark?"

Paul could clearly see the eagle with its rigidly outstretched wings over a swastika ringed in laurel leaves. He nodded.

"It would cost a fortune to have this paper manufactured. Not only that, but to have it look aged like this? Now, I'm no expert, but I'm willing to bet that if you have this analyzed, and not only the paper, the typewriter that was used and the ink on the ribbon can all be dated and verified as being produced in Germany during the early nineteen-forties."

Paul was taken aback by the whole conversation. Howard was leaning back in his chair, his hands behind his head and a huge grin on his face, while Rosen went back to the files. It was ludicrous.

"Is this bizarre, or what?" said Howard, almost chuckling.

"The only thing I find bizarre about this whole situation is your attitude, both of you."

Rosen looked up at Paul for a moment and then returned to his work. "Come on, Paul, aren't you the least bit curious about what's in these files, what all this research adds up to?"

"Assuming that they're legitimate, which I don't believe they are, the research is thirty years old; it's worthless—"

"And I suppose that in a few years Watson and Crick's research will be too old for you. Well, we might as well throw out Pasteur's work, too; it's just too out of date."

"You know goddamn well what I mean!" Paul was trying to keep from shouting. Rosen seemed oblivious to the whole conversation. "They experimented on *human beings* for God's sake. Do you know how naive you sound?"

Howard sat up quickly, placing both of his forearms on the desktop. "Now who sounds naive, Paul? Those people are dead. You said it yourself: thirty years. And if any good can come of their dying it just might be through these files. I don't give a rat's ass if it was the fucking Nazis killing Jews or Jews killing Germans. If by using this research I can cure one person of epilepsy, Alzheimer's or autism, then these people won't have died in vain. Bottom line, Paul: If any of it is scientifically sound, I'm going to use it."

Paul didn't have anything else to say, Howard had pretty much pulled the rug out from under his arguments. He walked back to his chair and sat down.

Howard turned to Rosen. "How long do you think it'll take you to translate those, Ger'?"

"I couldn't finish all this if you gave me a year," Rosen responded without looking up.

"I don't need it all." Howard took one of the files off of his desk and approached Rosen. "Look, you see how each file has a summary at the end, Infante's speculation about the result of each vivisection?" Rosen nodded. "What I need is one page for each file containing the sketches of the brain hemispheres and the summary underneath."

Rosen nodded again. "Sure."

"I also want a few complete files done, including the best account you can give me of the actually procedure itself as well as the testing process, any operations where he had complications, and about a dozen that I'll pick out from the sketches. What do you think?"

Rosen set down the file in his hands and pushed up his glasses. Across the room Paul nearly grinned. "Well, Dr. Phillips, as much as I'd love to work on this project, I have a lot of work to do already. I honestly don't know how much time I could actually devote to this without sacrificing my own studies."

Howard reached up and rubbed his forehead as he thought. "Who's the head of the Germanics department over there?" he said, referring to the University where Rosen was doing his graduate work.

"Dr. Elwell."

"What if I talked to Dr. Elwell and he allowed you to do this work for me as part of your degree?"

"Then I'm all yours," Rosen said with a smile.

Howard slapped him on the back. "Far out."

"Listen, Howard," said Paul as he stood up, "I have to get back to the ICU."

"Hey, thanks for stopping by, Paul. This whole day has been kind of incredible."

"Yeah, well I've been mulling this over and I'd just like you to keep a couple of things in mind. I know you only have the best of intentions, but you need to think about having your name linked with the Nazis and also the fact that if the guy who did this is the one you talked to, then he's still alive and you don't know what he's capable of, okay?"

"You worry too much, Paul. I'll be fine. Do you want me to let you know what kind of stuff Ger' comes up with? It should be right up your alley."

Paul objected to the thought of human vivisection as being right up his alley, but he knew what Howard meant. "Sure."

"Take it easy, Paul," he heard Howard say, and he felt the slap of a hand on his back as he stepped out into the hall.

Walking back to intensive care, Paul couldn't get the image of Howard out of his mind. Maybe he had a point about the victims, but it still seemed wrong. Just then his beeper went off. Howard and his Nazi doctor would have to be relegated to his subconscious for now; he had patients who demanded his full attention.

4. 6 December 1975, 6:47 a.m.

"Hello?" Howard said into the receiver when the phone rang, but he knew who it was.

"Hello," said the unmistakable voice.

Howard switched on the lamp by his bed and propped himself up. He'd had a difficult time getting to sleep in anticipation of the call, but was now wide awake. A fleeting thought that he should be recording the conversation passed through his mind before the voice spoke again.

"Dr. Phillips?"

"Yeah, this is Phillips."

"I trust you have had a chance to acquaint yourself with the files I sent to you?"

"Yeah, I have. And I think you have a little explaining to do. I had an expert look at them and it seems that they date from World War II Germany."

"That was not a wise thing to do," the voice said evenly. "Do you not remember my warning to keep the contents of the files confidential?"

"Look," said Howard, "I don't read German and if I'm going to be translating a couple of thousand files I'm going to need a little help."

"Then you believe in their authenticity." The voice sounded excited.

"First things first. Where the hell did you get a hold of them?"

"What did you think of them—"

"I asked you where you got them." Agitation put an edge on Howard's voice.

For a few moments all Howard could do was listen to the buzz from what he figured to be an overseas connection. Then the voice cut in: "They are part of my research."

"Jesus Christ, do you really expect me to believe you're a fuckin' Nazi?"

"I am a doctor."

"Gimme a break, buddy. How in the hell do I know *what* you are? Unless I get a name—and it better be a good one—you could be any crackpot calling me."

There was another long pause.

"Well, Doctor?"

"I am taking a great risk by even speaking to you. There are people who are genuinely interested in those files and who would think nothing of killing to get them. Please remember one thing, Dr. Phillips: *you* are in possession of the files now and it is *you* who are at the greatest risk. I have only to tell these people that you have the files and they will no doubt kill you in order to obtain them."

"That won't cut it, Doctor. Unless I know who you are and who else wants the files I have absolutely no reason to believe you."

"I'm afraid that is just not possible."

"Then I guess I'll just have to take my chances with your friends."

The voice paused again. Howard was not about to hang up, so he waited.

"Have you ever heard of Josef Mengele?"

"You're not going to tell me you're Mengele?" Howard said incredulously.

"No, but I worked with him and now he wants my research. I am afraid he will stop at nothing to get it."

Though he was trying to keep up a determined front, it was all a little unnerving and Howard was having a hard time writing off the threats this guy was making.

"So why give it to me?"

Another pause. "I thought you had a chance to look at it?"

"Okay. I like what I see so far. If it pans out the way it looks on paper, we could be looking at a Nobel. But why me?"

"I want that Nobel prize. I want people to know that I am not a beast; those children would have died anyway. Am I to be looked down upon because I used my position to the greatest advantage for humanity? Would mankind really refute my genius because of a few people who are already dead?

"I am the world's most preeminent neurosurgeon and yet I am forced to live in exile, my research gathering dust instead of taking its rightful place among the great scientific discoveries of the century." The voice was ranting now. "My work must be recognized and I must be given the credit I deserve, the credit I have earned."

When the voice ran out of gas, Howard thought for a moment. If the guy's research did work, it could cut years off of the experimental stage of his own. Or it might push his work in another, more important, direction. There really wasn't much of a precedent in a case like this so he was going to have to go on instinct.

"Okay, Doctor, when do you want to meet?"

"In a few days I will be leaving the country for America. I will contact you when I arrive. Good day, Dr. Phillips. I look forward to meeting you."

The line clicked off in his ear and Howard stared at the receiver for a few seconds before hanging up the phone. He sat in bed for a while thinking about the events he had just set in motion, then he shook his head and went out to the kitchen for some coffee.

5. 8 December 1975, 1:36 p.m., Tel Aviv, Israel.

Aharon Halevi was rarely in the Tel Aviv office as most of his time was spent on assignment. Currently, he was wrapping up a case and making plans to take some time off when Chaim Yashar walked into his makeshift office.

The Mossad were fairly informal and most of Halevi's superiors were also his friends. Yashar pulled up a chair and sat across the small desk from him.

"Aharon, we've received a few phone calls from South America and I'd like to put you on the case."

Halevi feared for his vacation, but if he were reassigned he would manage. Work always came first. "What's the story?"

"It seems that someone, anonymous of course, thinks he's seen a Nazi in Buenos Aires."

They both laughed.

"Anyway, the name this person gave us is Zindell. Apparently he was at Auschwitz until the end of the war, but we can't seem to dig up anything on him. You being our expert on Nazis, I thought you might be able to come up with something that could help us."

"I was kind of hoping to get in some vacation soon; it's been a couple of years now."

"I know. But right now all I need is a little research so I can make some informed decisions. It shouldn't take more than a couple of days. What do you say?"

"Sure, Chaim."

"Good. Come see me in the morning then."

The next morning in Yashar's office Halevi gave him the rundown on what he had discovered about Zindell.

"Our files have nothing on him, so I got on the phone with one of our agents in Berlin and he was able to get into Spandau and question a recently captured guard from Auschwitz. Auschwitz was a big place, but we got lucky: he remembered Zindell.

"With a little digging I was able to come up with his SS number and work assignment but that's about all I could get on my own. He actually worked at Birkenau which, as you know, was a few miles away from the main camp at Auschwitz. This is interesting because Birkenau is where most of the gassings took place.

"Then I listened to the tapes of the calls and what we didn't have, the unknown caller filled out in spades: physical description, addresses for work and home, aliases—I guess he goes under the name Infante now—and a complete account of all the alleged atrocities he committed at Birkenau. Whether it's true or not . . ." Halevi shrugged.

"Good work, Aharon; do you think you can get him?"

"That's not the problem; it's what we do with him after we get him. We have no corroboration. So far I haven't been able to come up with a single reference to him in any of our testimonies, and if we don't have any witnesses we couldn't bring him in even if we wanted to. If he *was* a doctor at Birkenau, either he didn't perform any of the selections or everyone who saw him went to the gas chambers."

"What about the guard? Perhaps a deal could be worked out?"

Halevi shook his head. "The guard said he knew *of* him, but has no knowledge of what he did in the camp."

Yashar pressed his hands flat together as though he were praying and placed the tips of his index fingers on his lips, thinking. A moment later he looked up at Halevi. "Any suggestions?"

"I would like to go down there and confirm that it's him."

"Good, good," said Yashar, nodding.

"And if it is?" Halevi asked.

Yashar's head was still nodding slightly, unconsciously. "Take the appropriate measures," was his response.

Halevi and his partner David Meyer caught the next plane to Argentina by way of Paris and New York. Once in Buenos Aires they rented a car and drove out to Olivos, an upper-class residential section of town. It was four o'clock Wednesday morning. Meyer was sitting in the driver's seat next to him and they were looking out at the house of one Konrad Zindell, M.D., Nazi.

They were waiting outside the address that the caller had given and would tail their suspect all day. If things checked out, they would hold an "interview" with him to establish his identity later in the evening.

Shortly before six in the morning something unusual happened. The suspect didn't come out of the house as expected, but instead pulled up in a car and proceeded *into* the house. As soon as the man stepped out of the car, Meyer turned to Halevi and smiled; the description was exact. Halevi couldn't help smiling back.

A large hedge surrounded Zindell's house, virtually shielding it from the street. It was meant to keep out prying eyes, Halevi suspected, but it would work to their advantage; once past the front gate, no one would be able to see them. The hour was also early enough that few people would be up. Now was the perfect time. Halevi glanced at his watch; if everything went smoothly, they could catch the next flight home.

They both pulled on thin leather gloves. Halevi adjusted the Uzi under his coat and nodded at Meyer and they both stepped out of the car. Meyer went around back and Halevi eased cautiously through the front gate. All of the curtains were drawn except those in the front room. Zindell was clearly visible, examining papers which appeared to be laid out on a table. Halevi walked through the gate and ducked in behind the hedge and made his way to the side of the house. As soon as he saw Meyer give the high sign he responded with hand signals of his own. They would both kick in their respective doors in thirty seconds. If the man inside wasn't Zindell or if there were other people present, they would be able to leave peaceably, the man never knowing who they were. But if he *was* Zindell, they didn't want to take any chances.

The front of the house was offset from the gate and Halevi could wait by the door without being seen from the street; it was as if someone had planned the house with him in mind. As the second hand of his watch swept up to twelve, Halevi kicked in the door, brandishing his Uzi. Zindell already had his gun pulled when Halevi entered the room but before he could decide whether to use it, Meyer came up from behind. Zindell handed his weapon over to Meyer.

"Sit down, Zindell," ordered Halevi in his best German.

The man's face went white, registering utter shock. It almost made Halevi laugh. Did they really think that no one knew about them hiding in South America? When Zindell tried to feign ignorance by speaking pathetically-pronounced Spanish, heavily laden with a German accent, Halevi couldn't help himself and he expelled a short burst of laughter. Zindell turned to Meyer but got no reaction at all.

Halevi walked over and stuck the stub of the Uzi barrel in Zindell's chest. "Sit!" This time Zindell obeyed.

"There must be some mistake," Zindell pleaded in German, his hands held out. "My name is Muller; you have the wrong man."

A small coffee table in the middle of the room was strewn with documents. Halevi ignored Zindell as he looked them over, everything from a Hitler Youth membership card to SS identification papers, complete with picture. Zindell was a fool; he should have destroyed these years ago. Halevi turned back to Zindell and held up the photo. It matched perfectly: he was the same man as in the picture but thirty years older.

Zindell sagged in the chair, a look of total despair etched across his face, utter frustration. Halevi turned and went into the kitchen. He rummaged through the drawers until her found a large knife. As he was leaving, his eye caught the old-fashioned ice box that Zindell used instead of a refrigerator. He went back and searched through the drawers again, this time lifting something else and slipping it into his pocket.

When he reentered the living room Zindell had his head in his hands. He looked up and his eyes met the knife Halevi was holding. "What are you going to do to me?" Zindell said, his voice cracking with fear.

Halevi nodded to Meyer and Meyer grabbed hold of Zindell's arms. Halevi reached into Zindell's coat pocket and removed his wallet. Sure enough, the phony ID said his name was Kurt Muller now instead of Infante. Halevi shook his head in disbelief at Zindell's feeble attempt to disguise his identity. He carefully replaced the wallet and nodded at Meyer who wrestled Zindell's right arm over his head.

Halevi stuck the knife through both Zindell's jacket and shirt just above the armpit and, careful not to cut him, ripped through the material down to his waist. He set the knife down on the table and opened up Zindell's clothing. He could see the neat scar where the tattoo that identified Zindell's blood group when he joined the SS had been removed. It was the last piece of evidence that Haveli needed.

He nodded and Meyer released Zindell, who straightened himself out as best he could. Halevi walked around behind the man but Zindell continued to look forward. As Meyer moved to the front, keeping his Uzi trained on the former SS doctor, Halevi took the ice pick he had found in Zindell's kitchen from his pocket. With his left hand he grabbed Zindell's hair and pushed his head into his chest, and with the other hand thrust the ice pick into the base of Zindell's skull.

Chapter Five

1. Monday, 5:43 a.m., Telsen, British Columbia.

The sound of alarms woke Paul Raymond from a dead sleep. It was still dark. No one had come in or out of his room since Steve had left and for the first time in days he didn't feel drugged out of his mind. He thought about getting up but instead, as soon as the alarms stopped, he simply sat up on his bed and waited. Phillips would be back.

Paul had been gagged and blindfolded on the day of his abduction, tied up when he regained consciousness in the van, and had all of his bonds removed when he entered this room; that was when Phillips had come in. Howard had looked like shit. But that was probably to be expected what with having to kidnap people as part of his work.

Before then Paul hadn't actually seen Howard since 1976, but had followed his rise and fall in the news and medical journals like everyone else. The Nazi research had evidently been unusable and wasted a lot of lab time before Howard had abandoned it and gone on to develop uradrine. Now he said he supposedly needed Paul to operate on him, but wouldn't tell him why. That was the last real thing Paul could remember. He had been heavily sedated the rest of the time.

About fifteen minutes after the alarms shut off Paul heard a noise and then the door opened. A large silhouette filled the doorway as Paul squinted into the light.

"Dr. Raymond?" said the figure.

"I'm awake."

"Do you mind if I turn on a light?"

"No."

The light came on and the door closed. The figure turned out to be a large man in army fatigues. His pants billowed out where they were tucked into his tight-laced boots and the sleeves on his shirt were short, displaying well-muscled arms. One hand rested on the butt of a gun holstered around his waist and the other held an envelope.

His features were large and his hair short. His skin was tanned and he sported a thick, well-trimmed mustache. Unlike the younger men who had abducted Paul, he looked like he was in his early forties. Wasting no time, he walked right up to the bed. "I have a letter for you."

Paul looked into his eyes; the man seemed very calm and self-assured. He took the envelope, thinking it might be a letter from Steve, and opened it. Inside were three single-spaced typed pages. He looked at the last page but there was no signature.

"It's from Phillips," the man said.

"If I'd known that, I never would have opened it."

The man laughed and then sat down in a chair a few feet from the bed. "Kind of a pain in the ass being here, isn't it?" He seemed completely relaxed as he pulled a booted ankle up onto the opposite knee. Legs crossed, he continued: "The doc says you've refused to cooperate and I don't say as I blame you much. Not the most pleasant way to spend a weekend. But here's where we are: he wants you to read the letter and I told him you would. So what do you say?"

"I heard an alarm earlier."

"Just a drill," the man said without missing a beat. He draped one arm over his leg, apparently waiting to field any other questions.

"And what if I told you I wouldn't read it?"

"Look, Doctor, I don't know what Phillips wants you to do and I don't really care. But I know he's got your kid and he won't hesitate to kill him." He put his leg down and leaned over, elbows on kneed and hands clasped. "What he wants is outlined in the letter. Once you read it, I can walk out of here; you haven't compromised yourself and my job is done. So what do you say?"

"Why doesn't he come here and talk to me himself?"

"I don't know," he said, hands held out, palms up. "Maybe he's shy."

The strangest feeling suddenly came over Paul; he felt like laughing. The guy's manner was very disarming and it was all he could do to remember where he was and why. He looked down at the letter and then back up at the man; the man was nodding. Paul drew in a deep breath and exhaled slowly as he contemplated the paper in his hands. Maybe the guy is right, he thought; reading the letter wouldn't commit him to anything. And it probably wouldn't hurt to find out exactly what Howard wanted. So Paul began to read.

The three pages outlined in minute detail the bilateral stereotactic surgery that Paul was expected to perform. With Phillips under local anesthesia, a hole would be drilled on each side of his skull and a thin probe would freeze the nerve bundles that were causing his dyskinesia. All the hows were there; what was missing was the why.

This type of surgery was done almost exclusively to treat Parkinson's disease, but hadn't been used for over twenty years. It was a feeble attempt to destroy the nerves responsible for the uncontrollable tremors associated with the disease. No surgeon who still had a license would perform this operation now. Paul thought hard and couldn't remember seeing any signs of Parkinson's in Howard, but then he had been pretty well drugged up.

Was this why he had been kidnapped? Surely he wouldn't be forced to perform a surgery that was so out of date and had such a marginal chance for success. The more Paul thought about it the more troubled he became.

"Okay. I'm done."

"Great," said the man, standing up. "I want you to know I appreciate the cooperation." Paul held the letter out to him but he waved it off. "No, he wants you to keep it."

Paul shrugged and tossed it on the bed next to him, then watched as the man walked out and the door closed it behind him.

"Did he read it?"

Walther Brandt casually locked Raymond's door and began walking down the hallway. He wanted the doc to sweat it out a bit. "Sure. What did you expect?"

"Did he say anything?"

"No."

The two men walked in silence until they reached the reception area where they turned and faced each other.

"Listen, I have no idea how you let those two get away, but I want them found."

"I've got most of my men on it right now." Brandt looked at his watch. "We should have them by eight at the latest."

"They never should have escaped in the first place."

"Relax; they can't get off the compound."

"You also said they would never be able to get out of the building. And now they have a set of keys!"

Brandt hitched up the holster around his waist and fingered the handle of his pistol. Sometimes the old guy really pissed him off. Not that he would ever show it. Emotions were what got men killed. Calm and cool was the way to avoid making mistakes. "The keys won't open the gate," he said. "They're not going anywhere."

Brandt turned and headed for the front doors indicating that the discussion was over. "I'll let you know when we have them."

Outside it was beginning to get light. A heavy mist was falling and the sky looked dark and threatening. Brandt put the thumb and forefinger of his right hand in his mouth and whistled loudly. The soldier who had captured Steve the day before came running over.

"Any word?" asked Brandt.

"No, Sir," said the soldier at attention.

"Does Ramey have the radio set up yet?"

"In the back parking lot, Sir."

"Good. Go ahead and return to your post."

Brandt hoisted himself into his Jeep and drove around to the back of the building. Though he hadn't gone on the assignment, he had masterminded Raymond's kidnapping. He'd sent his two best men on it and they had done admirably. But when the kid and his girlfriend had stumbled onto the Institute grounds Brandt had made his first mistake since coming here: he had decided to put a couple of new men on guard duty and give them a little experience. Now one of them was partially blind and the other would have to have his face sewn back together.

He supposed that he had agreed to play messenger boy in order to atone for his error in judgment. But he planned on catching those two no matter what it took. He could not afford to be embarrassed again.

Brandt pulled in beside the radio truck and talked to Ramey for a few minutes. There were three groups of men on the search. One group was combing the perimeter, the other two the woods behind the Institute. No word as of yet, but Brandt was confident that there would be soon. There was no way for them to escape.

For a minute he stared blankly at the drizzle on the windshield, then turned his Jeep around and headed back to camp.

2. 6:07 a.m.

Two hundred yards into the woods Steve could hear the water; thirty more yards and he could see it. The Georgia Strait ran between Vancouver Island and the mainland of British Columbia. In all the confusion of the past few days, he had forgotten how close to the coastline they were. But there was no way to travel along the beach. Steve and Janet stood on the precipice of a twenty-foot cliff and watched as the frothy gray water of the Strait lapped against the black rocks below.

Remembering that the fence was to the north, Steve turned them in the opposite direction, staying close to the shoreline while heading south. The rain was falling heavily as the sky lightened to what was little more than a shadow of daylight, and after only a few minutes they were both completely soaked.

Steve was constantly glancing to his left looking for movement. The problem was that *everything* was moving. Rainwater fell from the trees in giant dollops, bombarding the forest floor and making the undergrowth come alive. The sound was deafening and as they plowed through the brush it drowned out their footfalls in an eerie simulation of silence. Despite their good fortune in escaping the building, Steve firmly believed that they would be captured at any moment. So far, though, they hadn't seen anyone.

For a long time Steve and Janet didn't speak to each other; there wasn't much to say and in the noise of the rain they would have to shout. Steadily they moved through the forest. "Watch your step," he said a couple of times as Janet tripped over exposed tree roots but his voice seemed swallowed up by the forest as soon as it left his mouth. He was sure she couldn't hear him.

He let Janet lead; somehow that just felt right. The land south of the Institute had a gentle downward slope to it and after a half hour he heard the sound of rushing water. It wasn't the sound of the strait to their right, and he had unconsciously tuned out the din of the rain; it was something else. As they drew closer the roaring became even more pronounced and Janet finally broke away from Steve and ran ahead through the trees.

"Look," she said, as he stepped onto the rock-strewn bank. "A river."

They both stood near the water and rested. The river was only about thirty feet across but it was moving at a pretty good clip. Decision time.

"What do you want to do?" said Janet.

"Jesus, I don't know. Come on, let's sit down for a minute."

They walked back into the woods, each with an arm around the other's waist, and had to make their way upstream a few yards before they found a fallen tree to use as a backrest. Steve's clothes were heavy with water; even his vest had soaked through. They sat down and he watched Janet as she combed through her wet hair with her fingers and pulled away the tendrils that had plastered to her face. His own hair was tied back and hung like a wet rope down the back of his neck. Janet had missed a strand that ran across her forehead and Steve removed it for her.

"Thank you," she said automatically.

"You're welcome."

Steve moved closer and slipped his arm around Janet. The rain dripping off of her face made him want to kiss her and he did. They hugged each other tightly.

"Steve, I'm really scared."

"Me too, hon'," he said. And for the first time in days Steve really felt it. As he sat there, cold and wet, hungry and miserable, he began to replay in his mind all of the unbelievable events of the past week. Mercifully, Janet interrupted him.

"What are we going to do?" she wanted to know.

Steve didn't know. "What are our options?"

"We're already soaked. Should we just cross the river right here?"

"I thought about that, but if we can't beat the current we could be washed out into the strait. I don't like the sound of that."

They still had their arms around each other and Janet squeezed him. "If we go too far upstream," she said, "we might run into a search party."

Steve nodded. "If we stay in the woods, though, they won't be able to spot us as easily. I think we should look for a good place to cross, and at the first place we think is safe we'll do it."

"Okay."

Neither made a move to get up. Steve's legs relished the rest they were getting and he was sure that Janet's were doing the same.

"I love you," she said.

"I love you so much." Steve held Janet in his arms and unexpectedly was overcome with emotion. Suddenly he began to cry. His throat tightened up and tears began to roll down his cheeks along with the rain. Janet pulled his head down onto her shoulder and he found himself not resisting. He *wanted* to cry; it felt good, cathartic.

He cried for his dead mother, and with relief at finding his father, with love for Janet and fear for her life. When the tears finally stopped, his lungs hitched as he drew in a deep breath.

Steve saw the concern in Janet's eyes and hoped that he hadn't undermined her resolve. "I'm sorry."

"Don't be," was all she said.

He took a couple more breaths to regain his composure and then stood up. Janet followed. "I still want you to go first," he said. "Okay?"

"Are you sure?"

"Yeah. Just be careful."

The river twisted in several directions before it took a decisive turn southward. Once they were above the bend the water looked fairly smooth. They talked it over and decided that they should try to cross there. Steve helped Janet into the water first, staying behind her and holding on as they waded into the current.

The bank dropped off quickly and before they were halfway across, the water was up to Steve's waist. The smooth rocks on the riverbed were slimy and gave way easily beneath his feet. As a result he had to walk with exaggerated slowness, lifting each foot no higher than necessary to take a step and then using all of his concentration to make sure it was secure before taking the next. His steps felt leaden, and the cold and the constant constriction of his muscles made his legs feel as if they were burning up. The current was still powerful under its deceptive smoothness and he found that he had to let go of Janet to keep his balance.

They were just past the midway-point in the river and Steve was busily studying the woods for soldiers when he felt the rocks beneath his right foot begin to give way. An involuntary grunt escaped his throat, soft, but loud enough for Janet to hear. She turned around just in time to see Steve's body being picked up by the rushing current, and she reached out her hand to him. Instinctively he grabbed it and suddenly they were both swept away.

His grip on her wrist felt tentative but she had a good grasp on his. He was working furiously to regain control of his body in the water. "Hold on—" he yelled, but before he could get the rest of his words out his head was plunged beneath the surface and his arm was nearly ripped from the socket. He was suspended in the middle of the river, and the water was now rushing over him at a frightful speed. But Steve was still holding on to Janet's hand, his body twisting underwater like a windsock. He hadn't had time to take a breath and his lungs were already starting to burn.

He squinted his eyes open in the current and was surprised at how clear the water was. He could see that Janet's foot was caught on a tangled mass of branches and knew that she wouldn't be able to free herself as long as he was holding on to her hand. He was just about to release his grip when a thought flashed through his mind that terrified him: what if he let go and she still couldn't get her foot loose? She would drown while he was carried downstream, helpless to save her.

As fast as he could, Steve began pulling himself along Janet's arm as though it were a rope. The look on her face as he passed her was one of terror, her mouth open and her eyes wide with fear, forcing him to look away. He grabbed on hard to her armpit with his right hand and reached with the other for her belt. He caught it on the first try and quickly latched on to it with both hands. Next he hooked his left arm around her crotch and hoisted himself up so that he had both arms wrapped around her right leg. Then, with something akin to a shinny, he worked his way along her leg to the twisted limb that had ensnared her.

A loop of branches on an underwater log, aided by the current pulling at her body, had tightened like a vice around her foot. Steve tried with one hand to wrest her free but he didn't have enough leverage. Decision time again. He couldn't hold his breath any longer and he doubted whether Janet could either. He would just have to trust that they could both make it to the riverbank alone. He let go of her leg and, with a hand on each branch, pried them apart.

As soon as he saw her foot slip through he let go, frantically trying to get his head above the water. Once his head broke the surface his lungs began to pull at the atmosphere in great sucking gasps. He heard Janet coughing before he saw her and it took some of the edge off his panic. Steve twisted himself around in the water until he could see her, only a couple of yards downstream from him. They were fast approaching a large bend in the river; if they swam toward the outer edge they would be in slower-moving water and could easily make it to the bank.

Steve pointed to the eastern edge of the ninety-degree corner.

"Swim for it!" he yelled. But his lungs were weak and his voice even weaker and the shout amounted to no more than a whisper. Janet was looking at him but her eyes told him that she had not understood so he took a couple of hard strokes and caught up to her.

"Over here," he shouted, this time acknowledged by a nod. "Go."

Janet took off and Steve followed her and at the last second they veered off into the eddy that swirled away from the river as it hooked west. They pulled themselves out of the water and lay on the rocky beach, their breathing coming hard and heavy. Steve was on his back, looking into the gray sky; the rain had stopped. When he sat up he heard Janet's teeth chattering.

"Are you all right?"

"Yes," she said, rolling over and putting her arm around Steve's chest. "Thank you for getting me out of that. I couldn't . . ."

"It's okay now."

"Almost."

"What do you mean?"

"We're still on the wrong side of the river."

Sure enough. After all of that effort. Just how close they had both come to drowning Steve didn't know, but now it seemed like a lot of risk for no result.

"God, I'm freezing," Janet said.

Steve put his arm around her and could feel her trembling. "Look, we should get going. If we're moving we'll stay warmer."

"What about this?" she said, motioning toward the river.

"As long as it's going south we can stay on this side."

Steve stood up first and then helped Janet to her feet. Her arm around his waist and his over her shoulder, they walked on.

3. 7:35 a.m.

About a mile upriver, still well hidden by the woods, Steve spotted a bridge. He assumed it was part of the road that led to the Institute. Janet began to make a move for it but Steve put his hand on her shoulder and she stopped, first looking at him, and then back toward the road.

"What—" she said, but he cut her off by putting his finger to his lips. They both stood, frozen and breathless, as a Jeep sped past them over the bridge. They waited a few moments more before Steve spoke. "I think it's okay now," he said.

After a few cautious steps they walked out onto the bank and ran for the abutment. They had only gone a short way when they first heard the voices.

. . . And then the damn thing moved! Jesus H. Christ, I thought old dickless here was gonna shit his drawers—

Knock it off, Dobson. If we don't find those two, you'll have more than a damned snake to worry about. Brandt just drove by, you know.

Steve and Janet had barely enough time to make it underneath the bridge and when they made it they froze. It was a crude wooden structure but the cross beams looked strong enough to hold any kind of vehicle. The heavy planking of the bridge deck had only separated slightly in a few places and Steve could see the flicker of shadows as the men crossed them, their boots falling heavily as they walked. He counted three men.

Yeah, I know. But if he wouldn't a put those two shit-fer-brains on guard duty last night we wouldn't be out here freezin' our asses off right now while he's out joy ridin'.

That's enough, Dobson.

Yeah, Rob, I don't want no trouble.

Jesus, you pansy—

Move it, you two. We're supposed to find them by eight.

Hang on, you guys. I gotta piss like a racehorse.

The sound of a belt unhitching was followed by a stream of urine arcing over the side of the bridge. A few seconds later the stream slowed to a trickle, was followed up by two strong squirts, and then stopped.

Hey, wait up . . .

The voices trailed off, and as Steve and Janet sat on the rocks that were wedged underneath the bridge, a wave of fatigue settled over Steve. Suddenly he didn't want to move, ever again. He wanted to sit—no, sleep—right here under the bridge and wake up to find Janet next to him in bed, in her apartment. None of this would have happened: no Phillips, no Columbia Institute, no gung-ho G.I. Joes, no running and being wet and cold and—

"Huh? What?" Steve was roused from his stupor to feel Janet shaking his shoulder.

"I have to go."

"Yeah, okay. I guess we shouldn't stay here too long." Steve had been staring at the water as it frothed over the rocks, letting himself be lulled into a kind of waking sleep.

"No, that's not what I mean. I have to go pee."

Steve smiled but the look on Janet's face told him that he better snap out of it quickly.

"Yeah. Me too. I'm going to take a look first, and then we can find a spot."

"I'll stay down here," she said, already pulling her shirt out of her jeans.

"You sure?"

She nodded.

Steve eased out from underneath the bridge and studied the area. He looked hard down the road leading up to the bridge, and across to the other side of the river where the soldiers had gone. Then, he climbed over the bank and ran into the woods.

When he spied a suitable tree he ducked behind it and emptied his bladder. But his relief only made him more acutely aware of the vacancy in his stomach. It began to rumble with a vengeance. Janet poked her head up a minute later and Steve waved her over to the woods.

"I think we should go across the bridge."

"But *they* just went that way."

"I know, but I think we should follow the road and see where it leads. We'll have to go kind of slow, but if we stay hidden I don't think they'll find us. They'll probably be combing the woods over by the coast."

"All right."

They made the crossing without incident, this time Steve leading the way. The rain had completely stopped by now but the sky was still dark and the thick dirty clouds seemed as though they were resting on the treetops. In the ensuing quiet, every step they made echoed unmercifully, and a couple of times Steve had to stifle an urge to tell Janet to walk more quietly. But he knew it wasn't her fault; he was making as much noise as she was.

After a mile or so Steve felt a tap on his shoulder. He jumped. Janet was pointing to a small sentry post up along the road, complete with red-and-white-striped boom gate.

They took a wide berth around the guardhouse and before long they could hear sounds. Steve felt a little more relaxed; their steps would not be heard. He saw a few buildings through the trees, but it was not until they had reached the outer edge of the grassy skirt surrounding it that he and Janet were held breathless by the arresting sight of the camp.

4. 8:00 a.m.

Standing on the edge of the woods, looking out onto the camp, Steve became conscious of Janet's breathing next to him. The sound was comforting, and he reached out and took her hand in his.

Twenty feet in front of them stood a huge fence, strung on both sides with barbed wire, that enclosed two rows of wooden barracks. The fence posts looked like steel girders that turned suddenly outward at the top. They were insulated, and at the base of each one was painted a red lightning bolt; the fence was electrified.

Off to the left it looked as if the river ran right by the camp, but its artificial evenness made him think that it was more than likely a canal. Along the northern side, to their right, another sentry post like the one further up the road sat just inside the gate.

Steve took a step back and led Janet deeper into the woods. Now that he knew what they were looking at, they didn't need to be so exposed. When they had walked fifty yards or so they saw a guard tower set in the corner of the camp, and upon closer inspection, could see one on every corner. The towers looked unmanned at the moment, making Steve feel slightly more at ease.

When they realized that there was no way to continue along the eastern side of the camp without being seen, they doubled back to a bend in the road between sentry posts and crossed there. Now they were able to steal their way along the western wall of the camp beneath the cover of the woods, crossing several trails that led out to the strait along the way. A better look at the enclosure showed two rows of ten barracks each inside the barbed wire. Though they could see a few men walking around, the place seemed deserted; the sounds of machinery they heard were coming from beyond the camp.

The road than ran down the center of the camp led up to the front of a large building situated just inside the southern end of the electric fence. The building spanned the entire end of the camp and had a twelve-foot chimney on one end. The road turned in front of the building and led out past a gate in the far corner. Beyond the camp, outside of the enclosure, were a dozen or so more wooden buildings, an occasional man walking between them the only activity that could be seen.

Steve wondered for a moment what this conglomeration of buildings was for, but even then from their vantage point in the woods they could detect the smells of breakfast wafting through the air. Chief among them were coffee and bacon, but he thought he could also imagine eggs, toast, jam, pancakes, and maple syrup—

"I'm starving," said Janet.

"Me, too. Look," Steve said, formulating a plan as he spoke. "I don't see anyone around and we have to get something to eat. Why don't you stay here and I'll see . . . I don't know, whatever I can see."

He knew he shouldn't. He knew they should run away from there as fast as they could, and try to find a way out. But as soon as he saw Janet's head bobbing in agreement, his mind was set. Quietly he stole out from the cover of the trees and drifted toward the long rectangular building from which emanated the scents that had him salivating.

When he reached it, he took a look around at the front. There were two small steps leading up to the door, which was set in the very center of the southern side of the building. Unfortunately, the end of the building where he was standing had no windows; had there been one, he could have just peeked inside. As it was, he would risk more exposure by looking in the side windows because he would still be in full view of the adjacent building. Still, he hadn't seen anyone since they had stopped.

With trepidation Steve stepped around and looked in through one of the dirty windows. He could see a dozen long wooden tables with chairs all around and, at the far side of the building, a steam table, literally steaming with heaps of hash browned potatoes, scrambled eggs, and bacon. Two big coffee urns and a stack of dishes were at one end and trays of silverware at the other. The urge was too strong; he couldn't have gone back now even if he had wanted to.

After making sure there was still no one around, he went to the door, took the two steps up and pulled it open. For a moment he was overwhelmed. Steve was so hungry he thought he would be able to feast on the smells alone. His stomach was doing flips and twists as he scanned the room for any sign of life. When he didn't see any he ran up to the table and grabbed a plate. Although the eggs and bacon looked good, he knew that they didn't digest well and so he started in on the hash browns.

"What are you doin' in here?"

He had just picked up the huge aluminum spoon when a voice from behind him struck him like electricity and he dropped it as though he had been shocked. Blood flushed his face and the sweat began to flow. In his excitement Steve hadn't realized how warm it was inside.

He turned to see a bald middle-aged man standing in the doorway, tufts of white hair ringing his head above his ears. The man was about five six and had a round protruding stomach that suspended his dirty white apron like a skirt. Steve was moments away from running, but something kept him in place: the man was smiling.

"I thought you'd be out with the rest of 'em, hunting for whoever it is they're hunting for." Without giving Steve time to respond he continued, "Say, I haven't seen you around here before. You new?"

"Yeah," Steve said, trying with all his might to control the urge to bolt through the door.

The man was still smiling, showing teeth that were yellowed and stained. "Just get in last night?"

"Yeah." This guy was making it easy.

The cook, which was what Steve figured he was, picked up a white coffee cup from a green dishwasher rack, flipped it right side up, and began to fill it at one of the urns.

"Say, you be careful now. I hear that a couple of new kids got tore up pretty bad."

"Yeah. I heard about that, too."

"Sweet Jesus!" The cook lifted a fat finger off of the black spigot, stopping the steaming flow with his cup half full. "How do you like that? I work my ass off for ten years around this place and I have to find out what's goin' on from the gomers. You been here a day, and you already know. How'd you find out?"

"Well, it just happened right after I got here."

The cook's bushy white eyebrows came together in a furrow as he finished filling his cup. "I thought you said you got here last night."

Steve's heart was beating so fast he expected it to jump out of his chest at any moment. "I guess it just seemed like night. It was still dark out this morning when I got here."

"Sure," said the cook, looking as though he were trying to convince himself. Then he snapped out of it and back into his yellowed grin. "Well, don't just stand there. Dish up while it's still hot. Won't be for long." He put one hand on his hip and with the other tipped back a large gulp of coffee. "Hell fire, they don't tell me a goddamned thing around here. I'm cookin' for sixty men and I don't find out till I'm done that none of them are gonna be eatin' because they're out on some kinda man hunt."

Steve grabbed the handle of the spoon and began dishing up the hash browns. He looked back over his shoulder at the cook and watched him gulp down more coffee. But just as the cook was checking his watch, a large black man walked out of the doorway at the end of the mess hall.

"I finished the dishes, sir," the black man said in a monotone that sounded somehow familiar to Steve.

The black man was at least a foot taller than the cook. He was wearing tan slacks and a matching vest that looked as if they had once been part of a three-piece suit. His white shirt was rolled up at the sleeves and worn open at the neck. What interested Steve, though, was the man's head. His hair was shaved off on one side and a section of skull the size of a golfer's divot appeared to be missing, though the skin of his scalp was covering it.

"Get your coon ass back in the kitchen, boy, before I get my pistol and blow it off!" The cook was screaming at the top of his lungs and Steve could only watch in amazement as he turned back and said, with his regular good-ol'-boy voice and gleaming yellow teeth, "Say, why don't I get you some *catch-up* for those spuds?"

The black man shuffled off into the kitchen with the cook following at his heels and shouting after him. "Move it, boy! You stay the hell away from there, you hear? It's bad enough I have to work with a goddamn nigger without havin' to look at one with my mornin' coffee . . ."

Steve put down the spoon and used the plate as a scoop, piling it high with steaming potatoes, then turned and ran for the door. He launched himself off the top step and was almost to the woods when he realized that he had forgotten to check if anyone had seen him leave. He mentally shrugged; it was too late now. When he reached Janet he didn't even have time to open his mouth before she had grabbed a handful of hash browns and was stuffing them into hers.

"Hey, wait a minute. Let's get out of here first."

Instantly the door to the mess hall burst open, the cook hopping down the stoop with a bottle of Heinz in his hand. Steve froze. Janet was intent, but she didn't stop chewing. The cook looked around, his brow furrowed and his free hand back behind his head scratching at his neck. He shook his head and turned to go back inside. "Hell fire!" he said, going in through the door. "I thought I told you to stay in the kitchen, you son of a bitchin' . . ."

"Let's go," said Steve, scooping up handfuls of the greasy potatoes. He couldn't remember any food ever tasting this good. They were only able to make it twenty yards before they sat down and devoured the entire heap.

Just past the group of buildings where the mess hall was located was a small stand of trees that separated the camp from a large farm. Two big barns stood at right angles to each other in the foreground. Beyond them, several large tractors were out tilling soil while thirty or so men worked removing the remnants of this year's crops. Off in the distance to the east were other buildings that Steve could not identify.

"I just thought of something," Janet said.

"What?"

"We haven't run into the fence. I know there was that wire around the camp, but what about the fence that's around the Institute? Do you think the institute owns all of this?"

"I don't know." Steve hadn't really thought about it, but Janet was right. Was it possible that the Institute owned all of this land? "But what exactly is *all this*? It looks like something out of World War Two, a Nazi concentration camp."

They were silent for a few minutes and then Janet spoke. "What should we do? If we keep running like this they're going to find us sooner or later. You said the cook told you there were sixty men?"

"Yeah. That's what *I* got out of the conversation at least."

"What if we hide in one of the barns until it's dark?"

"I don't know." He hedged.

Janet took Steve's arm and turned him toward her. "They're out searching the woods right now. They're not going to think to look right in their own buildings."

He knew she was right. They had run out of ideas; there was nowhere else to go. He hadn't had very much sleep the night before, and with the potatoes in his stomach the thought of lying down was irresistible.

"It doesn't look like there's anyone close by, but we'll have to run out in the open to get there," Steve said.

"We should walk. It might look suspicious if we're seen running."

The walk to the barns was as nerve wracking as it was uneventful. The building closest to them had its large barn doors open and Steve and Janet quickly ducked inside. The cement floor had been swept clean. At one end was a threshing machine, and at the other was a table that spanned the entire end of the building. Tools were arrayed in orderly fashion on it and against the wall, and tires, fan belts and cases of oil were stacked in neat piles along the back wall.

Janet grabbed Steve's hand and led him back to the doors. "No place to hide in here."

Even before Steve had pulled the door on the second building open wide enough for him and Janet to slip through, he had smelled the sweet odor of cow manure and hay. Once inside he could see another set of doors that opened onto a fenced pasture where a dozen or so cattle were grazing. The barn was twice the size of the garage next to it and, remembering the pile of bacon and eggs he had seen, he thought there must be pigs and chickens as well.

The ladder that led to the hayloft was clearly visible against the back wall and Janet led the way. When they reached the top they could see through the opening down into the barn. Though the loft had been stocked for winter, more bales had been removed from the far side. Behind them was a solid wall of hay that reached out almost to the edge of the loft. They crossed a plank bridge that led to the other side, rearranged a few bales and then lay down.

The loft was much warmer than it had been outside and Janet stripped off her wet jacket while Steve did the same with his vest and shoes. She pressed herself up tightly against him and when he looked into her eyes she kissed him hard. They tugged and pulled at the rest of their clothing and laid it down in the hay. Their naked bodies latched together and they coupled with an urgency and desire that left them both drained. Afterward, wrapped in each other's arms and covered with Steve's vest, they fell asleep.

5. 2:19 p.m.

Steve was awakened by a pain in his foot and as soon as he opened his eyes he could see that someone had been kicking it. That someone was a soldier who was now standing at the edge of the loft, talking to someone below.

"Tell Brandt we found 'em. Looks like they've been fuckin', too."

Steve quickly looked at Janet and then rolled over to shake out his clothes. Janet came awake as the soldier turned around: "What—"

"Let's go, you two."

The soldier seemed relaxed, leaving his weapon hanging at his side and waiting patiently while Steve and Janet dressed. Their clothes were still damp and felt miserable going on. Then the soldier followed them across to the ladder and down into the barn. Sunlight streamed in through the back doors and Steve checked him watch; it was 2:30. Once outside he could see that the sun had only come through a break in the clouds. Waiting for them were four other soldiers. Two were smoking cigarette's, one was hitching up his pants, and the other let out a whistle at the sight of Janet. Steve felt her arm slip around his waist but she looked unwaveringly into the eyes of the man who had whistled. No one said a word.

Up above them, in the thick clouds, they heard the distant rumble of thunder. A few minutes later the jeep they had seen pass over the bridge pulled up, and out of the passenger seat jumped the cook.

"Well, I'll be damned. That's him. I knew it. I knew there was something wrong with that fella as soon as I laid eyes on him."

"Okay, Art," said the man who stepped from the driver's side. "Why don't you wait in the jeep? I think we can handle it from here."

Art complied but was shaking his head and muttering, "I knew it," on his way back.

All of the other soldiers had come to some semblance of order and were paying close attention to the driver of the jeep as he stepped forward. He was a big man, older than the rest and a commanding presence.

"What do you want me to do with them?" asked the soldier who had discovered them.

"Go ahead and put them in quarantine. I have to run back up to the hospital now. You just make sure there's somebody in there who knows what the hell he's doing, okay?"

"Yes, sir."

"I don't want any more mistakes. You read me?"

"Yes, sir."

Once the Jeep was out of sight the soldiers relaxed. One lit up a fresh cigarette.

"All right, boys and girls, lets move it," said the leader, and they began walking back to the camp.

𝕭𝖗𝖆𝖟𝖎𝖑, 1979

4 February 1979, 6:18 p.m., São Paulo.

Sunday is hot. On the street below Walther Brandt's room waves of heat rise from the pavement along with the sounds of traffic. But Brandt hears none of it; he is asleep on his bed. What Brant hears is a knock on the door. Not on the door of his room, but the door of his home, his parent's home, his childhood home in Montevideo, Uruguay.

It is not 1979 for Brandt but 1959. He is eight years old. His mother lets two men inside. They ask for Walther's father and when his father enters the room they say he is a something called a Nazi. They accuse him of torturing people, of sending them to something called a gas chamber. They call him a murderer. Walther's mother takes him in to the kitchen but he can still hear every word. They say his father's real name is Kessler or Hessler. His father tries to tell them that they are mistaken but now they are screaming at him in a language Walther does not understand. Only later will he learn it is Hebrew.

When they finally leave, Walther and his mother come out of the kitchen. Walther's father walks slowly now with his head down. He shuts himself in his study and doesn't come out for dinner. Walther asks his mother what is wrong with Papa, but she says he is busy with work. It is just after his mother tells him it is time for bed that they both hear the noise. It is a loud noise coming from his father's study and it frightens Walther. His mother screams. Then she cries. She runs past him to the door of the study and he follows her. When she opens it they both see his father slumped over on his desk, what's left of his head in a pool of blood, a gun in his hand. Then his mother screams again.

As Walther Brandt sat up on his bed he could feel the cool sweat run down his forehead; the dream always made him sweat. His left eye stung but he barely noticed. He stood up and walked over to the window. It was open but the air that circulated through the room felt like it was emanating from an oven. Yet even though the sun would be up for another three hours, the worst of the afternoon heat was over.

From his hotel room he could see most of the city, the largest in Brazil. It was hot and dirty and smelled like shit, just like the rest of South America, and he hated it. It hadn't been his idea to come down here. As far as Brandt was concerned, he would just as soon never go south of the equator again. But he always followed his orders; that was what made him so valuable.

Right now he was waiting for the most important assignment of his life. If he succeeded—and considering his record so far there was no reason to think he wouldn't—he would be able to write his own ticket. *He* would be giving the orders. They had promised him that much.

Brandt locked his fingers behind his head and stretched. The flight from West Berlin had only arrived that morning and he was glad for the rest. He yawned and turned back to the bed when a knock came to the door. Calmly, he hefted his namesake P-38 from the shoulder holster he was wearing and silently walked to the side of the door.

"Yes?"

"I have a message from a friend."

"Slide it under the door."

A folded slip of white paper came through the generous space beneath. Keeping the pistol trained on the door, Brandt slid the paper across the dirty wood floor with his toe before picking it up. He read the note and then walked over to the table, unceremoniously dumping it in the ashtray and lighting it with a disposable lighter. Brandt didn't smoke, but he always carried a lighter.

"Señor?"

"It's open."

A salt-and-pepper-haired native stuck his head in the room. He looked at the gun and then back up at Brandt before he stepped inside and shut the door behind him. When Brandt was sure that he wasn't carrying a piece, he put his gun back in the holster.

"What do you have for me?" he asked, getting right to the point.

"You speak English?"

"Spanish is fine," said Brandt, effortlessly switching over to the language of his childhood.

"Gracias, señor."

The native walked over to the table where Brandt was standing. He took a sheaf of papers from the pocket of his tan windbreaker and handed them over. Brandt glanced through them quickly. Most of it he had seen before and none of it had apparently changed. "Well?"

"He will be traveling to Bertioga in the morning."

"Are you sure?"

"Positive. He is going to be staying with some friends. Their name is Bossert, a man and woman. They have a house on the beach."

Brandt smiled; this was perfect. But he kept his emotions in check as he formulated his plan. "I'm going to need a few things," he said finally.

"Our friend says you are to have whatever you ask for."

"Good. To start with I'm going to need a boat, a sailboat, six to seven meters. Seven and a half would be better. I have to be able to sail it myself, but I don't want a catamaran—it has to be big enough to sleep in."

That native took out a pad and pen and began scrawling down Brandt's request.

"Then I'll need a wetsuit and scuba gear with at least a couple hours' worth of air in the tanks. Have them in the boat and ready for me when I get there."

"Where do you want to pick the boat up?"

"Have it waiting at the marina at Santos." Brandt looked at his watch. "You should be able to get there tonight. I want to set sail at five tomorrow morning."

"Anything else?"

"Yeah, a bed sheet, white, and a box of one gallon Ziploc bags. Don't bring me anything smaller."

A brief look of curiosity came over the native's face for an instant and then subsided. "I've also been instructed to purchase a plane ticket for you."

"Anything, as long as it gets me out of this dump."

"Where to?"

Brandt didn't even have to think about it. "The United States."

Monday morning, before the sun was even close to coming up, Brandt had driven the one hundred and thirty kilometers to Santos, but before he went to the marina he drove down the coast a few kilometers between there and Bertioga. When he had found the cove he was looking for he stopped. The foliage grew right up to the water line. He took one of the green duffle bags from the back seat and, making his way down as close as he could, hid it in a secluded spot near the water. Then he drove back to Santos.

There were no problems at the marina. He was traveling as an American businessman on vacation using the name Kevin Adams. The boat was perfect, a seven and a half meter sloop with a small inboard. The scuba gear was down below in a tiny sleeping compartment and without hesitation Brandt pulled up anchor and set sail for Bertioga.

In another duffle bag, a long slender one that he had brought with him, were four items: a pair of high-powered 38x100 binoculars, a Heckler & Koch PSGL 7.62mm semiautomatic rifle fitted with a Steyr ZF69 telescopic sight, a lightweight Walther PPK pistol, and a small collapsible fishing knife. Along with these items, he tossed in the box of Ziploc bags that had been left for him.

He sailed far enough out to sea that he could make his approach to the house from almost due East. He plotted his course to put himself directly between the house and the sun; no one would be able to spot him until he was already in position. He had staked out the house and the shoreline back in November for just such an eventuality. Now it was here.

He dropped anchor just as the sun lifted above the horizon, and reached in the duffle bag for the binoculars. He was just about two kilometers offshore, far enough away not to attract attention, but close enough to get a good look at the target.

The Atlantic was calm and Brandt was grateful; the heat at high noon and beyond was going to be enough of a battle of endurance. About 11:00 a few more boats could be seen in the waters off Bertioga and it made for good cover. To keep himself cool he would dip the bed sheet in the water and lay it over himself while he kept his vigil on the tiny two-bedroom beach house.

At 2:30 that afternoon, the woman of the house went around to all the windows and closed the shutters. The target had arrived.

The rest of the day was uneventful. The woman left once at 5:30 that evening, returned a half hour later with a grocery bag, and then took a walk along the beach around eight. At no time was the target alone. Nothing happened after that but Brandt waited until midnight before pulling up anchor and making for the nearest unoccupied dock. Most of the properties along the beach were summer homes and it was surprising how many of them were not being used.

Brandt tied off at a house he had reconnoitered earlier in the day. It was fairly well hidden by foliage and although he could have spent the night inside quite easily, it wasn't worth the precautions it would necessitate. Instead he was content to set the alarm on his watch and crash in the sleeping chamber of the sailboat.

His plan was to get the target alone in the house, swim ashore, dispatch him, and swim back toward Santos. If his mission couldn't be accomplished here, he would try somewhere else. Brandt hadn't earned his reputation by being impatient.

The next day was the same as the one before. At sunrise he donned his wetsuit, sailed out, made his approach along with the morning and waited. It was obvious that the target was still staying with the couple. Several times as they were leaving to take a walk along the beach he could see them talking animatedly with someone inside the house. But a beach walk didn't give him enough time. At the end of the second day and the next morning of the third, Brandt repeated his rituals.

Wednesday at 3:00 in the afternoon the target finally appeared. Brandt threw off the moist sheet that covered him and sat up, looking through the binoculars. The man was sixty-eight years old with a full head of gray hair and a thick bushy mustache. He had just come out of the door along with the couple who owned the house and the three of them were walking down the beach together.

He was wearing white shorts, no shoes, and a light-blue short-sleeved shirt. Brandt put down the binoculars and picked up the rifle. He sighted through the scope but knew he wouldn't take a shot. He would use the rifle only if he would be able to get away cleanly. His instructions were explicit: remain undetected. If he shot now, he would certainly be spotted in the sailboat.

The group turned and began walking toward the house. Lawn chairs were brought out. The woman went into the house and returned with a tray of ice cube-filled tumblers and a pitcher of drink. At no time was the target left alone. Brandt was preparing to raise anchor and head toward the shore when he saw the old man take off his shirt and gingerly wade out into the breakers. He could barely contain his excitement.

Brandt hurriedly put on the rest of his diving gear and looked through the binoculars again. The man was now chest deep, arms out to his side, relaxing in the water. Beautiful. He took his PPK and slipped it into one of the Ziploc bags, leaving enough air in the bag so it would fire, and tucked it into his belt. Time, he was taking too much time. Brandt dumped the rifle and binoculars overboard, along with the duffle bag, then hoisted the air tanks onto his back. The man had started swimming.

Brandt tied off the sail and cut the anchor line, and as the boat lurched off for parts unknown, he slipped into the water. He checked his regulator, adjusted his mask, and then headed for the figure in the water that was already swimming out toward him. Brandt was submerged with about a thousand meters to travel and, using all the strength he possessed, covered the distance in good time, surfacing only once to check his bearing.

The water was only about twenty meters deep and very clear. The swells were small, making Brandt a little nervous, but once he reached the target he could relax; at close range he would have several opportunities. An air bubble in the Ziploc bag threatened to float his gun to the surface when he lifted it from his belt, but that was good; it meant that the shell had enough oxygen to fire. If he missed, there was always the knife.

He pressed the gun to his hand around the plastic and waited beneath the shadow of the swimming man.

When the target stopped and began treading water, Brandt made his move. Carefully he floated toward the surface, held just below the man's kicking feet, and reached up with his free hand. The target came down easily. He flailed a little but Brandt had his gun to the man's head and fired off a shot almost instantly. Blood streaked the water around him as he released the body and let it float to the surface.

He could have just drowned him, but that was not the objective. It had to be known that he had been assassinated. The fact would not come out right away, possibly never. Those around the man would try to cover it up but that didn't matter; *they* would know.

When he surfaced a few meters away, the sight of two men swimming out to the body jogged Brandt back into action. He stripped off the plastic bag and let the pistol sink, then submerged, swimming north. He would return to the cove for the green duffle bag waiting there. In it were his clothes, the P-38, and a one-way plane ticket to Seattle.

Chapter Six

1. Monday, 2:45 p.m., Telsen, British Columbia

Janet felt utterly defeated and clung to Steve as they approached the entrance to the camp. The sentry opened the gate immediately and the party walked through in silence. On the left was the large building with the chimney, and once past it they were ordered to stop near the end of the second row of barracks. On the side of the building was a large hand-painted sign that read: QUARANTINE.

"Okay," said the leader opening the door. "In you go."

Janet took the two steps up into the building, Steve followed her, and the door was shut behind them. It was well lit inside; the wooden shutters on all the windows were open. To the left of the entryway a doorway led to showers and toilets. The doorway on the right took them into a room with thirty or so bunks, each made up with blankets and a pillow.

Janet stopped when she saw the three men in the room. Two were on the right-hand side, lying on adjacent bunks. One looked around sixty years old, the other in his thirties. They wore dirty canvas jeans and flannel shirts, and their faces were bearded but clean. Janet had heard them talking when she walked in but now they just stared at her and Steve. The third man was at the far end of the room on the left-hand side and looked like he was in his mid-forties. She was instantly suspicious of him and when she looked up at Steve's stubbled chin she realized why. This man was clean-shaven. He wore slacks and a sport shirt, and barely acknowledging their entrance.

Steve reached past her and pulled a blanket off of the closest bunk, wrapping it around her before he grabbed one for himself from the next bunk. Janet was continually touched by the fact that Steve always thought of her first, even in the direst of circumstances. She led him to a bunk near the door on the right and sat next to him. They huddled together to ward off the chill that had seeped through their damp clothes.

"I'm so sorry I brought you up here," said Steve.

She kissed him and said, "Steve, don't."

Janet knew that Steve would blame himself for everything if she let him, even his father's abduction. He felt responsible for her and tried to protect her, but she knew it was really the other way around. She didn't think Steve knew their lives were on the line.

She had seen all of the human brains in the specimen jars. The obstinate receptionists, the black dishwasher—she could put two and two together. If they didn't get out of here, they were going to wind up as human vegetables on someone's operating table. If it made Steve fell better to keep things from her, that was fine. He was emotional; he seemed to feel things more deeply than she did. It was probably better this way.

There were times when she thought she might feel things as acutely as he did, but for a different reason. Steve seemed to look at the world very literally, take things as they came, on their own terms. She never took things at face value, always looking for the subtext, the hidden agenda, reading between the lines. This was probably what had initially drawn her to legal work and what made her acutely aware of what was happening now.

The firm she worked for specialized in criminal law. She'd read the casebooks, she knew about the inexorable barbarity of the human race firsthand. People killed other human beings for innumerable reasons; jealousy, passion, pride, and anger were romantic notions but more often than not the real motives were much baser, things like spite, bravado, sexual excitement, and boredom. The relative ease with which humans committed murder, and their truculent brutality, made Janet always expect the worse of her fellow man.

And here was Steve, her beautiful Stephen, trying to protect her. She had grown to love him more than he would ever know. Now that they were together, she would be damned if she was going to leave his side again.

He gave her a hug and then yawned. "God, I'm tired."

"Why don't you try to sleep?" she said.

"What about you?"

Janet shook her head. "I'll be fine."

Steve stretched out beside her, still looking exhausted from their early-morning trek. She was too keyed up to lie down, the humiliation of being roused without her clothes only minutes before playing over and over in her mind.

When she looked down the row of bunks at the two men, they were sitting up and both of them were staring at her. The older man smiled and nodded to her. God, she hated that. Why couldn't they just leave her alone? Steve had his eyes closed and was breathing quietly. She glanced over a second time and was mortified to see that the old man had stood up. She looked back down at Steve but his eyes were still shut.

Janet felt a twinge of fear as the man walked toward her. Anger welled inside of her to combat it. She was furious that women were raised to be frightened in any unusual situation, and even more so that she was herself. She would feel better if Steve was up, but she refused to wake him.

"Well, it's gettin' to be pretty crowded in here," the man said. The younger man, still in his bunk, snickered. Janet looked again to Steve but didn't say a word as the old man sat down on the bunk next to theirs.

"Hi there, I'm Eli Neuman. Over there is my son Danny." The younger man waved. "So, what brings you two here?"

"It's a long story," she said trying to stare him down. But he wouldn't go away.

"That's okay, we've got nothing but time."

"I suppose you think that's funny. Well I don't." She could feel Steve sit up beside her. "We're prisoners here and right now we just want to be left alone."

"Just thought things might be easier if you knew somebody."

"I don't want to know who you are. I don't care." She felt her body tremble and Steve put his arm around her tightly but she couldn't stop herself. "Jesus, we've been kidnapped! We're here against our will! Now, why don't you just leave us alone!"

The hurt was evident in Neuman's eyes. He stood up. "I'm sorry you feel that way, Miss. We're all in the same boat. I didn't mean to imply otherwise."

"Hey," Steve said to her as the man began to shuffle away. "What's going on?"

She could fell the tears welling up behind her eyes. Damn, she thought, she was supposed to be the strong one. If she didn't control herself quickly she was going to wind up bawling on Steve's shoulder like a typical woman.

"Wait," Janet called out. "I'm sorry. I didn't mean to . . ."

The man turned around warily. Janet looked at him apologetically, trying to convey her frustration, and he came back. "Just thought you could use a friend to talk to," he said with a wink. "Someone who knows what goes on around here."

Janet suppressed a grimace at his condescending manner; she wasn't going to let him get her again. Steve seemed to be fully alert now and offered his hand when the man sat back down. Neuman shook it firmly.

"My name's Steve, and this is Janet. How much do you know about what goes on here?" Steve asked eagerly.

"Pretty much everything. Danny and I've been here a long time now. We actually helped build the place. Course we didn't know that at the time. Once the fence went up, they decided we oughta stay for good. That was fifteen years ago."

"That's incredible," said Steve.

"How'd you folks come to be here?" Neuman asked.

"My da—"

"We were picked up for loitering," Janet said, cutting him off. There was no reason to give out any more information then was necessary. Not until Janet knew who they were dealing with.

Fortunately, Neuman laughed and Steve seemed more interested in what the old man had to say then why she had cut him off. "You've really been here that long?" Steve asked.

"Yeah. Danny was just eighteen then. Down south of here, just at the end of the big fence, there used to be small town, only about two thousand people or so, mostly out-of-work loggers and their families, like me. Danny's mother died when he was fifteen," he added.

"Well, this young fella, big guy, tells us that he's doin' some construction up north a ways and wants to know if anyone needs a job. Ten bucks an hour to start. So, what are we going to tell him? That he can keep his money? Hell, no. Just about every man in Marysville—that's what the town used to be called—they took this fella's job.

"We started at the hospital and worked our way south. The barbed wire? That didn't go up until we were already fenced in."

"They just kept you here?" said Janet, not sure that she could believe any of the old man's story.

Danny had left his bed and walked over to join them. He was huge and reminded Janet of the man who had been driving the Jeep earlier. "Hi, I'm Danny."

Steve shook his hand and introduced himself and Janet. Danny smiled at her and nodded while Eli continued.

"They herded us at gunpoint into these very cabins that we had built for them."

"What about your families?" Steve asked. "What about the rest of the town?"

"When they finished up the big fence they ran it around the town, slapped up the barbed wire, and the next thing you know we're all prisoners. They put signs up out at the highway sayin' that the road was washed out and they tore it out, the whole thing. Not a trace of it left."

Janet shuddered. She and Steve were sitting very close together, their legs over the side of the bed facing the two men. They still had the blankets covering them and she felt him reach under her blanket and take her hand. Steve's touch was comforting, and with Eli and Danny here she found herself feeling relieved in spite of her fear.

She took a casual look around the room, her fingers entwined in Steve's. Over in the corner the other man seemed to be hanging on every word that Eli Neuman was saying.

"That's when the bad stuff started happening They had the women in one cabin and the men in another and they started taking us out a few at a time. Lots of folks didn't come back. The ones that did weren't the same. They had their heads shaved. It seemed someone was pokin' around in their brains."

"That's what must have happened to the man I saw in the mess hall," Steve said excitedly. "He looked like half his brain was gone."

"Yeah," Eli said with a snort. "They don't waste time puttin' your skull back on. They leave your head all soft on top so they can squash your brains if you give 'em any trouble."

That brought Janet back into the conversation. "What happened to *you*?"

"We faked it," said Danny. They all turned to look at him, but he only nodded.

"How would you do that?" Janet finally asked, and Eli continued.

"Well, we watched for a while and sort of figured out what they were doin'. They had people sort of—I don't know—trained to do certain jobs around the place. We were some of the last to go and so we took Danny's knife and shaved her heads as best we could and slipped out a window. Then we walked over to one of the cabins that wasn't quite finished yet and started doin' a little carpentry.

"Well, right away one of the guards comes over and tells us that we're supposed to be over finishing up the workshops. So we high-tailed on over there and nobody knew different. Pretty soon our hair grew out like everyone else's and as long as we kept our mouths shut we were fine."

"Why didn't you try to escape?" Janet asked.

"I helped put in those fences myself, little lady. The barbed wire one is 'lectrified. I don't even know how a person would begin to get over *that*, if you could get that far at all. Those boys with their guns are all over the place."

"The towers were empty when we came in," she said.

"Sure, everybody's out workin' durin' the day."

"Why the 'quarantine' sign out front?" said Steve.

"This is where they put the new prisoners, the ones that are waitin' to go get operated on."

Janet was shocked. "Why are *you* here?"

"We got caught," said Danny.

Eli let out a long sigh and the conversation lulled for a moment.

"What about him?" Steve said quietly, with a nod toward the other man in the room.

"Hasn't said a word since he got here. I tried talkin' to him, but he won't have any of it."

"So what happens now?" said Janet.

"I expect we're all on the list to be gomers."

Steve's face lit up. "That's what the guy in the mess hall said."

"What?"

"Gomers."

"It's what they call the ones that have been operated on," Eli explained.

"Yeah," said Steve. "It's hospital jargon. It means Get Out of My Emergency Room."

"Always reminded *me* of *The Andy Griffith Show*," said Eli.

Danny was smiling now, as well as nodding.

Janet was horrified that everyone seemed to be taking all of this so casually, even Steve. Didn't they realize what kind of danger they were in? All of her worst fears had been confirmed. She didn't know what the connection to Steve's father was but it was clear that they had better act fast or it would be too late.

No one said anything for a long time and eventually Eli stood up. "Well, I guess we've bothered you two enough. Dinner's not until five and you'll probably want to get a little rest before—"

"Wait," said Janet.

Eli stopped and waited, but Janet hadn't really known what she wanted to say. She just knew she didn't want them to go yet. As hard as it would be, she would have to trust them. She couldn't see any other way out. Now Steve was looking at her and she blurted out what was on her mind. "I think we should try to escape."

She felt Steve squeeze her thigh. Danny's eyes were sparkling and a big grin spread over his face. Eli simply rubbed his chin and nodded but didn't sit back down right away. "How?"

"I don't know, exactly. I thought we could talk about it with you. You know the layout of this place as well as anyone, probably better." Janet had thrown in that last bit to stroke Eli's ego and it had worked. Eli sat back down.

2. 4:55 p.m.

For the past two hours Janet, Steve, Eli, and the taciturn Danny had been kicking around ideas for escaping. At one point Danny pulled a slat from one of the unused bunks and, with his knife, carved out a crude map of the Institute property. It was bigger than Janet had imagined, running not only to the gate on the eastern border but out to the highway, and then south, past the acres of farmland to the annexed town of Marysville.

They had problems in settling on a plan, though. Eli explained to them that the easiest way to circumvent the fence would be at the point where the Little Telsen River entered the Institute property, but Steve insisted on going back to get his father.

"That's suicide, plain and simple. Those kids with the guns? They don't mind usin' 'em, you know. Sometimes I think that's the only reason they're here."

"Look, I know where he is. I was there. We almost had him out. I even know what room he's in."

Eli wasn't convinced. "Never mind gettin' him out—how you gonna get in to him in the first place?"

"I don't know yet. We had a set of keys, but when they caught—"

"They're itchin' for someone to pull the trigger on. You'll never make it."

"I'll take my chances." Steve was adamant.

Their talking, for all its passion, was very subdued. Janet had been bothered by the third man across the room, who was straining to hear their conversation, and suggested they keep their voices down. Since even Danny and Eli didn't know who he was, they had agreed.

"You plannin' on doin' this alone, are you?" asked Eli.

"What do you mean?"

"I was thinkin' about her."

All of the men turned to Janet. "She can head for the fence with you—" Steve suggested.

"The hell I will," Janet said in a loud whisper. A cloud of anger had been forming around Steve, and she hoped she would be able to dissipate it. "Why don't we all try to get out of here the quickest way we can," she said. "Then we can call the police and they can get your dad." Janet could tell it wasn't working; Steve was frowning and seemed to be pouting.

Suddenly Eli spoke up before she had a chance to warn him off. "I just don't think you're takin' these fellas very serious—"

"Well, you two sure as hell don't seem too worried about being gomers for the rest of your lives!"

That brought the proceedings to a screeching halt. The third man, who seemed to be losing his interest at this point, was all ears again. The only one of the group who didn't seem embarrassed was Steve, who was still fuming. Janet didn't know whether to try and comfort him out of his anger or not, fearing that he might blow up at her.

Eli spoke up. "Fair enough," he said, to Janet's surprise. "But I want to be able to understand how we can—"

"Here they come," said Danny.

Janet listened closely and watched as Eli and Danny turned somber. "What is it?" she asked.

Eli motioned his head toward the other end of the room. "Go ahead. Take a look for yourself."

Janet took Steve's hand and he followed her. It was dark out now; the bare bulbs above them must have been on during the day because she hadn't noticed the change. As they approached the window she could see banks of lights flooding the area in front of the main camp building as well as the gate.

There were six tables lined up along the front of the building with two people, not guards, at each. Every table had on it a large steaming pot and stacks of bowls. She and Steve had to press up close to see the gate open. When it did, people started to walk into the camp. It was their steps, she realized, that she had heard earlier.

Each person walked up to a table and took a bowl, then held it out and had it filled from the pot. Janet watched in amazement as each ate his bowlful and deposited the empty dish in a tub, which she hadn't noticed before. Soon there were armed guards milling around, keeping their prisoners in line and ordering them back to their barracks when they were finished.

She watched in sickened dismay as endless streams of lifeless humans walked past. There were men and women in equal numbers, mostly black. They looked dirty and unkempt, the women with crudely-cut matted hair, and men with beards. Their eyes were sunken and their skin was sallow, and they wore clothes of every type, jeans and T-shirts, dresses, suits, and pajamas. They were all different ages, some young, some elderly, most between thirty and fifty. But it wasn't until a group of tiny children marched by, their eyes as dull as slate, that Janet had to tear herself away from the harrowing scene.

Steve put his arm around her from behind. "Are you all right?"

She looked up and saw that the third man was looking at her and she turned to walk back toward Eli and Danny. Steve put his arm around her waist and she leaned into him. They were halfway back when the door slammed open, startling her.

Three soldiers entered the room, two carrying trays of food and the other content to stand by the door, feet apart and hand on his rifle, in a stance of dominance. Janet and Steve moved out of the way as the two walked past them and set their trays on a table at the far end of the room. No one said a word as they turned back to the door.

Eli stood up and was walking around the end of the bunk when the soldier closest to him stiff-armed him square in the chest and knocked him to the floor. "Outa my way, Gramps."

What happened next was so quick and took Janet so much by surprise that she simply just stood for a few moments after it was over, trembling in fear of her life.

In one smooth motion Danny was up off the bunk and launching himself at the soldier. The sudden movement caused the man to turn slightly so that Danny caught him square in the chest, lifting him up off his feet and wrapping him in a picture-perfect football tackle. The scream on the way down ended in a loud air-expelling grunt as Danny's muscular frame pinned the soldier to the floor. Danny was up on his knees straddling him, his left hand gripping the man's neck as most people might grip a garden hose, his right hand cocking back and looking for all intents and purposes like a sledge hammer, when a rifle butt cracked into the back of his head.

Janet had screamed without even realizing it and she felt Steve clutch her as Danny fell in a heap on top of the soldier. The other soldier rolled him off with the heel of his boot and helped his partner up while the gunman trained his rifle on Janet, Steve and Eli, but none of them were moving.

"Son of a bitch," said the soldier, staggering to his feet. As soon as he was up he leveled a booted foot at Danny's face and kicked him hard. Danny's head snapped around and blood and saliva spewed from his mouth. Janet turned her head and buried her face in Steve's shoulder. When the smell of the hot food reached her nostrils it made her stomach turn.

She looked up as the soldier was about to kick Danny again, but the gunman grabbed him by the arm. "Knock it off. You're not hurt. Let's get outa here."

"But that son of a bitch knocked me down, goddamn it."

"Come on, I said. Move it."

"Son of a bitch knocked me down," he whined to his partner but his partner was already walking toward the door and he followed reluctantly. "Son of a bitch."

It seemed like none of them breathed until the door had been shut and locked. Eli crawled on all fours over to his son, taking a handkerchief from his pants pocket and dabbing the blood from Danny's face. He looked up at Janet and Steve. "Okay," he said. "We'll do it any way you want. I'm not gonna be a gomer and neither is my boy." Eli looked at Danny and then back at them. "Can you help him? Is he gonna be alright?"

"Sure," said Steve. Janet was still in a daze; she was breathing rapidly and noticed Steve was doing the same. "Just let me—"

"Wait!" boomed a voice from across the room. Out of nowhere the third man appeared. Eli was just about to lift Danny's head when the man grabbed is arm. He stepped around Eli and took out a penlight from his shirt pocket. "We don't want to move him until we're sure his neck isn't broken."

Danny was lying face up on the floor and the man spread Danny's eyelids apart with his thumb and forefinger, looking into his eyes one at a time with the light. Then he felt gently around the back of Danny's neck with both hands. When he seemed satisfied he looked up at Steve. "Come over here and help me lift him onto the bed." Then to Janet: "Take the pillow off of there so he has a flat surface to lie on."

Steve walked over to help and when Janet was finished the man called her over as well. Then he looked at Eli. "Do you think you can help us lift him?"

"Yes," Eli answered.

"Good. I want you to hold on to his shirt underneath is arm so that his arm stays by his side. And I want you to take his leg," he said to Janet, "okay?" Then he turned to Steve. "Can you get that side by yourself?"

"Yeah."

"Good. I'm going to take his head. Now it's important that we all lift together so there's as little movement as possible."

"Are you sure we should move him?" Steve asked.

Janet couldn't believe it. It was obvious the man had some kind of medical training and here Steve was questioning him.

"The blow he sustained missed the vertebra," said the man calmly, to Janet's relief. "It caught him clear up by the occipital lobe. I don't think there's any problem with moving him, but I still want to take precautions."

The man counted to three and they all lifted Danny up and carried him slowly, the man cradling Danny's head expertly with his hands, and then set him on the bed.

"He should be fine, sir," said the man to Eli. "It looks like the bleeding has stopped. If you want to wash him that would be fine, but I don't want you to move his head until he wakes up, okay?"

Eli nodded. "Yes. Thank you, Mister. Thank you for helping my boy." Then he put a hand on Janet's shoulder and looked over to Steve. "Thanks to all of you."

While Eli was heading to the washroom to wet his handkerchief Steve spoke to the man. "Are you a doctor?"

"Yes."

"I thought so. I'm sorry about what I said back there. I didn't mean to . . ."

"That's all right. I just though he would be more comfortable on the bed. He'll have a sore neck when he wakes up, but he really should be fine."

"My name's Steve Raymond, and this is Janet Newell," Steve said, offering his hand. But the anticipated hi-it's-nice-to-meet-you did not come. Instead, the look on the doctor's face became one of total confusion.

"Are you Paul Raymond's boy?"

"Yes," Steve said cautiously.

When the man finally introduced himself it was their turn to become confused.

"My name's Phillips," he said. "Dr. Howard Phillips."

3. 5:03 p.m.

Paul Raymond was sitting up on his bed at a moveable table and eating dinner: a withered hot dog resting in a stale bun, baked beans, corn, and cold coffee. With every bite of the vapid fare he became more pissed off. He hadn't seen Howard but the once, and he had been barely coherent at the time. Then there was the big guy; Paul hadn't made up his mind about him yet. Why was Howard sending in this jarhead instead of talking to him face to face?

The worst part about the whole deal, though, was Steve. Paul wondered how he was going to be able to protect him. Throughout the day, the gravity of his situation became more and more evident. Howard was playing some sort of game with him; he was obviously desperate. The letter he had delivered to Paul made absolutely no sense, but the threat on Steve's life certainly did.

It looked hopeless. If the threat was serious, then Howard might kill Steve no matter what Paul did. Unless Howard was bluffing, they didn't stand a chance. There was only one way to go at this point: Steve's way. As soon as Paul conceded to Howard's demands, Howard would have no further use for either of them. So his only course of action right now as to take no action. Refuse to do anything.

Paul looked down at his food again and pushed it away. He just wasn't hungry anymore. He was lying back down on his bed and closing his eyes, trying to think of something else, when the door opened. Into the room walked an old man in a white lab coat and Paul sat up to face him. His shoulders were slightly hunched and he had a strained look on his face. Paul waited in silence until the man spoke.

"Dr. Raymond, I must apologize for the most unpleasant way in which we were forced to procure your services."

"Who the hell are you?"

"That is not important now. I run the Institute here. If there is anything I can do for you—"

"Yeah, there is. You can give me my son and let us get the hell out of here."

"Of course. Just as soon as you have performed the surgery."

"Who the fuck do you think you are?" Paul stood up quickly and the old man took a reflexive step backward. "First I'm kidnapped and drugged—then there's my son—and now you expect me to perform some bullshit surgery? Go fuck yourself, buddy. You and Phillips both."

The old man had recovered enough to reclaim his lost step. "I had hoped you would not take that attitude, but I must say I am not surprised considering your reluctance to cooperate with your friend Dr. Phillips."

"Phillips isn't my friend."

"Apparently."

Paul sat back down on the bed. He was tired of this whole scenario and, as though to illustrate the point, he yawned. The old guy looked a little ill at ease and finally pulled up a chair. It wasn't until he was seated that the slight tremor Paul had noticed in his right hand became more extreme.

"I did not come here to argue with you. I came here to discuss the surgery. I have taken the liberty of scheduling it for tomorrow."

"Didn't you hear what I just said? I'm not doing a goddamn thing until you let us go."

"I must say I *am* disappointed by your attitude."

"Well, you're just going to have to learn to live with it."

"I am afraid I will not be able to do that, Dr. Raymond. But if I can't, then neither will you." With that the old man stood up and walked away. Paul was still puzzling over his last statement when he pulled open the door. Four soldiers filed into the room and headed straight for Paul. They gathered around the bed while the old man wheeled in an IV stand, two full bottles of clear liquid suspended from its hooks.

"You know what pain receptors are, don't you Dr. Raymond?"

Paul felt his heart rate increase and he didn't like it. He thought about rushing him but the old man pulled up well short of the bed, and besides, he would never be able to get past his khaki entourage.

"Look, I don't know what you're trying to pull—"

"Pain receptors, Dr. Raymond. You must remember from your medical school days. Nerve endings in the brain that, when fit with the exact molecule, induce symptoms of extreme pain, not unlike that of intense heat or, say, severe muscle cramps. Only the pain never goes away; it continues as long as the chemical is administered into the patient's bloodstream or until the patient loses consciousness."

"Tell me something I don't know."

"Very well, then. We are about to take you out of the realm of theory, Dr. Raymond, and into the world of practical application. To say that you are familiar with pain receptors, I take it to mean that you have studied their effects on helpless laboratory animals, never really experiencing and gauging the effects of the results for yourself. Now you will have that opportunity. I think you will find this demonstration most enlightening."

"I don't believe this shit! If you think threats like this are going to work you're a lot stupider than I thought." That one hit the old geezer where he lived. Paul could see him clenching his teeth, his face reddening, and decided to twist the knife a little more. "Any first-year med student knows that the only way to treat Parkinson's is with chemotherapy. The surgery you want me to do"—Paul was guessing that the old guy was behind all this; he knew Phillips was smarter than that—"was discontinued in the sixties. Only an idiot would try something like that now. You're wasting your time with me—"

"Shut up, you! Hold him down!"

Instantly, eight hands clamped onto Paul and pinned him to the bed. He tried to break free but he might as well have been paralyzed for all the effect he was having on his captors. Leather straps were brought out and his legs and arms were fastened to the collapsed railing on both sides of the bed. The only thing he could move with any degree of freedom was his head.

"Now, I shall ask you one more time: Do you wish to cooperate?"

"Go fuck yourself!"

"As you wish."

The old man wheeled up the stand to the bed and slipped on a pair of half-lenses that had been dangling from a lanyard around his neck. The two IV bottles fed into one tube and the old man held the end of it with the pinky of his right hand. Then he swabbed the crook in Paul's elbow and deftly inserted the IV. Once he had taped it securely to Paul's arm he stepped back.

"In the first bottle is saline solution, in the second, pain. The chemicals must be diluted, otherwise you would pass out almost immediately. Now, I'll give you one last chance to cooperate."

Paul was silent, staring at the ceiling, as the old man started the intravenous drip. The chemicals felt warm going into his arm and within seconds he felt as if his whole body were heating up. The degrees of warmth, discomfort and pain came in a blur. His body was on fire now and Paul was writhing beneath the restraints. He couldn't see the flames, but they were there. He could feel them licking at his flesh and burning him everywhere, from his skin down into his bones. But he would not cry out. He wouldn't give the bastard the satisfaction.

"How are you feeling, Dr. Raymond?"

Paul opened his eyes. The soldiers were gone now. He wanted to yell at the old man, curse him until his voice went hoarse, but he knew that as soon as he released a breath to talk he wouldn't be able to hold back the anguish and it would rush out in a torrent of wails and capitulation.

"It appears that the dosage is not quite right." With a twist of the valve the old man sent a red-hot spear into Paul's brain. That was when the screaming began.

4. 5:15 p.m.

Walther Brandt watched the entire affair from the back of the room and it sickened him. Killing someone was one thing; torture was something else again. He had more respect for a man than to make him suffer.

For an hour or so Zindell had Raymond screaming with pain and more than once Brandt had to avert his eyes. It wasn't that he couldn't take it; he just didn't see the need. Raymond took everything Zindell dished out without giving in and Brandt felt a twinge of concern for the man. Some might have thought Raymond stupid, but Brandt didn't think so. Maybe he was just trying to protect his kid. Whatever the reason, it didn't matter; the guy had balls.

Finally, Zindell reduced the drip to the point where Raymond was at a continual moan. He hissed something unintelligible at Brandt on the way out and then left him alone with Raymond.

5. 5:20 p.m.

Steve was stunned. Things were happening faster than he could keep up with them. "Wait a minute," said Steve. "The doctor I met at the Institute said *his* name was Phillips."

Phillips smiled. "Is that what he called himself?"

"Yeah. I just assumed . . . I mean, I *thought* there was something wrong with him—he was too old. You're about the same age as my dad."

"Sure, we went to school and did our residency together at Johns Hopkins."

"You developed uradrine."

Phillips nodded slowly and Steve could see that he had said the wrong thing. He tried to get back on the subject. "So who is that guy?"

Phillips walked over to the opposite side of the room and sat on a bunk. He propped up a pillow and leaned back against it, his legs extended. It was clear he was still keeping an eye on Danny. His face became pensive and Steve silently watched him, not sure whether they should have followed him.

Eli came back from the bathroom with a wet handkerchief and used it to clean the blood from Danny's face as Phillips began to talk.

"Have you ever heard of Konrad Zindell?"

Steve walked over with Janet in tow and sat across from Phillips. "No. Who's that?"

"That's the man you met. Zindell was a Nazi. He was a doctor—at least that's what he called himself—who worked under Josef Mengele at the extermination camp at Auschwitz. Well, he did experiments on twins there, radical brain surgery, just like he's done on the people around here, except that the twins were killed right afterward. Now he's keeping them alive for some kind of longitudinal study, looking the long-term effects of the surgeries."

Steve could hardly believe that the old man he'd met was a Nazi relic from World War II, and he and Janet both listened raptly to Phillips' account.

"Zindell spent a few years hiding in Europe after the war before escaping to South America with his research. Well, eventually Mengele found out where he was and wanted to get Zindell's work by blackmailing him. He said that he would expose Zindell if he didn't hand over all of his surgical reports. That's when I get a call.

"The next thing I know Zindell shows up in Baltimore wanting to work with me. He already had someone fly to Germany and get pictures of one of Mengele's henchmen. Then Zindell pasted them to his own papers and when Mengele's man came to pick him up, the Israelis were already waiting there and shish-kabobbed his brain with an ice pick. Zindell got off scot-free. The only one who knew was Mengele, but who was he going to tell?

"Four years I worked with Zindell to find a way of brain mapping using his research. Four years I spent programming his data into a computer, only to find out that it's impossible."

"What happened?"

"A little thing called AAD, that's what."

"Alternate-area development," Steve blurted out.

"Very good," said Phillips. "You a doctor like your pop?"

"Not yet. I'm still in my first year of medical school."

"What's alternate-area development?" Janet said.

Steve looked to Phillips but he nodded back. "It means that when areas of the brain are damaged—" Steve began.

"Or missing," added Phillips.

"—the brain cells nearby will sometimes take up the functions of the damaged or missing areas."

Janet nodded.

"What that means in a theoretical sense," Phillip continued, "is that not all individual brain cells have individualized functions. Zindell's whole theory was wrong. He thought he could determine the exact function of each brain cell simply by its location in the cerebral cortex, but that's just not possible. Like a fingerprint, everybody's brain is different."

"When I confronted him with this he blew up. He said I was trying to undermine his research and use his study to get a Noble Prize for myself. Finally he said he didn't need my help and went off to Canada to do more experiments. I went back to my original research and you probably know the rest."

"Once I had been fired from John Hopkins I got a letter from him. He said if I was willing to help, he would let me study with him. I laughed at first until I found out the hard way that I'd been blackballed. The idea of never working again was unthinkable, so eventually I took him up on his offer."

"Why does he need my dad?"

"He's got Parkinson's."

"I thought so!" said Steve.

"Yeah?"

"Yeah. I saw the tremor in his hands when he introduced himself . . . as you."

"He thinks he has a foolproof operation that will cure him but he needs your pop to do the surgery. At first I went along with it, but as soon as I saw what they did to him I went back to Zindell and told him I didn't want any part of it. When I refused to help him strong-arm Paul he locked me up in his little concentration camp."

"What *is* this place?" said Janet.

"Zindell has a partner named Brandt who has some Nazi, Aryan race thing he runs out of here. They've got soldiers, guns, the whole nine yards."

Steve was well aware of the camp's resources. "What do you think will happen to us?"

"They're probably keeping us on ice till Paul does the surgery."

"I told him not to," said Steve.

"No shit?" Phillip's face clouded over in thought for a moment. "So he knows you're here."

"Yeah."

"How did they ever get a hold of you two?" Phillips asked.

"I found a letter that you . . . Did you write a letter to my dad?"

"Yeah," Phillips said, grimly, "But he didn't respond. I don't think your pop likes me very much."

"Hey, Mister," Eli suddenly shouted from across the room. "I think Danny's wakin' up."

Phillips was off his bunk and at Danny's side in an instant. Danny moaned and put his hand up to his head.

"Take it easy," said Phillips. "Don't try to set up. Just lie there."

"I feel sick," Danny said, his eyes still closed.

"You've had a concussion. Just relax for a while and the nausea will go away. Right now I want you to move your feet for me. Can you do that?"

Danny's booted feet swished back and forth like windshield wipers. "That's good. Thanks." Phillips looked up at Eli. "He'll be fine."

While Phillips was attending to Danny, Steve looked over to the food that was on the table. "Do you think we should go over and eat?" he asked when Phillips had finished.

"Good idea."

Janet asked Eli if he wanted her to bring over a tray for him and Danny but he shook her off. "No. I'll come over and get it when Danny's ready."

Steve, Janet and Phillips sat down at the table and stared for a moment at the small pot of orange-yellow gruel.

Janet grimaced. "What is this?"

"Well" said Phillips "it's a little something Zindell concocted to meet every growing zombie's daily requirements. I think there's corn in it."

Janet dished up three bowls and gave each of them a spoon. Phillips merely poked at his food while Steve and Janet tried not to look as if they were having a contest to see who could finish first. When they finally pushed them away, their bowls were clean.

Danny was sitting up in his bed now and Eli turned to Phillips. "Danny says he's feeling better—he wants to know if he can come over an' eat something. That okay?"

Phillips nodded.

On the way to the table Danny had one hand up to the back of his head and was turning it, testing his neck.

"Are you sure you're all right?" asked Janet.

"Yeah," he said, trying to smile. "I'm hungry."

Danny and Eli had started on their meals when Phillips cleared his throat. "I was listening to you guys talking before, about escaping." Phillips' eyes were pinpoints and he paused for a moment, looking at each person around the table.

"We didn't really get very far," said Steve. "I was thinking that I should try to get to the Institute on my own. Then you four could try for the fence by the river."

"Never get out of the camp," Eli uttered though a mouthful of gruel.

"I think we could," Phillips said, his head bobbing and his eyes now seemingly looking inward. Danny and Eli stopped eating and everyone looked to Phillips. "I have a plan."

6. 6:28 p.m.

Paul's brain was white with heat. Just when he would get to the point where the pain was so unbearable he though he would lose consciousness, he was brought back to a state of mere torment. Most of his ability to reason had left with the first screams but now he seemed to be getting some of it back.

The room was coming back into focus, too, and he could see someone standing over him at the IV stand. The fire was gone and gradually his senses returned. Paul could feel the straps against his arms and the wetness between his legs and he could smell the sweat on his body. But the pain was entirely gone; not even a trace remained. The difference was so remarkable that he wondered fleetingly if the pain had even been real. Then he heard a voice from beside him.

"Dr. Raymond? Dr. Raymond, can you hear me?"

"Yes," he said, surprised at the sound of his own voice.

"I just thought I'd shut this thing off while Zindell's gone."

"Who?"

"The old guy. His name's Zindell."

Paul's head was cleared now as he looked up to see the man who had given him the letter from Phillip yesterday. "It's you? What are you doing here?"

"I thought we should talk."

"Is there any way you can take these straps off first?"

"I'm afraid I couldn't do that."

"Could you at least turn off the saline drip?"

"What's that?"

"The other bottle on the IV rack."

Paul watched as the man slowly turned the valve and then pulled up the chair that Zindell had been sitting in earlier. The man sat down with his customary ease and looked into Paul's eyes.

"We haven't been introduced. My name's Walther Brandt."

"What do you want, Mr. Brandt?"

"I think you should do the operation."

"What the hell for?"

"Maybe it's just me, but you didn't look too comfortable just now."

Paul didn't respond.

"I'm sorry. It's just that I may be in a position to help you and the two kids get out of here."

"Two? What are you talking about?"

"Your son and his girlfriend."

Paul shut his eyes. Steve hadn't told him that Janet was here, too.

"And why should I believe you? How do I know you're not going to tell him everything I say?"

"You don't." Brandt sucked his lower lip into his mouth, formulating his argument. "Just listen to what I'm proposing, Dr. Raymond, because I'm only going to say it once. If you tell anyone here what I've said, I'll kill you myself. And that's not a threat, it's a promise. I don't have a problem with killing people. What I *do* have a problem with is Zindell.

"What he hasn't told you is that he wants you to do the operation on *him*."

Things were coming together for Paul now. "He's going to kill me after it's over. Steve and Janet, too."

"That would be my guess."

"Fuck him. I'll just refuse."

"Not for long. Even a sadistic bastard like Zindell gets tired of torturing people. I heard what you told him earlier about the operation. It sounds to me like if you're too much trouble, he'll kill you and get someone else."

"Then why the hell did he bring me here in the first place?"

"Looks like you're his first-round draft pick. You must be good." The remark did not seem disingenuous.

"So I'm just shit outa luck?"

"There might be something you could do about it."

"And what would that be?"

"You're going to be in his brain?" he said with a shrug. "Fuck him up."

"What? Lobotomize him?"

"No, no, nothing like that."

"Then what are you talking about?"

Brandt put his hand between his legs and scooted the chair closer to the bed, then leaned in, lowering his voice. "I have some of his notes—I took them from his desk and made copies. He has a way of making people docile by operating on their brains. When he's done, they do what they're told and don't argue. He's been doing it for years. *I* just want you to do the same thing to him. Don't kill him, whatever you do. Just fuck him up."

"And what's to keep you from killing me afterward?"

Brandt leaned back now, his voice resuming its former volume. "You're just going to have to trust me on that one. If you do, I'll make sure you and the two kids get out of here. Just tell me you'll do the operation and I'll have you out of those straps before I leave. I'm not going to turn this shit back on," he said, thumbing to the IV stand, "but Zindell's going to be back and he will."

"And what do you get out of all of this?"

"That's my business. The less you know, the better. If you don't want to do it it's no skin off my nose, but I don't want you to be under any illusions either. If you don't do it, you're gonna die. The kids, too. And there's nothing I can do for you at that point."

Paul laid his head back and closed his eyes. He had no idea whether he could trust Brandt, but at least if he agreed to do the surgery he would be a lot more comfortable. Up until that point, he could always back out. It was their game, and he was going to play it by the same deceitful rules that they did. He needed to make a decision and this would give him the time. "Okay," he said, eyes still closed. "Tell him I'll do it."

Canada, 1985

Walther Brandt made his way easily down the Institute corridor to Zindell's office. In his left hand was that evening's edition of *The Telsen Register*, folded up to page three. The compunction he felt after reading the article that was facing out would make it hard for him not to simply snap Zindell's neck when he saw him. Instead he rapped once on the door with his knuckle and entered without waiting for a response.

"What do *you* want?" said Zindell over the top of his half-glasses.

Brandt tossed the paper onto his desk. "Here, I thought you might like to see this."

While Zindell read Brandt looked around the room. Against the back wall were two glass cases. One contained a variety of skulls, several of them human, and even with his limited medical knowledge it was obvious to Brandt that the jars of murky liquid in the other cabinet contained human brains. The walls displayed pictures and documents that meant nothing to Brandt, but over in the far corner was something that

201

did: the boxes, five wooden crates, stacked one on top of the other, where Zindell kept his original Auschwitz files.

"Why should I care about this anymore?" the old man said, even though, as Brandt had noticed, he had read the entire article.

"Look, I just thought you might be interested, that's all." Brandt should have known better than to expect any kind of gratitude.

"Are they going to find anything they do not know about already?"

"No, it was a clean job."

"Then get out of here and leave me alone."

As soon as Brandt's hand touched the doorknob, Zindell spoke. "Take your paper with you."

Brandt showed no signs of duress as he gently took the newspaper from Zindell's hand. Once out in the hall his own hand went automatically to his pistol as he imagined what it would feel like to splatter the old man's brains across the back wall of his office. Problem was that with Zindell gone, it would only be a matter of time before the whole thing came to a grinding halt.

Zindell was smart. He played his cards close to the vest. The nuthouse was just a front for his experimental hospital, and most of the patients who were admitted here either wound up as prisoners or got tossed into the pit. Brandt knew more about the operation than anyone else, but even that was almost nothing. Zindell was a liaison with the public and everything that was shipped in for Brandt's soldier's was under the guise of being for the hospital.

Of course Zindell owned the entire five miles of coastline, too, and no one but he knew where any of the titles were or who would get the property once he died. So even though Brandt had free reign over the soldiers, Zindell had him by the nuts.

What the hell, thought Brandt. At least he keeps his nose out of my business, I should be grateful for that. So why is it that I want to kill the fucker every time I see him?

As he was walking past one of the empty rooms, Brandt spied a garbage can. He opened the door, tossed the newspaper into the can, and hurried back toward the entrance. He was already late for his meeting.

The story that had run in *The Register* that evening was of international interest and had been reported in nearly every newspaper and on every television and radio in the world. As they didn't have a reporter in South America, *The Register* had elected to go with a wire service account:

REMAINS IN BRAZIL
THOUGHT TO BE MENGELE

EMBU, Brazil — Thursday Brazilian police exhumed the remains of a man who was said to have died here in 1979 and began the lengthy task of analyzing the skull, bones, and shreds of clothing that police believe could belong to Josef Mengele, the Nazi death-camp doctor and the world's most wanted fugitive.

Josef Antonio de Mello, director of the Sao Paulo morgue, held the skull for hundreds of onlookers to see when the remains were disinterred at Embu, 27 kilometers from Sao Paolo, Brazil's largest city.

Mengele, who would be 74, is accused of sending hundreds of thousands of people, mostly Jews, to their deaths at Auschwitz concentration camp, and for his sinister experiments on those not sent to the gas chamber.

Brandt drove his Jeep lazily through the woods back to the camp. He liked the summer because the sun stayed up so much longer. Even in the thick forest south of the Institute he didn't have to turn on his headlights.

When he crossed the bridge that took him over the Little Telsen River his tires chattered beneath him and he smiled. Even with Zindell, at this point in his life he wouldn't have wished anything different for himself. He was happier than he had ever been before. When the guard at the gatehouse saw his Jeep rambling up, the cross arm rose immediately and Brandt returned the salute he received on his way through.

Once he reached the barbed wire of the camp, he had to slow down so that the gate could be opened. He was proud of his achievement: the camp was a scale model of the one in Dachau, Germany during World War II. The ten barracks on each side of the large avenue running down the center were currently holding about two thousand people and had room for about two thousand more. The prisoners were reasonably well cared for, fed three times a day and bathed once a week. Their quarters were squalid, but overall it was nothing like the death camps. When Brandt reached the end of the avenue he swung left in front of the administration building, which contained his living quarters, his office, and the camp brothel. Then he drove past the other guardhouse and out through the side gate.

Just south of the camp were the buildings that comprised the living quarters for his men. There were five barracks that held twenty men each, and five other buildings that housed the mess hall, the laundry and storage depot, the club house (complete with big-screen TV and VCR, pool tables, couches and chairs, and a small bar that was opened for special occasions), the armory, and the meeting hall.

He pulled his jeep up in front of the meeting hall right next to the brand-new van that he had finally persuaded Zindell to purchase, hauled himself out, and went inside. It was beautiful. Against the far wall behind the podium was a huge portrait of Hitler, flanked by two German war flags, their giant swastikas making Brandt's pulse quicken with pride.

He loved Germany, his real homeland, and had pledged his life to restoring it to its former glory. After his father . . . was gone, he had had a long talk with his mother. She told him how his father had served Hitler and the Reich, and, after the war had been lost, how the Jews had persecuted his father, telling lies about him and making him ashamed of all that he had accomplished in the service of the Fatherland. The story of how his father had succumbed to their vile hatred made Walther cry. But his mother slapped him in the face, telling him that German soldiers didn't cry and that he should carry on as his father would have wanted him to.

After that the decisions were easy. He would kill Jews, as many of them as possible, and create a new Reich where his German countrymen could flourish. He began as a freelance hit man in West Germany, perfecting his craft under the guidance of his father's peers, who had procured him most of his contacts with the Arab states. But although the work was plentiful, he was distressed by the anger and resentment that still existed for the way of life for which his father had died.

It was through this network of his father's friends that he first heard of Zindell. Zindell had just purchased a gigantic piece of coastline in Canada and needed to outfit a small unit of men to protect the place. He wanted Brandt to command them, but Brandt wanted more. They haggled fiercely and Zindell finally agreed to Brandt's terms on the condition that Brandt do a job for him. Both upheld their ends of the bargain and inside of a year everything had been built, the hospital to Zindell's specifications, the rest to Brandt's.

Brandt tried not to think about Mengele, but every so often the memory crept into his mind. Sometimes he thought he had *lost* his mind back there. He had been so hungry for the opportunity to start his own version of the Fourth Reich that he had done something he could never forgive himself for: he had allowed himself to kill a German. It wasn't just because he was German; Menegle was a fellow countryman who had made tremendous strides in ridding Europe of the hate-monger Jews.

As he walked up the aisle of folding chairs he noticed how many of them were empty. Although the hall seated a hundred, Brandt only had twenty-eight men at the moment. But there would be more, many more. Seven months ago the machinery had been put in motion, ensuring that Germans would once again rule the world. After he had realized how difficult it was to find men for him who could meet his strict specifications, Brandt had dreamed up his own version of *Lebensborn*.

After intensive negotiations with Zindell, Brandt's breeding program had finally come to fruition. A maternity ward was set up in the hospital and six women who had been chosen from widely diverse sections of British Columbia and the northwestern United States were kidnapped. They were all of pure German descent, and they all vanished from their homes without a trace, just like half of the other prisoners in the camp. Zindell cracked open their skulls and did his thing, and before long they were ready for breeding. Five of them were pregnant now—Brandt had been forced to put one of them into the camp brothel when Zindell discovered she was sterile—but with more acquisitions they would have enough pure German stock to carry on forever.

All of his men were culled from various white supremacist groups around the Northwest. Where Brandt's thinning-out process was most brutal was genealogical descent and attitude toward Germany. Brandt insisted that each of his soldiers have some German blood and that their views of German—not just Aryan—supremacy be synonymous with his own. Over the years, he had only been able to find twenty-eight. Of course there were always some who didn't work out, like the two he had to take care of tonight, but for the most part, his instincts proved correct.

There were sixteen men seated in front of him, ten out on guard duty, and two in manacles and leg irons on the floor. They had only been with the outfit for a month or so, but they had already been making grumblings like they wanted to leave. And that just wasn't possible.

Zindell had chosen Brandt and Brandt had accepted because of the secretive nature of their respective interests. Zindell did not want encroachments on his experimental medicine and, likewise, Brandt did not want governmental interference with his experimental society.

Their goals meshed perfectly. While Zindell was doing long-term studies on the prisoners, Brandt was able to utilize them as workers in the fields and in the machine shops. Half of them were patients who had been committed to the Institute and the other half were people whom Brandt's men had kidnapped like thieves in the night, Negros and Orientals mostly; Jews were harder to spot.

Brandt's end of things was strictly non-profit which was another reason he couldn't do without Zindell: the old man was loaded. Not only was he making money off the nuthouse ruse, with many families paying long after the patients were dead, but he had some secret bank account that was ticking out cash to the tune of almost ten thousand dollars a month.

Secrecy. That was the main thing. And it was what he was here in the meeting hall to take care of. Once someone had entered the inner sanctum, he could never leave.

The men rose as Brandt stepped up to the podium, their arms raised in the Nazi Party salute. He saluted back to them and they were seated.

"I asked you to meet with me here tonight because of Carrigan and Asbury." He nodded to the two men in chains and walked around to sit on the platform, the prisoners between him and his men. "Yesterday they came to me, together, and told me that they thought they didn't belong here and that they would like to go back to the States. As you know, that can't be done.

"A few of you remember when this happened before, back in '80 or '81. But the rest of you have arrived here since then and I make it a point to be as honest and open about what we are trying to do here as I can. We're beginning again; we're starting over; we're creating a new German race. What we're not doing is shouting it from the mountaintops; there'll be time enough for that later. Right now, there's no room for fanaticism.

"In a few months a new generation will be born and our destiny will be assured. I want to thank all those who participated. But you can't create something like this if word gets out about what you're doing. It's stupid to think otherwise. Those fools in the States who wear their white hoods and burn crosses—they'll never get what they want because they're idiots. When they break the laws of the country they live in, they let themselves get caught. Stupid."

Brandt stood up now and unsnapped the leather restraints on his holster, resting his hand on the grip of his P38. "I don't really know if anyone else has been thinking along the lines of these two here and I don't need to know. What I *do* know—and what I want *you* to know—is that it can never happen. You can't leave. I told you that from the beginning and I meant it. I never lied to you." Brandt saw several heads nodding and had to stifle a smile.

"Carrigan and Asbury said that they understood, but that I couldn't keep them here against their will. I agree. I would never be able to trust them. I think that's all I have to say. Does anyone have any questions?" heads shook all around.

Carrigan and Asbury were face down on the floor. Each was gagged and blindfolded, his legs bent at the knees, hands and feet chained together almost touching. Brandt pulled his P38 from the holster, placed the barrel at the base of Carrigan's skull and fired, a drop of blood spattering onto the boot of one of his men.

"Sorry, Ted."

Asbury was squirming against his restraints in a mad panic to free himself and screaming into the gag, but Brandt calmly lowered his gun and dispatched him as well. He replaced the pistol in his holster and looked up at his captive audience.

"Demonstration's over. Marshal, Benson, dump them in the pit."

Chapter Seven

1. Tuesday, 3:15 a.m., Telsen, British Columbia

Brandt had been true to his word: as soon as Paul agreed to perform the surgery, the restraints had come off. Brandt had left for a few minutes and then brought back the notes. What they showed was nothing more than a spruced-up lobotomy, which Paul would be more than happy to perform on Zindell. Brandt, however, was a different story.

Over the past two days Paul had come to trust Brandt, and he found himself thinking that under different circumstances they might have been friends. These thoughts worried him. Paul knew that after the surgery he would be killed no matter what Brandt promised; it was stupid to think otherwise. He had to go on the assumption that he would never make it out alive. But as much as that hurt, it still wasn't as bad as thinking about Steve and Janet's fate.

After stewing in his anger for a while, Paul finally came to a decision. As long as he was going to die, he might as well die trying to escape. If he had to grab a gun away from one of the guards, he would do it, and worry about the rest later. A feeling of immense relief came over Paul and he supposed that it must be like the one felt by people who decide to commit suicide: at least the deliberation was over.

Wind from the storm that had kicked up during the night shuddered the windows, driving the rain hard against the tiny panes. Paul had not been able to fall asleep for the past few hours, but now that he was straight in his mind about what he would do, his body took over and he began to sink into a restful slumber.

Sometime later, another vigorous gust of wind followed by a loud clap of thunder woke him with a start. He opened his eyes and thought for a moment that he was back in his bedroom in Seattle; it had all been a dream and now Steve was coming in to tell him that he had overslept. But what came into focus instead was one of the pig-shaved posse.

Paul sat up and rubbed his eyes and ran his hand through his hair. It was greasy; he hadn't had a shower in days. His clothes suddenly felt grimy and when he looked up at the gunman he felt dirty all over.

"I need a shower."

"What?"

This guy's power of reasoning was obviously directly proportionate to the amount of hair on his head. "I said, I need a shower."

"Tell it to the doc. I got orders to take you there."

"I have a better idea. Why don't *you* 'tell it to the doc'?"

Another gust of wind. Paul looked outside and saw only blackness behind the glare in the window. Thinking it should be lighter out, he glanced at his watch and noticed it wasn't Daylight Savings anymore. While he was resetting the time to just before 7:00, the muzzle of the gun came into his line of sight.

"I said it's time to go."

Paul looked the kid over and decided he could take him. He couldn't have weighed much more than 150 soaking wet. Unless this guy had a partner waiting outside, Paul was going to stay right here.

"Jesus Christ," the kid moaned. "I haven't got all da—"

Paul made his move. He stood up quickly, pushing the gun away with his hand and achieving the desired effect: the kid stumbled backwards and fell on his ass.

"You're going to have to do a lot better than that gun to scare me, punk. Now you tell whoever gives you your orders that I'm not going anywhere without a shower and a hot meal." The part about the meal was an afterthought, but it made him realize just how hungry he was.

Now the kid scrambled to his feet, putting the barrel of the gun to Paul's neck, but Paul leaned into it. "Go ahead and shoot, kid. You'll be doing me a favor. But I wouldn't plan on living much past noon, if I were you. I don't think Brandt would be too impressed by your marksmanship."

The kid's eyes were bulging and his face was screwed up with blind rage. Then he stepped back. He aimed the gun down at Paul's legs. "What if I just—"

"You do and I can guarantee you'll have to take another shot, because I swear to God I'll kill you." They were both silent for a moment and then the kid turned to leave.

"Fuck!" Paul heard loudly from the hall, and smiled.

A few minutes later, two men in white entered the room, followed by the kid. This time he had brought along a friend, a real bruiser. The friend wasn't much taller than Paul, but he had certainly put in a lot more time on the Nautilus machines.

"We need to move you to another room, sir," said one of the men in white.

"What for?"

"You'll be able to take a shower there, and then someone will bring you breakfast."

"Now you're talkin' my language. I'm all yours, boys," he said, presenting his arms to the men in white as though he needed help to walk. When they took his arms he chuckled.

"Shut up, fuckhead," the kid threatened as the trio passed by him. This only made Paul laugh harder.

The big guy reached for Paul but the exasperated attendant on Paul's left was able to shrug him off before he caught hold. "Hey! Knock it off! Will you guys please just back off?"

They obeyed, but Paul couldn't help flashing the kid a wink as he passed through.

"You're mine, motherfucker," he heard behind him as he stepped out of the room.

Paul took a quick glance down the hall before entering the other room directly across from his, but there was little to see. The new room was smaller and the slit of a window looked out on another building. The arrangement of the bed was the same, but to the left was another door.

"The shower is in through there, sir," said one of the attendants, pointing. "One of us will be here if you need more towels or soap or anything. When you're done we'll bring you breakfast."

Paul shut the door behind him, stripped off his clothes and cranked up the shower. For a long time he simply stood under the stream of hot water and let his body relax. The constant strain of not knowing what was coming next had taken its toll on him. He would be operating in a few hours, though; he could be fairly certain of that. He lifted his face from the water and lathered up, rinsed and shampooed.

He was toweling off when someone knocked. He wrapped the towel around his waist and opened the door. "Here are some clean clothes, sir," said the attendant.

White boxers, white socks, blue slacks, and a white dress shirt. They weren't exactly Paul's size, but they were in the ballpark, and they were clean. He ran a virgin comb he had found in the medicine chest through his hair. He was tempted briefly by the disposable razors and shaving cream—he preferred an electric razor—before opting to leave his burgeoning beard alone. The smells of food finally brought him out.

Paul ate ravenously, devouring the pancakes, bacon, eggs, and hash browns. Afterward he sipped hot coffee.

"All right," he said to the attendant as he set down his empty cup. "Let's go see the doc."

The two delinquents were waiting outside and followed as the attendant led him down the hall. The other attendant met them in the lobby and Paul was able to get a much better grasp on the layout of the place as they rounded the reception desk. He tried to get the receptionist's attention but she ignored him and he was ushered through a connecting corridor that led to the other building he had seen earlier.

Straight through the doors was a wide alcove backed by a large, garage-type door, and on the left was an elevator which they entered; the gun club stayed behind. Paul was sure that there would be no place he could escape to once he was on—he looked to see which button the attendant pushed—the third floor.

The elevator opened and Paul smelled the odors of chemicals, which indicated laboratories, research laboratories. Only one attendant got out with him and they hooked around to the right and down a few doors. The attendant knocked and the old man, papers in hand and looking over his half-glasses, opened the door.

"That is all for now. I will call you when we are ready."

The attendant walked off and Paul stepped inside. Zindell sat down behind his desk and Paul took a chair.

"I am sorry about the business last night but you left me no alternative. I had to ensure your cooperation."

"Sure," Paul answered with subdued sarcasm. "And you still trust me to operate on you?"

Zindell was leaning back. "It is not exactly a matter of trust, Dr. Raymond. I am reaching the apex of a long and fruitful career, one that Parkinson's has effectively ended. I have relatively little to lose. Now, you may have decided that you as well having nothing to lose at this juncture, but I assure you that this is not the case. I fully intend to release you upon the completion of your work here."

"What about Steve and Janet?"

"They shall be freed as well."

If these people around here wanted to take Paul for a complete idiot, that was fine with him. He'd play it for all it was worth. He just needed to make sure that he didn't give away his intentions too soon.

"I don't know whether to believe you or not, but it doesn't look like I have much to say about it either way. Why don't you just fill me in on the surgery?"

"Good, good." Zindell sat up and began shuffling through papers. "You will need to be fully briefed."

God, if this guy didn't ease back on the spy talk, Paul thought he would burst out laughing.

"I took the precaution of testing you by outlining the outdated Parkinson's surgery."

"And I passed."

"Correct."

Paul remembered the details in the letter from Howard, and now he wondered why Howard wasn't here. "What happened to Dr. Phillips?"

"He has gone back to the United States. We had a disagreement on exactly how to persuade you to stay."

Interesting. Maybe Howard had a conscience after all? Doubtful, but it was a nice thing to consider.

Then Zindell outlined the actual procedure: brain implantation. In order to provide the dopamine that the brain of a Parkinson's patient lacked, the theory went, other cells could be implanted into or near the striatum, and these cells would make contact with nearby neurons and begin to store and release appropriate amounts of dopamine. Though adrenal tissue from the patient could be used, Zindell wanted something more suited to the task at hand. New growth required embryonic tissue.

"Do you have the necessary cell colonies?" Paul asked dubiously.

"As much as I need. If the specimens I have are not suitable, more can be obtained. Please don't hesitate to keep me apprised."

"Sure," said Paul, trying to imagine where they had come from and not sure he really wanted to know. "What about the craniotomy?"

Zindell went on to show Paul x-rays, CT scans and an angiogram of his own brain that had been recorded earlier, giving him the specifications of the procedure he wanted done. The sections of tissue that Paul would have to remove according to the notes Brandt gave him would never be exposed, but all he had to do was nick a few nerves or suck up a little gray matter and Zindell would be a human vegetable.

"Does everything seem clear to you?"

"Perfectly. When do we start?"

"In a few hours."

Zindell looked pleased with himself and it made Paul uncomfortable. It was as though Zindell could read his mind, read his thoughts, daring him to "fuck him up" as Brandt had so eloquently put it. But the feeling passed as soon as Zindell stood.

"Before I take you upstairs to the operating rooms, I would like to show you around our research laboratories here." Zindell opened the door and stepped out into the hall. Paul followed.

They walked past the elevator and to the first door on the right. Zindell took a small ring of keys from his pants pocket and unlocked it. When Paul stepped inside he was met by an incredible sight. His lab back at the University Hospital was one of the most modern and high-tech in the country and yet it looked like a garage sale compared to this.

Computer-controlled neurophysiology equipment filled the room. Everywhere there were monitors, their green-glowing screens blipping and moving and giving the whole lab an underwater effect. Zindell turned on the fluorescent overhead lights and the equipment was even more impressive.

"It is not very often I have the chance to share what I have built here with someone who can truly appreciate it."

"I recognize most of the equipment, but it looks different."

"The entire output of our research here, Dr. Raymond, is computer controlled. Instead of bulky graph paper, everything is recorded onto computer disks. A special system will allow me to pinpoint any number of progressions at the touch of a button."

"How do you do visual comparisons?"

"My computers will overlay multiple images, or, depending on how many monitors are needed, I can split-screen as many graphs as necessary."

Paul's jaw nearly dropped as Zindell exhibited his technological wonders. There was a sleek electroencephalogram console with two monitors directly in front of him. To the right were two of the latest in three-dimensional imagers and off to the left was a huge bank of computers, maybe twenty in all. Windows to an adjoining room looked in on some older neurometric translators, electrophysiology amplification equipment and biofeedback gear, all outfitted with their own monitors.

"It's too bad the older equipment can't communicate with the new stuff," Paul said with genuine concern.

"It can now. One of my assistants has developed a program which gives my computers the ability to translate CT scans and PET scans both into three-dimensional images."

"That's fantastic. How does it work?"

Zindell was beaming as he demonstrated the outer frontier of modern medical science. Soon both men were engrossed in shop talk and, despite Paul's initial disdain of Zindell, he found himself totally caught up in the lab like a teenager checking out a friend's new car. It wasn't until one of the assistants burst into the room that Paul snapped out of his trance and suddenly felt embarrassed about himself.

"Doctor, we have an emergency downstairs. We need you right away."

Zindell frowned. "What is it?"

"Cerebral hemorrhage."

"The one we did yesterday?"

"Yeah." The assistant ran out of the room.

"Please come with me." Zindell walked out of the lab and Paul followed him across the hall. He took out his keys and could barely unlock the door; his tremor had seriously increased. "I will have to ask you to wait in here until I return. I will be back shortly."

"Okay," Paul said with a shrug.

The lights came on in a neatly kept chemistry lab, big black lab tables sitting out in the middle of the room like islands. The door shut and Paul heard the keys jangle as Zindell locked him in.

Paul pulled out a stool and sat down at one of the lab tables. In contrast to the glitz of the other lab, this was where the nuts and bolts of science took place. Against one wall were shelves from floor to ceiling filled with sparkling-clean beakers, test tubes, pipettes and Petri dishes. The six lab tables were outfitted with two sinks and two feeds each of oxygen and propane.

Opposite the door was a large hood, a ventilated, glass-fronted enclosure where vaporous chemicals were kept. At the end of the room were glass cabinets containing bottles, boxes, jars, and cartons filled with all manner of elements necessary to complete any experiment. Inventory taken, Paul turned his attention back to the surgery, and sagged.

There was no way out. He could not allow himself to hurt Zindell; he realized that now. He hated himself for being so malleable but he just wasn't the hero type. Oh, he could kick some ass at the hospital when necessary but that was always in the context of saving lives. The idea of actually killing someone, even lobotomizing Zindell on the operating table, was so repulsive to him that he knew he would never be able to do it.

Who are you kidding, he asked himself. You're no paragon of virtue; you're just afraid of dying. That was it, really. And the fact that Steve and Janet were here only made it worse. He felt responsible for them and the thought paralyzed him. He had no plan, no ideas. He was going to accept whatever was meted out to him. He was reactionary, not an instigator. He hated himself for it, but he knew he would do exactly what Zindell asked of him, and then wait until he let him go or offed him.

Paul was staring straight ahead at the cabinets, and when the idea appeared full-blown in his mind he almost didn't believe it. From across the room he could see what looked like a brick of moldy cheese in a large glass dome. Sodium. Sodium metal, to be exact. His breathing quickened. It was all there—every aspect of his escape, right in that glass dome, if he was willing to take it.

He suddenly realized he didn't know how long Zindell had been gone. Would he be back soon? God, he had to decide now. His previous calm at choosing to do nothing was entirely gone. If you're going to do it you'd better do it now. He couldn't decide. His hands shook. What the hell was he going to do?

"Fuck it," he finally said, hopped off the stool and ran across the room.

2. 7:00 a.m.

The alarm clock jolts Steve awake and he reaches over quickly to swat it off. He sits up in bed and surveys his room, just glad the whole nightmare is over. He tries to remember what classes he has today but he can't. The three calendars he had hanging up are gone.

Steve gets out of bed and grabs a pair of jeans off the chair. They are soaking wet. He drops them to the floor as if they have burned him. He pulls out a dresser drawer and water sloshes

out over the side. He runs, naked, for his father's room. Before
he can get there his mother stops him.

"Steve! What are you doing out of bed?"

"Mom, is Dad all right?"

"He's sleeping. Now, why don't you go back to bed?"

"I have to see him."

"Steve, I don't think that's a good idea. Please go back to
bed, dear."

"Mom," he fairly screams, "Dad's in danger!" He runs
past her and into the bedroom. His father seems to be sleeping
but Steve is compelled to make sure. He walks around to the
side of the bed. His father's eyes are wide open. Steve looks up.
His mother is gone now. His father doesn't appear to see him
so he touches his shoulder.

"Dad? Are you awake?"

His father sits up, his eyes wide with fright. Steve has to
take a step back.

"Dad . . . Dad?" He screams it now. "Dad!"

His father turns and looks to him. Steve calms down
slightly and tries again.

"Dad? Are you all right?"

His father opens his mouth and blood pours out onto the
sheets. Steve screams and backs away. His father's jaw is
working up and down like a puppet's as more and more blood
pours out. Steve screams and backs away . . . more blood . . .
screams and backs away . . . more blood . . . screams and
backs . . . more blood . . . screams and . . . more blood . . .
screams . . .

Steve was the first one to wake up. He didn't remember
what he had dreamt last night but he could still feel it clinging
to him. Janet was next to him in the same bunk and he slung
his arm over her and hugged her tightly. It was close quarters
but they preferred it that way. Janet only had a single bed in her
apartment and they always slept nestled together.

He rolled back to look at his watch and then wished he hadn't; it was going to be a long morning. The plan that Dr. Phillips had come up with was as good as any they were going to get an opportunity to use. They had hashed everything out the night before. Eli said there would be the fewest guards at the camp at lunchtime and they all agreed that that would be the best time to try. That also meant that he still had a long wait ahead, and a long time to think about it.

A huge gust of wind threatened to take the barracks off its foundation and something Steve hadn't considered suddenly demanded attention: the weather. The rain he was hearing in the back of his mind stepped up for review. Would more people stay in camp if it was raining? Guards, too?

He looked around and saw that Phillips was still asleep. They would need to talk later. Danny and Eli were sleeping as well.

"What are you doing?" It was Janet in a groggy voice.

"I was just checking to see who's awake," Steve answered.

Janet rolled over and looked up at him. "Are you worried?"

"Yeah. I wish it was time already."

Steve lay back and Janet rested her head on his chest. They had both stripped off their damp clothes underneath the blankets of the bunk and Steve had set them down on the next bed.

He was keenly aware of Janet's breasts against his skin and the smell of her hair. He breathed her in deep, grateful for the distraction. A few minutes later Steve sat up and slipped on his jeans. They were *almost* dry, and he thought wryly that they would probably be perfect by the time he was heading outside into the rain. He laid Janet's clothes on their bed and walked past the doorway and into the bathroom. To the right was a trough urinal where he relieved himself. Along the wall next to the door were three sinks and behind him were three stalls. On through another entryway were the showers, a square tiled room with a dozen or so showerheads.

Steve buttoned his pants and walked into the showers. He turned on one of the faucets all the way and a tiny stream of orange water leaked out. Then he turned it off and left. On his way out Steve met Danny, and they silently exchanged smiles and nods as they passed each other. Back in the sleeping quarters Janet was sitting up fully dressed. Phillips was rubbing his face in his hands and Eli was still snoring.

Steve sat across from Janet and yawned. As soon as Danny passed them she jumped up.

"Can you keep them from coming in until I'm done?"

"The stalls have doors."

"Great," she said and hurried away.

"Looks like we got quite a squall out there." Eli was awake now.

"Do you think this is going to change anything?" Steve asked.

"It'll probably work to our advantage," said Phillips. "The fewer people out on the compound the better."

"Until then we just wait," said Eli.

Phillips nodded. "Watch them when breakfast comes. Then if there's something we missed or if you have any questions we can talk it over so everybody's sure."

When Janet returned Steve was stretched out on the bunk. She sat down next to him and he filled her in on what she had missed. For the next twenty minutes everyone was silent with his own thoughts, even Eli. Then breakfast came.

The routine was the same as it was the previous night and, Steve hoped, the same as lunch would be this afternoon. Three men in dripping ponchos and mud-caked boots entered the room. The two with the trays of food went to the table and exchanged them for last night's while the man with the gun stood in the doorway. They left without incident and everyone slowly headed for the table.

Breakfast consisted of the same corn-based gruel they had been given the night before. As they began eating, Phillips was the first to speak.

"I don't know how much any of you have thought of this—I know we've been talking about the plan a lot and we've all been pretty jazzed—but once we're outside of the wire there's every reason to believe that we'll be shot on sight."

If the menu hadn't killed appetites by now, Phillips' statement did. Spoons went down all around.

"Well, I have to admit," Eli began, "that I didn't really think much about dyin' before. I just figured that they'd force us to have the operation and that would be it. It wasn't until the little lady here got me to thinkin' and, well . . . I think I can speak for Danny"—Danny nodded—"that we'd just as soon die tryin' to get out of this place as be gomers."

"Good. I just wanted to be sure that all of you had a chance to think about that. How about you two?" he said, turning to Steve and Janet.

"I've got to get my dad out of there," Steve said.

Phillips looked to Janet and then so did Steve. When everyone had their eyes on her she paused for a moment before speaking. "Does anybody here really believe for a second that we won't be killed if we stay?"

This was followed by a pregnant pause during which the only movement at the table was Danny shaking his head.

"All right, then," said Phillips. "Let's kick some ass."

3. 8:41 a.m.

Paul snatched one of the test tubes off the shelf in the back and ran to the farthest sink from the door. He would have to guess at the volume of the water the sink held and also how much flow he would need to make it spill over in about three hours. He did a hurried mental calculation, unsure if it was anywhere near correct, and turned on the tap, filling and refilling the test tube as he adjusted the water until the flow was as close as he could get it.

Next he looked for something to stop up the drain with. He was opening drawers with little luck. There were rubber stoppers but they all looked too small. In desperation he finally wadded up some paper towels and packed it tightly into the drain. It would have to do. Then he moved the spout so that the water quietly flowed down the side of the sink with no splash.

Paul went through most of the drawers again to look for a knife and grabbed the closest thing to it, a metal ruler. He gently lifted the glass dome off of the sodium and picked it up with some paper towel. After setting it on the table he sliced off the layer of oxidized metal like mold from a brick of cheese.

Paul gouged out a piece of the freshly exposed metal about the size of the head on a wooden match and tossed it into the sink. There was already about half an inch of water in the bottom and as soon as the sodium hit, it began skating wildly on the surface, sparks and flames issuing from the contact points. In about thirty seconds the metal had completely reacted with the water and dissolved.

To keep the brick of metal from being blown across the room the moment the water reached it, he clamped it to the lip of the table. The bulk of the metal was over the sink and would no doubt make a hell of an explosion, but would not have quite the destructive power Paul was looking for. Everything was ready as he sat on a stool in front of the propane feed that was nearest the door. He placed his hand on the spigot, leaned in as though he were simply resting, and waited.

As it turned out it was another fifteen minutes before Zindell returned. As soon as Paul heard the keys in the lock he stood and pulled back from the table, in the process turning the spigot to the propane. He walked quickly and breezed past Zindell the instant the door was opened.

"I wouldn't think you'd have too many emergency situations here, unless you have more patients than I thought,"

Paul said. He was well out into the hall and trying to distract Zindell as much as possible.

Zindell took a cursory glance around the lab and Paul thought his heart was going to stop dead. Then he flicked off the lights and locked the door. Perfect. The plan was back in full swing, only this time Paul would have a distraction to help him, coming in the form of a major-league explosion.

Paul had only seen the two assistants, and the fact that one of them had had to come and get Zindell the minute there was an emergency indicated that there probably weren't any more. Also, there were no gunmen present; they were probably not allowed above the first floor. After the explosion, he would have to improvise.

"I have enough patients that they keep me busy," said Zindell.

"How long before the surgery?" His distraction successful, Paul moved back to the subject at hand.

"A few hours. I want to take you upstairs now to the OR and give you a chance to acquaint yourself with some of the equipment that you may not be familiar with."

Paul ran his hand through his hair. "Okay. If it's as high-tech as the lab, though, I'll be impressed."

"You will be, most assuredly."

The elevator was standard stuff. Paul watched closely for any deviation in operation but it was about what he had expected. If the door to the stairs was locked he would take the elevator as a last resort. He didn't know what was on the second floor, but it seemed like a good place to hide out while everybody was busy sorting through the blast.

The doors opened and the two men stepped out. Paul looked off to the right.

"I have two wards down there," Zindell said. "The operating rooms are this way."

Paul's pulse quickened as Zindell led him down the hallway to the left. By the time the old man pushed through the swinging doors to the scrub room Paul was in a near panic.

He had made an egregious error and was utterly helpless now that the whole thing had been set in motion. He hadn't even considered the possibility: the operating room was directly over the lab.

He had simply forgotten that there might be people above or below the lab. Had he thought of it he was almost certain he would not have set the bomb, and now that he had, it was too late.

"Are you all right, Doctor?" Zindell could tell something was wrong.

"Yeah. I'm just worried about my son." A convenient catch-all for now.

"Please try and concentrate on the surgery. When you are finished, I promise you will be reunited."

In the afterlife, Paul thought to himself, then tried to ignore Zindell. If he said anything, it would be over. He would never have a chance like this again. Paul couldn't be certain when the bomb would go off—sometime after the next two hours. That was all the leeway he could be sure of.

From where Paul was standing he could see through a large plate-glass window into the operating room. One of the assistants, gowned and gloved, was already making preparations inside. In the outer area were the scrub sinks, sterile towels and scrub suits.

Zindell was saying something when Paul interrupted him. "I think we should start the operation as soon as possible."

Zindell shook his head. "I'm understandably cautious as things are without—"

"Look," said Paul, trying to be as tactful as possible. "I'm here because you have faith in my abilities. I also have faith in my abilities. I'm a neurosurgeon. It's what I do for a living. Now, I've gone over the operation, as you've laid it out, in my mind and I've prepared myself in the same way an athlete might. At this point I really don't see that anything beneficial can be gained by waiting. I'm ready right now."

Zindell took a thoughtful pause and Paul had absolutely no idea what his reaction would be. "Very well," he said. "But there is still the matter of the equipment."

"I assume there'll be others scrubbing in?"

"Yes. You have already met my two assistants. They are excellent."

"Good." Paul looked back through the glass partition. "Then they should be able to answer any questions I might have while you're being prepped."

Zindell picked up a phone and made arrangements for the embryonic tissue to be sent up as soon as possible, and then calmly ordered two armed guards to the OR.

"Jesus Christ, you expect me to work with a gun in my back?"

"That is the way it must be. I will be immobile during the procedure and I must be assured that you will cooperate to the end."

"But you and I both know what will happen if I don't."

"Nevertheless, you will be under guard during the procedure."

Paul was visibly upset now. He hadn't allowed for this. The whole plan was going to blow up in his face, literally.

"I can see this bothers you," said Zindell. "If you like, we can postpone until the original start time."

NO! he wanted to scream.

"Uh, no, I don't think that's necessary." Paul was pulling himself together as he spoke. Time was critical. He wanted the surgery to be over before the big bang. Delays were not good. The less chance they had to stumble onto his little surprise, the better. "How much time do you need to prep for surgery?"

Zindell looked concerned for a moment and then answered. "As soon as the guards arrive I will go to pre-op and then I will be ready in about thirty minutes. That should be enough time for you to scrub and get situated in the OR."

"What about the guards?"

"What about them?"

"They're not going to be in the OR."

"No. They will wait in here."

After his two pals from the goon squad showed up, Paul scrubbed and went into the operating room. He was given a brief rundown of Zindell's surgical procedures and special equipment by one of the two assistants, who introduced himself as Joel. Joel and his partner Chris were the only two people who helped Zindell run his little hospital, and both would be assisting Paul with the operation.

When half an hour had transpired, a freshly-shaved Zindell was pushed into the OR in a wheelchair, his bald head dimly reflecting the overhead lights. He was wearing a white cotton shirt and a pair of gray trousers. They looked loose and comfortable and not as necessarily embarrassing as a hospital gown. Zindell stood and then took his seat in the operating chair. Paul would be using a local, enabling Zindell to remain conscious during the operation on the pretext that Paul might have some questions. Paul suspected he would most likely be doing a bit of backseat surgery.

A high-resolution video monitor was adjusted for Zindell, and the camera above the operating theatre was turned on. Next, Zindell was given the local and his head was bolted into the brace. His chest was strapped but he instructed Joel to leave his arms free to move.

"Turn on the intercom," said Zindell, and Joel walked over and flipped a switch near the door. "Can you two hear me out there?"

"Yes, sir." The quality of the intercom made the voice sound like the person was actually in the room next to Paul.

"If anything out of the ordinary happens in here, if you see me struggle or yell, I want you to kill Dr. Raymond immediately. Do you understand?"

"Yes, sir." Paul could almost hear the smiles on their faces.

"You couldn't have told them that in private?" he said to Zindell.

"I want to make sure we understand each other."

"Believe me, we do."

Paul outlined the area on Zindell's scalp where they would be going in, and soon the operation was underway. Chris would join them when it was time for the transplant of the embryonic tissue. Getting into the brain through the skull was fairly routine, as far as any neurosurgery went. The second half of the procedure was anything but.

Zindell seemed fascinated with his own brain as he guided Paul through the procedure, having him place the transplanted nerve tissue adjacent to the corpus striatum. Although this was still an experimental procedure, it was clear to Paul from Zindell's precise and exacting directions that he knew just what he wanted done. Paul also knew that this type of experiment in animals had been met with some success. He had even read the literature on human patients in Sweden, but he had never preformed the transplant himself.

Everything went well. The actual results however, would not be known for some time, time that Zindell would obviously not wait before disposing of his surgeon.

After closing Paul stood back while the two assistants helped Zindell out of the chair. Paul snapped off his gloves, ran his hands though his hair and then rubbed the back of his neck. An errant gaze fell upon the gunmen waiting in the outer room. They wore expressions of utter boredom and Paul had forgotten about them during the past few . . .

He checked his watch and felt his throat constrict with something like panic. The bomb should have already gone off by now. The operation had lasted over three hours and should have easily fallen within the parameters of his estimation. Had someone found out what he was trying to do? Was Brandt waiting in his room to kill him?

I don't have a problem with killing people.

He hadn't "fucked up" Zindell; the old man was going to be fine. He might still have Parkinson's, but otherwise he should be completely normal.

"Nice work, Dr. Raymond." Zindell, his head gauzed, was sitting in his wheelchair already.

"I only hope I'll be around to see the results."

"I'm sorry that won't be possible. Gentlemen, please come into the operating room."

The gunmen pushed open the doors and flanked Paul. "Gee, now why doesn't this surprise me."

"Take me to recovery," Zindell ordered Chris.

"What about Steve and Janet?"

"Put Dr. Raymond back in his room."

As Zindell was being pushed by, Paul reached for him. "I asked you a question you Nazi son of a—" The gunmen had Paul slammed up against the wall and his breath knocked out of him almost before he realized it had happened.

"That is all, Dr. Raymond. Your services are no longer required." And with that Zindell waved his hand and was propelled forward.

"I should have scrambled your brains when I had the chance."

Zindell lifted his hand and the chair stopped instantly. "Ah, but you didn't, did you?" When his hand fell the chair continued out the door.

"You fuck—" was followed by a rifle butt to the stomach and Paul was then taken out of the room with a gunman at each arm and his toes dragging behind him on the smooth floor.

Canada, 1990

1. 4 September 1990, 9:38 a.m., Telsen, British Columbia

Bill Tuttle woke up at six a.m. as usual. He put on his work clothes as he did every morning and then ate breakfast. Bill was a farmer—had been all his life. He spent each day out in the fields whether tilling up soil, planting, or harvesting his crops and today was no different. Farming was all Bill knew and life was good.

Lately, however, he had been having dreams, strange dreams with strange people in them. He wasn't sure when they had actually begun, but he felt as if they had been going on for some time and he just hadn't realized it until he was awake. Once he became aware of the dreams, he would try to conjure them up at night before he went to sleep, and until now he had bee unable to. But today they were clear in his mind and the visions of his newfound dreams fascinated him.

There was always a woman in his dreams, the same woman. He still didn't have an exact idea of what she looked like but he knew it was the same woman every time. Then there was the boy, two if them maybe, and a girl; he didn't know for sure. But all of these images parading through his mind were slowing up his work. He tried to concentrate on the clod of earth beneath the blade of his hoe, but the visions wouldn't go away.

Bill looked up at the sky. The sun was bright and the morning still cool. It would be a hot one this afternoon. He turned his attention back to the soil beneath his feet and had begun to go at his work with renewed vigor when the hoe in his hand stopped. There were more images now.

A table, not the one where he ate every day, but smaller. It was in a different room, too, and he was pretty sure those other people were there. Bill felt funny now. He felt as if something were wrong with him. He had never had this much trouble working before; he was a good farmer and enjoyed working. He liked to work in the fields. But something felt different now and he didn't like that.

He attacked the soft, crumbled earth beneath his feet, throwing himself into work, desperately trying to keep the images out of his mind. But the dream stayed with him; it wouldn't let go. Only it wasn't like a dream. Not really. It was as if he knew those people, as though he had actually done all of those things that he saw himself doing with them. But if it wasn't a dream, then what was it?

The picture of Anne flashed in his mind again. He saw her standing over the sink doing dishes, her hair pinned up high on the back of her head, pushing away a few loose strands with the back of her hand. Wait a minute! He had just called her Anne, hadn't he? How did he know her name? Now Bill was a little scared. Something was happening to him that he had no control over. Something was putting people into his mind, people he didn't know. But then he realized he *did* know them.

His head was swimming and he could barely stay on his feet; the people were bombarding his brain. Patrick, Mike and Jenny were sitting around the TV, laughing, but not at him. He was right there with them, his arm around Anne. And then suddenly he knew.

The memories—that was what they were, he finally realized—came flooding back into Bill's mind so fast that they pulled his hands up to his head. The hoe fell to the ground with a clatter and Bill took a step back, tottering on his wobbly legs. One of the men with guns came running up to him, and at that instant he remembered who they were, too.

2. 2:49 p.m.

Zindell entered the operating room wearing his surgical scrubs and a white hood, the white mask over his face covering everything but his eyes. He turned when the doors to the OR opened. It was Howard Phillips and Zindell's two assistants wheeling in a gurney bearing his patient.

The subject, a 55-year-old white male, was under light sedation and would undergo general anesthesia once he was prepped for surgery. Zindell checked the number tattooed on the inside of the subject's lower lip against the number on the file he had taken from the research laboratory. They matched. The subject was in very good health and, although he would never admit it to anyone, Zindell knew that it was the work Brandt had them doing that kept his specimens in such good physical condition.

Of the nearly three thousand subjects that were stored here, only about a hundred had shown signs of alternate-area development. It wasn't enough to warrant any drastic measures, but enough for Zindell to be concerned that his theories might be in danger, that his work of a lifetime might end up as worthless as Mengele's. It was not a pleasant thought.

His assistants were now lifting the subject onto a specially outfitted operating chair that Zindell himself had designed. The chair was sparingly padded and bolted firmly to the floor to reduce extraneous movement. It swiveled in every conceivable direction, each lever twisting down tightly and locking in place to prevent even the slightest motion during surgery.

As Zindell went into the adjoining scrub room to sterilize his hands, a surgical-steel brace that fastened to the chair was being positioned around the subject's head. His chin was set into a stirrup and then four steel spikes that circled his head were adjusted inward until they just touched the skin of his freshly shaven scalp. Now Phillips moved in to secure the skull. He screwed the spikes in tight, imbedding the tips into the bone, just above the eyebrows in front, and above the ridge at the base of the skull in the back. With the head firmly secured, the subject was strapped securely into the operating chair.

When Zindell reentered the OR, one of the assistants handed him a sterile towel and he dried his hands while watching the video of the three-dimensional brain scan that had been taken of the subject earlier that day. The space in the cerebrum he had removed over ten years ago was now a little more than a dimple, the lobe having reshaped and filled in where the vacancy had been. When Zindell was gloved and ready he approached the operating field.

Zindell stepped up onto the hydraulic platform behind the subject and sat down. A few minutes later Phillips was gowned and gloved and joined him. The procedure this time would be much simpler than the initial entry into the cranial cavity; the portion of the skull that had once protected the area he would be working on had been discarded after the first surgery. For a moment he reminisced about the old days in Germany and the surgical saw he still kept in the bottom drawer of his desk. Things were much more precise now; they used stainless-steel power drills, perforators, and rongeurs to remove the bone. And of course, these days the idea was for the subject to live.

The chair was then adjusted with the upper body at approximately a 45-degree angle, and the curtains were draped in such a way that only the top of his head above the spikes was visible. His scalp had been thoroughly washed and Betadine, an orange sterilizing agent, was painted on. As Zindell expertly made the initial incision a thin line of blood appeared and one of the assistants moved to keep the operating field clear using a low-pressure suction device.

After folding down the three-sided flap of skin and muscle, Zindell and Phillips stopped the flow of blood with a row of hemostats. Once these metal clamps were in place an assistant irrigated the dura with saline solution and suctioned off the remaining blood. Next, Zindell used a small scalpel to slice through the dura and sutured it out of the way, repeating the procedure on the thin mesh of arteries comprising the arachnoid layer. He had now exposed the brain. Just beneath the thin membrane of the subarachnoid space lay the folds and convolutions of the cerebrum, continuously bathed in cerebrospinal fluid.

Zindell gently peeled back the membrane and, activating the vacuum with his foot, suctioned off the excess fluid. Now he moved a low-magnification surgical microscope into place and began to remove actual brain tissue, sucking away little purplish globs down a slender plastic tube. He had been working for about ten minutes, carefully checking his progress against the original file, when the accident happened.

Without warning a tremor hit Zindell's right arm, spreading quickly down to his hand, and the sucker, seemingly with a mind of its own, plunged deep into the cerebellum.

"*Scheisse!*" he screamed, pulling his hand out of the subject's skull with such force that he almost knocked over the microscope.

Phillips and the assistant froze. Zindell threw the sucker to the floor and pushed the microscope out of the way. He slipped his glasses on and looked into the operating field. Blood oozed from the spot where the sucker had been, indicating that a vessel somewhere had inadvertently been resected.

Zindell stood now, his gaze moving back and forth from his trembling hand to the bloody pool that was already forming in the open cranium.

"You rotten piece of shit!"

Zindell thrust his hand down into the subject's skull. Blood spilled over onto the curtains as he extracted a handful of the gelatinous gray matter and flung it across the OR with all his might. It spattered against the wall, most of it falling to the floor, the rest sliding slowly downward.

When he turned back around Zindell was shocked. He had inadvertently exposed the source of all the blood: a tiny vessel squirting into the pit he had just excavated. Reflexively he retrieved the sucker from the floor.

"Quick" he said to anyone. "Hand me the probe."

He suctioned the blood and held out his hand. One of the assistants handed him an electric probe and he promptly cauterized the vessel with the hot electric tip. A thin tendril of smoke, smelling of burning flesh and blood wafted up to his nostrils. When he had finished he paused for a moment, pondering the damaged brain in front of him, knowing it was his own damned fault.

Zindell had been taking medication for several months now to combat the onset of Parkinson's disease, but the drugs were having less and less of an effect on his tremors. It seemed cruel: Dr. Konrad Zindell, the world's most gifted neurosurgeon, afflicted with an incurable neurological disorder. God, if he was out there, was trying to rob him of the glory that should be rightfully his, and it was pissing him off. Well, he wasn't about to sit here and take it; he would fight back.

Except for emergency cases like this, he had already ceased his experiments, devoting himself entirely to studying all the latest findings on Parkinson's. Eventually he had been faced with the only acceptable option: brain tissue transplantation. He must be able to achieve full recovery of all his fine motor function and total elimination of the tremor. If he didn't continue his work, he would consider suicide, but only as a last resort. Right now he just needed someone to do the surgery.

Phillips was out. Not only couldn't he be trusted, but he probably hadn't done any surgery in the last twenty years. No, the surgeon he used would have to be the very best he could find. It was sheer coincidence that the top neurosurgeon in the field was a friend of Phillips', and practiced close by in Seattle. It was time to call on the services of one Dr. Paul Raymond.

"Bring him out of it. Phillips, you close. I will want to see him in post-op, but only to see what kind of damage was done. He is no good to me like this. Call Brandt and tell him I need a couple of men for disposal." With that Zindell stripped off his gloves, threw them to the floor, and stormed out of the OR.

3. 5:19 p.m.

When Bill Tuttle woke up everything was dark. He strained his eyes to see what was around him, but there was only blackness, and the effort made his head scream with pain. He cried out, but either no one heard him or no one cared. He was strapped down so tightly that he could barely breathe. He wanted to know where he was and why he was in so much pain.

The last thing he could remember was the dream. No, the memories. Yeah. Memories. And the memory of the armed guards hauling him away. Those sons of bitches. Now he remembered that night—it seemed like yesterday—when the work had been finished and instead of letting him go home they locked him up in one of the huts. He never saw Anne or the kids again. When was that? How long ago had it all happened? God, it was like a nightmare.

But he could remember now, at least. They couldn't take that away from him again. He wouldn't let them operate this time. He'd fight, or kill himself if necessary. He tried to move but the restraints were rock solid.

Voices. At last he could hear voices. Then he could feel someone picking up his arm by the wrist. Why didn't they turn on the damn lights?

Instantly a flash of white-hot light burned into his retina. There was a glimpse of a shadow and then it was gone. A ghost of light danced in front of him. Then in the other eye, a blinding flash, fading back into darkness. He screamed but could not hear himself. Instead he heard only the muted voices around him.

"Hard to say how extensive the damage is."

"Can he move at all?"

"Sympathetic nervous system still seems to be intact."

"Voluntary function?"

"No, all muscular function has been lost. My guess is that the trauma to the cerebellum was so great—"

"When I want your opinion I will ask for it. Just get him out of here."

Wait! *Stop*, he yelled, but again he couldn't hear himself. Then the realization that the lights *were* on and that he simply couldn't open his eyes brought forth beads of sweat all over his body. He had clearly felt his arm being lifted, unrestrained, but all of his concentration wouldn't budge it now. Maybe there were no straps holding him down at all. His sweat continued to flow. He couldn't be paralyzed, could he? He could still feel.

He could feel the cold sheets of the bed against his arms, and the evaporation of sweat raising goose bumps on his legs. He could feel the gown he was wearing and could smell the medicinal odor of the room. And he could hear, too. Damn it, he could hear everything. He needed help.

A knock on the door.

"We're here for a disposal?"

"Yeah. Over there."

Disposal? What the hell was that? He could feel himself being picked up by the armpits and legs. The two who were carrying him smelled of outdoors, of rain and wet earth. He was put on a stretcher and then taken out of the room. Footfalls echoed in his ears as he gently rocked to their steps. Maddening. Now he started screaming in earnest. Over and over he screamed until the pain in his head forced him to stop. Where were they taking him?

Outside now, the rain pattered his face, against the thin film of fabric that covered his body, and against his eyelids. A soft breeze chilled him, making his teeth want to chatter, but they didn't. A door slid open and he was thrust inside. Must be a van, he thought, and the echo of voices confirmed it. The engine fired up and they lurched forward.

"Where do we take him?"

"The pit."

"The pit? What's that?"

"You've never been to the pit? How long you been here?"

"Coupla months. What is it?"

"It's a big cement bunker just over by the east fence. It was originally designed as a fallout shelter, but now they just use it as a body dump. Beats diggin' graves."

But I'm not dead!

Why where they doing this? This time his screaming was frantic. He begged and pleaded for them to stop but his cries never left his brain.

The constant drumming of rain on the roof of the van and the whine of the engine assaulted his ears, while gas fumes invaded his nostrils. The pain in his head cinched up another notch and he began to cry. Tears. They would see the tears. They had to. Then they would know he was still alive.

The van stopped. He was yarded out and the rain plastered his face. Bill Tuttle's tears would go unnoticed among the rainfall on his cheeks. He heard the sound of cement on cement and then there was the smell. It almost choked him and the slick, salty taste in his mouth made him want to puke but his stomach would not comply. He was picked up and then felt himself falling.

Something that could only be layers of bones broke his fall. Putrefying flesh: the smell seeped into his body the moment he came into contact with it. He thought he could feel maggots squirming against his skin and finally he passed out.

4. 7:57 p.m.

When Bill Tuttle awoke it was dark. The smell . . . was it gone now? Maybe he had dreamed the whole thing. He was lying face down, his head turned to one side. Somewhere to his right rang out a phlegmy cough. Thank God, he was not alone; it must have been a dream. This time the cough was louder, decaying into a sputtering series of hacks. He must be in a hospital ward. The throat cleared.

He could hear movement to his right; to his left, the steady drip of water. Had someone forgotten to turn a faucet off? The dripping was louder now. A loud crack

a bone?

filled the room, followed by a long wheeze and two short coughs.

Then he felt the hand on his flesh. A nurse, doctor,

the living dead?

a candy striper at the ready with a glass of water in hand? The touch was cold; it scratched. He felt several more hands and he knew he was still in the pit. The smell came back to him in the form of hot, stinking breath, followed by the damp, gurgling voice of a man.

"Aahh. A fresh one."

Chapter Eight

1. Tuesday, 11:45 a.m., Telsen, British Columbia

Wind whistled through the doorway and the door slammed shut as the soldiers entered the barracks with lunch. Steve had been on edge all morning awaiting this moment. The two men with trays were halfway down the aisle before the gunmen noticed someone was missing.

"Hey, where's the other guy—"

Danny had been hiding in the showers, and cut him off with a perfect tackle right at the kidneys. The gunman's body arced forward and hit the ground with Danny on top of him. He coughed up his weapon and the submachine gun slid to a halt beneath Phillip's foot. Phillips picked it up and somewhat awkwardly pointed it at the downed man.

"Just keep hangin' on to them trays, fellas." Eli, brandishing the knife, kept the other two from helping their partner.

The five of them had used Danny's knife to cut some blankets into strips, and Steve and Janet brought them out to tie up their prisoners. Speed was of the essence as Phillips had told them earlier. The quicker they had them under control the less time the guards would have to realize that Phillips probably wasn't going to shoot anyone. And the reality of a sixty-year-old man holding off two young men with a single knife was hardly intimidating. What they had in their favor was the element of surprise.

Steve and Janet took the trays from the two men and ordered them to remove their ponchos and lie face down on the floor. The men were still in shock and did as they were told. As fast as they could, Janet tied the man's hands and feet together behind their backs while Steve placed gags in the men's mouths. For a fleeting moment a thought entered his mind: he hoped that neither one of them had sinus trouble.

Danny had the gunman face down on the floor in a chokehold while Phillips kneeled in front of him with the gun pointed at the guy's forehead. His body was tensed in Danny's grip but he wasn't making a sound. When the two men were bound and gagged, Steve and Janet rolled them over facing each other and tied them together. Then, along with Eli, they hurried over to Phillips and Danny.

"So far, so good," said Eli to Phillips. "Comin' off without a hitch."

Phillips nodded and then placed the tip of the barrel so that it just touched the skin between the gunman's eyebrows. "Is anyone guarding the door?"

"Fuck you!"

Danny now had his arm full around the man's neck and tightened his grip. The man's face turned very red as his fingers clutched Danny's massive forearm.

"Unless you want your head twisted clean off," said Phillips, "I suggest you give me a straight answer, you dig?"

"You can take your nigger talk and stuff it up your ass."

Phillips flashed Steve a gee-I'd-really-like-to-empty-the-clip-of-this-gun-into-this-punk's-head-but-that-would-probably-attract-a-tad-bit-of-attention smile before standing back up. "Strip him." The shock that registered on the man's face seemed to satisfy Phillips for the moment.

The man's poncho and outer layer of khaki were peeled off and he was tied up wearing only his underwear. After he was gagged and seriously strapped to the leg of one of the beds they all moved to the door. Phillips turned to Janet. "Remember, if anyone's out there, tell them that someone's hurt and move back as soon as you can."

Danny ran with Janet into the entryway to stand behind her at the door and Phillips took his place just inside the sleeping quarters. Steve had argued that Phillips should be in the washroom but Phillips was adamant that Danny's presence would come into play long before anyone made it this far. Still, Steve was nervous.

"All clear," Janet shouted from the doorway and Steve breathed a sigh of relief, slipping his arm around her as she entered the room. "God, it's really coming down out there," she said. Steve could see drops of water on her face from just the brief glance out the door.

"I'm ready," said Eli, and everyone turned. He was now dressed in the gunman's clothes and holding out the baggy front of the jacket with both hands. "It's a little big, but the boots fit great." He rocked back on his heels and everyone laughed.

They all gathered together in the entryway and stood silent for a moment. Phillips un-tucked his shirt and stuck the slender handle of the machine gun into the back of his pants. Danny opened his knife and carefully concealed it in the sleeve of his shirt. Eli brought over the three ponchos, giving one to Danny and one to Phillips, and each of them slipped one over his head.

"This might be the last time we see each other," said Phillips. "If I don't get a chance to see your pop, Steve, tell him I'm sorry. For everything."

"Sure."

"I'll meet you two in the woods at the northern edge of the camp." Phillips turned to Danny and Eli. "We won't have a chance to talk after this. Good luck, and thanks for all your help."

"Aw, hell, if it wasn't for you three, Danny and I would be gomers as sure as I'm standing here. We owe you a lot, and anything we've done still don't seem like quite enough."

Danny nodded his agreement and there were firm handshakes and hugs all around. Philips was about to open the door when he turned around to Steve and Janet, who had stepped back away from the other three.

"Please get out as fast as you can the minute you see the gate open. If it doesn't happen, stay here. You've got hostages. I don't know how much time they'll buy you but . . . just . . ."

"Go on," said Steve. "Get out of here and we'll meet you in the woods."

Phillips nodded and pulled Eli's left arm over the back of his neck. Danny did the same with Eli's right arm and they hoisted them up between them. As Phillips opened the door a gust of rain-soaked wind flew in and then they were gone.

2. 11:52 a.m.

Wind and rain whipped around their bodies, ponchos flapping violently, and the ground was slick with mud. Howard pulled down on his hood to keep it from flying off and surveyed the area; there was no one else outside of the barracks in the whole camp. The guard at the gate kept a careful eye on them as they approached and Howard had to pound on the door of the tiny guardhouse before he would open it. When he finally did, the smell of electric heat and cigarette smoke whisked past them, and the buzzing drone of heavy-metal music could barely be discerned above the howl of the wind.

"What the hell are you doing out here?" the guard yelled.

"This man needs medical attention. I have to take him up to the Institute."

"Who the hell are you?"

The guard's gun was still slung around his shoulder as he held the door with both hands, bracing it against the wind. He didn't seem overly suspicious.

"I'm Dr. Phillips. It looks like we have a broken leg here. I'm going to be needing a Jeep."

Eli, his head hanging down, moaned as if on cue.

"I don't know anything about a Dr. Phillips," he shouted above another gust of wind. Then the guard closed the door and began flipping through papers on a clipboard.

"No," he said, his head poking back out the door. "I'm gonna have to call someone."

It was time for Howard to play his trump card. "Goddamn it, I have a man here who's hurt bad. I want a jeep and I want it now, before *I* have to call Brandt."

Bingo. The look in the guard's eyes was one of almost sheer terror and his back stiffened immediately.

"I'll have a Jeep sent around right away, Doctor."

The guard turned and was beginning to shut the door when Danny's hand shot between the gap and ripped it from his grasp. The door flew open wide and the guardhouse suddenly came alive with papers and other objects swirling around in the wind. The guard hadn't even reached for his gun and Danny was on top of him. His knife was out, but he didn't need it. His arm around the man's throat was all that was necessary, and Danny had him on the floor. Howard rushed inside after Eli and pulled the door shut, then ducked down and took the gun off the man.

"Here," he said to Eli. "Put this on."

Eli threw the strap around his shoulder and stood as though he were on duty while Howard and Danny gagged and bound the real guard.

"I think the gate is electronically controlled," said Eli.

Howard got up on his knees to look at the control panel. There were about fifty dials, knobs, buttons, and blinking lights. "Jesus, which one is it?"

"My guess would be this one," said Eli with a grin. He was pointing to a switch clearly marked "Gate."

Howard let his body relax. "Man, I was about to have a heart attack."

"Don't you go dyin' on us, now."

"Not me. What do you say we get out of here? You ready, Danny?"

Danny nodded.

Howard looked back to Eli. "Is the coast clear?"

"Yup."

"Then let 'er rip."

Eli flicked up the switch and the gate began to roll back behind the guardhouse. All three of them stepped out and ran for the fence. Howard squinted into the rain and could see Steve and Janet leaving the quarantine barracks. They would meet him in the woods, east of the gatehouse along the road, and together they would try to liberate Steve's father. That was the plan, anyway.

He tried to tell himself that it was the only thing he could do: he knew the layout of the hospital better than any of them and would be their best chance to rescue Paul. But he knew deep down that he was really doing it to atone for his sins; it was his fault that Paul had been dragged up here.

Besides, he almost didn't mind risking his life now that his days of scientific research were over. He hadn't done any real work at all since coming to work with Zindell, probably never would, and as far as he knew he was still blackballed in the U.S. No, his place was here, trying to right as many wrongs as he could.

Danny and Eli would be heading upstream and attempting to get through the gate where the river entered the Institute property. There was no reason they should stay, after having been forced to spend so much of their lives here as prisoners; the other three were unanimous on that score.

"Good luck," said Eli, and Howard gave him and Danny the thumbs-up.

Howard made his way as quickly as possible along the canal that ran the length of the camp. None of the barracks had windows on the end but he still felt vulnerable. Guard towers, even though they were empty, loomed above him threateningly. He stopped at the corner, looked back and saw that Steve and Janet had just left the camp. There was a guardhouse at the gate at this end of the camp and he checked to make sure the guard wasn't looking before making his dash to the woods.

3. 11:58 a.m.

Walther Brandt was breathing hard and fast and for the next minute he simply lay, relaxing, focusing on the blood rushing through his veins. He could feel his heart beating heavily in his chest and the beginning of a chill where the light sweat covered his body. Then he rolled off of the woman and stretched, his hands eventually coming to rest behind his head.

She sat up automatically, taking a basin of water and a washcloth from next to the bed, and began to clean him. When she was finished she sat motionless, awaiting his next command, but none came.

Brandt took a deep breath and pushed himself up. He grabbed a robe that was draped over the back of a chair and slipped it on as he walked toward the window. He wanted to rest for a few minutes before going at it again. He was using his own room instead of one at the brothel and of course his women never went into general circulation until he was through with them, anywhere from six months to a year depending on availability.

He put two fingers in between the slats in the blinds and gently pried them apart. It was a crappy day out. Zindell had said that the operation would start at noon, and it was about that now. He still had a couple of hours before he had to be back at the Institute to check up on Raymond's handiwork.

When he first noticed something odd he chalked it up to the driving rain, but the longer he looked the more positive he was that what he was seeing was real: the goddamn gate was open!

"I don't believe this shit," Brandt said loudly, and pounded his fist against the wall. He walked over to the chair and began dressing, completely ignoring the motionless figure on the bed. "What kind of fucking morons have I got running this place?"

He finished dressing and grabbed his poncho, which had been hung above the heater to dry, and stormed outside. He let his hood fly back behind him, and his hair became soaked with rain almost instantly. The tide of anger was rising inside him with every step that brought him closer to the guardhouse. When he reached it he ripped the door open, letting the wind slam it wide. Papers flew everywhere and he waved them out of his face. What he saw infuriated him.

The guard was on the floor, tied up with strips of blanket. Brandt pulled up his pant leg and took a dagger from the scabbard that was strapped to his calf. He severed the guard's bonds and then picked him up to a standing position with one hand.

"You want to tell me what's been going on here?" he said with all the restraint he could muster.

"Some guy named Phillips and two other guys . . . He said he was some kinda doctor. He said he was gonna call you if I didn't open the ga—"

"God damn it!" Brandt screamed, and heaved the man outside onto the ground.

The guard splashed into a puddle and was scrambling backward in the mud, crab-walking to get away, but in three strides Brandt was above him and picked him up by the front of his jacket. He flipped him around, one arm around the man's throat and the other around the back of his head. The guard flailed for a moment and then, with a sharp twist, Brandt snapped his neck and let the limp body fall into the water at his feet.

He walked back to the gatehouse and picked up the phone and dialed.

"I want forty men at the south gate in five minutes, understand? . . . Then do it!"

Brandt slammed down the phone and turned around. He ran his hands over his head to squeeze the water out of his hair and felt it run down his neck. When he looked at the body in the mud his anger dissipated. It was essential that he remain in control. He looked over to the quarantine barracks; with any luck some of them would still be there, but he wasn't hopeful.

Brandt marched through the rain, pulled the door open and stepped inside. When he laid eyes on the three men bound and gagged he turned and went back outside in disgust.

He locked the door and headed back toward the gate. Later, he would have to remember to collect any duplicate keys; nobody was going in there until next spring.

He was so sick of incompetence that there were times when he just wanted to kill the whole fucking bunch of them and start over again, but he had a few good men working for him and the feeling always passed.

Because of his hatred toward Zindell he had tried to bolster his troop numbers over the past few years by relaxing his strict standards. He wanted to send a message to the old bastard about who was in charge but, clearly, it wasn't working.

The choicest candidates were members of Aryan survivalist churches, but most of those were married and had families. There just wasn't that kind of room here, and so the bulk of his new recruits had come from skinhead gangs; they had the right ideology and most of them were single. The problem with them was that they didn't take well to authority, so Brandt would play to their violent natures and hand them each a machine pistol. That, along with the promise that they could keep their heads shaved and have access to the brothel, usually did the trick.

They weren't soldiers, though. Once they were free from outside distractions and cloistered within the camp, they responded admirably, but they didn't have the military instinct that Brandt needed in them. They were cocky with their guns and knives and consequently they made mistakes. In the past week, nearly every advantage he had hoped to gain over Zindell had vanished along with his prisoners.

Raymond better do what I told him, he thought, just as the first of the men began to arrive.

A few minutes later, forty poncho-clad soldiers were gathered around Brandt. Without exception, each was carrying an Ingram Mac-10 nine-millimeter machine pistol. They were looking with understandable uneasiness at the body that was face down in the mud.

"This is the situation, men: we have five prisoners loose on the compound. They've only been gone about five or ten minutes so they can't be too far away. They killed Linderman here. Wiley and a couple of kids from the mess hall bought it inside the quarantine barracks."

The continually darkening sky spasmed with light and Brandt let the rumble of thunder die out before continuing. "Where are my squad leaders?"

Eight men stepped forward.

"I want you to divide up into groups of five, four groups around the perimeter and four searching the interior. I don't want any of them to get near the Institute; do you hear me?"

The nods were quick and sure, and eyes were focused and determined. That was good. They would do better if they thought they were hunting for murders.

"I just have one more thing to say, so listen close, because if anybody fucks *this* up they're going to wish I'd killed them: I want the girl alive."

After another display of lightning and thunder Ramey raised his hand.

"Yes?"

"What should we do with the rest of them sir?"

"If they move, kill 'em. But I want the girl. Now choose your men and head out. Ramey I want you to assign the areas."

"Yes, sir."

In two minutes they were gone. Brandt held a man back to guard the gate and then headed for his jeep.

4. 12:03 p.m.

Eli stayed close behind Danny as they ran through the trees together. The brush seemed to part like the Red Sea in front of them but it wasn't because of his son's size; Danny had played in these very woods as a child and seemingly in no time they were at the point where the river entered the Institute property.

Eli wouldn't have believed it possible, but the rain seemed to be coming down even harder since they had made their escape. He was severely winded and took a few moments to catch his breath. He tucked his gun up inside his poncho and joined his son in taking stock of the situation.

Even during the summer, when the river was at its lowest point, it was doubtful whether anyone would be able to swim upstream even a short way. But now . . .

Eli guessed that the river had risen at least a foot from the additional runoff of the deluge, and the sheer volume and incredible velocity of the current made the river look terrifying. But if the river itself wasn't deterrent enough, the fence itself was impenetrable.

Eli hoped that he and Danny would be able to find a means of escape where the fence crossed the river. He hadn't actually worked on this part of the fence all those years ago, not that it would have helped if he had, except that it might have made him consider another plan. The designers had done their job well.

On both sides of the river, the fence ended above the flood line and made a ninety-degree turn, extending 15 meters or so downstream. Spring loaded sheets of fiberglass that could adjust to the height of the river stretched across the expanse like louvers, allowing debris to flow underneath but preventing anything from traveling upstream. There was no way to get over the louvers, either; they were strung across the top with coils of barbed wire.

The woods had been cleared away on both sides of the fence. Eli watched as Danny tossed a branch at it. The branch hit and fell to the ground and Danny gingerly touched one of the chain links with the tip of his knife. When he was convinced that the fence was not electrified he ventured a touch with his bare fingertips.

"Freeze motherfuckers!"

Eli's heart nearly leapt out of his chest. As they slowly turned around he heard his son whisper, "Wait for it, Dad."

"Hands on your head," said one of the two men with machine guns trained on them. Eli and Danny obeyed. The men approached until they were only a few feet away.

"All right, where's the girl?"

Eli and Danny looked at each other before Eli said, "What girl?"

"That's it, you two. Up against the fence."

Eli could see that Danny was not moving and began to stall for him.

"I don't think we could do that."

"Shut your fucking mouth, old man. Did I say you could talk? I'm gonna blow your fucking brains out, so you better do what I tell you."

"Now, there you go—that's just what I mean. Your logic's all screwy. The fact that you're going to blow my brains out is exactly the reason I *don't* have to do what you tell you."

In the second that the gunman was standing with a look of disbelief on his face, another soldier appeared out of the woods screaming at the top of his lungs. "Kill the fuckers!"

The two men were almost as startled at Eli had been earlier and they both turned. Danny immediately grabbed the closest one and had his knife at the man's neck using his body as a shield. The second gunman froze and Eli thrust his hand beneath his poncho for his own weapon. When the third man opened fire, Eli retaliated. Eli's poncho was laid open from within by his gun and in the few seconds before it was over the forest was riddled with bullets.

The strong recoil threatened to pull the gun from Eli's hands but he held on. He sprayed the weapon back and forth rapidly until both men had fallen and the clip was empty. His hands stung from the vibration. He dropped the gun and ran to Danny.

Danny was on his back, still gripping the bullet-ridden body on top of him. Eli pulled Danny's arm away and rolled the dead man off.

Some of the bullets had gone through the soldier's body into Danny. Another had hit Danny in the head, the trickle of blood pooling in one of his unseeing eyes. Danny was dead.

But there was no time to grieve; someone was coming. Eli snatched up the gun from the soldier who hadn't fired and disappeared into the woods. He took cover behind a tree and waited. Two more men walked cautiously into the clearing to inspect the bodies that were strewn about. Before the one who took his walkie-talkie from under his poncho had it to his mouth, Eli stepped out from his hiding place and fired.

His hands gripped the gun like a vice and with two short bursts he had killed both of them. Six bodies now lay before him, one of them his only son, and as the gun swung from his hand at his side he wept.

The others. He had to think only of them now. If he didn't, he just might stay here too long and get himself killed.

He stumbled forward, his eyes clouded by tears and rain. Wind battered him and he ripped off his tattered poncho as he walked over to the newly fallen men. He ejected the clips from their guns and put them in one of the oversized pockets of his jacket. He put one arm and his head through the strap of the gun, slung it around to his back, and then hoisted Danny over his shoulder. He might be an old man but he was damned if he was going to leave his son out here with these murders, a group which he could now number himself among.

A few yards into the woods Eli lay Danny's body in some undergrowth beneath a large tree. He knelt beside the body and pulled the hood of the poncho over his son's face.

"I'll be back, Son. I promise. I won't let you stay here all by yourself. But I have to help the others. I know you would understand if you were still here. I know you would. I know . . ."

Eli was taking deep breaths. He couldn't talk anymore and stood. Silently, he said his final goodbye and turned away. The fence was on his right. Somewhere in front of him were Steve, Janet and the doctor, so Eli took the gun off of his back and went looking for them.

5. 12:04 p.m.

Steve almost didn't see Phillips at first. He was standing like a statue with his back to them, the flapping of his green poncho dissolving into the waves of wind that were surging through the trees. They had barely reached him when he turned around.

Phillips' face was etched with seriousness. Rain dripped from his hood and his face. Steve had felt his own clothes sponge up the rain as soon as they had left the barracks and now he and Janet were both soaking wet, their arms around each other, shoulders hunched against the elements.

"Are you all right?" asked Phillips.

Steve looked quickly to Janet and then back. "Yeah, we're fine. Are you okay?"

Phillips nodded. "You realize we still have to get across the river, don't you?"

"Sure." Steve wasn't positive, but Phillips looked a little rattled. "But there's a bridge just up the road."

"I know, I know. Do you know of any other way across?"

"No, that's the way we came yesterday."

"I have to tell you guys, I'm not too confident about my ability to navigate through these woods."

Steve felt strange assuming command from the man who had chiefly planned and executed their escape, but he wasn't going to show his gratitude by ignoring Phillips' not-so-subtle hint. "I think I can get us back to the Institute but I'm going to need your help to get inside."

Phillips visibly relaxed. "No problem, just lead the way."

The three started off toward the river single file, Phillips taking the rear.

Because of the high winds, they didn't have to worry about their footsteps being heard, but it also meant that Steve had to check continually to make sure they were both still behind him. When the bridge came into view he stopped and the three of them huddled together.

"We should go across right now in case somebody happens to come along," said Steve. "We'll be totally exposed and I'd like to get it over with."

Steve took Janet's hand and they stepped out near the road. He looked both ways for any sign of soldiers and when he was satisfied that none were near, he ran with Janet across the bridge. Phillips followed close behind.

On the way across Steve was amazed at how high the river had risen. The place where he and Janet had hidden was now completely under water. Branches, leaves and other flotsam hurled by with amazing speed beneath the bridge. Once across they had barely ducked into the woods again when a Jeep drove by heading toward the Institute.

"Did you hear that?" said Janet.

Steve had been just about to continue deeper into the woods, "What, the Jeep?"

"No, I thought I heard gunshots."

"Me, too," said Phillips.

"Jesus, you think it's Danny and Eli?"

They stood silently, listening into the wind for a second, and this time Steve heard it, too.

"There it is again," said Janet. "What should we do?"

"We have to keep going." Steve put his arm around her and she held him tightly around the waist.

"I just feel like we should try to help them."

"I know," said Steve, "but we're too far away."

"Eli had a gun," said Phillips.

"That's right—"

All three of them turned when they heard the sound of footsteps on the bridge.

"Shit!" Steve blurted out as quietly as he could. "We've got to get the hell out of here, fast."

But he was too late. Bullets were zinging around him by the time Steve could take Janet by the wrist and run. In seconds the shooting had stopped, as soon as they were covered by the trees. Steve risked a glance back and he could see Phillips was still behind them.

Steve was scared now. He didn't know where any of the gunmen were. They were no doubt spreading out along the road while he was running blind. The worst part was that they were stuck in the narrowest part of the Institute property, trapped between the road and the fence.

He wasn't running as fast as he could, holding back slightly on his speed for Janet's sake. She was probably at the outer limit of her capacity, but he refused to let go of her. Luckily. They jumped over a moss-covered log and when Steve touched town in a patch of rain-softened earth, his foot slipped and he felt his entire equilibrium go. Janet held on tight and he righted himself without losing a step.

After a minute they slowed. Phillips was still behind them and he quickly caught up. The high winds had turned the woods into a mass of confusion. Leaves and needles were swirling wildly about them and they had to yell just to be heard.

"We have to get to the Institute fast," said Phillips behind them. "They've got the bloodhounds out now, and we can't afford to give them another sniff."

"Just make sure you can get us inside when we get there." Then Steve looked to Janet. "Are you all right?" It sounded funny having to shout it.

"I'll be better when we're out of here."

"Thanks for saving me back there."

She smiled and shook her head. "And I suppose you were running as fast as you could?"

He shrugged and smiled back.

Steve picked up the pace again and they were able to cover a lot of ground. But in an almost unconscious effort to steer clear of the road he suddenly realized they had drifted too far to the east. As soon as Steve caught sight of the fence he veered back toward the woods. Then there was more shooting; they had been spotted by guards along the fence.

Panic was rising in Steve. He wanted to scream; he wanted to piss his pants; he did neither. He kept running. He was trying to think about where they could hide when the Institute suddenly appeared through the trees. He was turning to tell the others when something plunged him into the undergrowth.

He was rolling over onto his back when he found himself looking into the blunt barrel of a submachine gun. Everything seemed to be going in slow motion now. He could see someone picking up Janet off of the ground and someone else was behind Phillips. Four or five soldiers were standing over Steve. There were guns everywhere.

Damn it! He didn't want it to end like this. His Dad was still somewhere in this fucking place. He let one of them pick him up by the vest. He really and truly wanted to cry and wasn't sure just why he didn't.

The gunmen moved in closer until the three of them were literally surrounded. Since the soldiers were in each other's crossfire Steve knew they weren't going to be killed. Well, at least they weren't going to be shot. Not right away.

One of them—he looked to be about thirty-five with big, black sideburns—let his gun fall to his side and started acing like the head honcho. "Wayne," he said to one of the anonymous ponchos, "split the rest of your group up and help track down the other two."

Five of the soldiers left, leaving five surrounding them. The head honcho pulled his hood off and turned his face to the sky, letting the rainfall wash him. When he lowered his head and his eyes met Steve's he looked crazed.

"Pull them away from her," he said.

Two men grabbed Steve and two grabbed Phillips. Janet tried to hold on to Steve but the honcho pried her away.

"Get your fucking hands off me!" Janet yelled. She jerked away from him with real force, but her wrist slipped easily from his wet hand and she sat down abruptly.

Honcho was laughing now, but Steve was still in a slow-motion dream, his mind trying with all its might to move his temporarily paralyzed body. What should he do? Honcho was on top of her now and she was kicking and screaming. He glanced over at the doctor. Phillips looked mad; his gun was still underneath his poncho and he couldn't get at it. The other soldiers were watching Honcho, and laughing. Steve's brain felt like it had just wound down and shut off for the day. Then the man hit her.

When the honcho slapped Janet across the face, Steve could almost feel the hot sting on his own cheek. Suddenly his brain was back up and running, fully stoked with rage and set on autopilot. He hit the honcho on the fly and rolled him off of Janet. He wound up on top of the guy, straddling him, and then, with a force from somewhere deep inside him that he hadn't known existed, he began to pummel the man.

First Steve launched into a flurry of blows to the face, before the honcho had even realized what was going on. Honcho's hands went up to protect his face and Steve beat on the man's knuckles with even greater force. When the hands came down Steve could see blood pouring from his nose. And his head, no longer resistant to Steve's fists, whipped back and forth limply every time Steve connected.

In the next instant Steve was knocked to the ground, this time on the receiving end of the blows. But his arms were no protection against two sets of boots and he found himself retching from kicks to the stomach and genitals, and reeling with blinding flashes of pain in his head.

He was barely aware of the gunfire that had preceded the end of the assault. The sound of his own blood roared in his ears and pain knifed through his body until, mercifully, he blacked out.

6. 12:05 p.m.

Paul was hauled out of the OR by the two gunmen, the kid on his right and the bruiser on his left. By the time they were halfway down the hall he could walk on his own and the kid released him with a mixture of contempt and disgust.

"I'm gonna enjoy killing you, buddy."

Paul said nothing. His one chance to escape, the bomb, had slipped by. Someone must have discovered it. What else could have happened? Doubts began to fill his mind: what if he had trusted Brandt? Had he ruined his only chance at survival? Second guessing was a foolish exercise, but Paul couldn't help himself.

They reached the elevator and the kid punched the button against the wall. They hadn't been waiting more than a few seconds before he punched it again.

259

"Hey, go check the stairs, will ya?"

The bruiser looked over to the kid wearily. "It's locked."

"I didn't ask you if the fuckin' thing was locked, did I?"

"All right, all right, I'm going," he said appeasingly, and walked off.

The kid beat on the button with his fist three times in quick succession. "Come on, you fuckin' piece of shit." Then he stood back behind Paul. Finally, it opened.

"'Bout fuckin' time. Hey, Frankie, let's go," he called out, and then back to Paul: "Get in."

The next few seconds were crucial. Paul hesitated as though he hadn't heard the command.

"Move it!"

Paul felt the gun touch his back. Now he had a bearing on exactly where the kid was. Bruiser wasn't back yet and the door was seconds from closing.

"What the fuck are you do—"

With as much force as he could gather, Paul swung his elbow and connected square on the kid's temple. The doors were closing, and as the kid was crumpling to the floor in a heap, Paul dove into the elevator. A couple of bullets snuck in before the doors shut and Paul could see the metal dimple toward him as the gun burped outside.

He was alone in the car. His heart was racing but when he looked up at the numbers it raced even faster. He wasn't moving! And then it hit him: he hadn't pushed a button! You idiot, he screamed to himself. Paul scrambled to the panel, terrified that the kid would hit the outside button and open the doors.

He mashed both hands against the four floor buttons and fell back against the rear wall. His bowels liquefied and sweat leaked from his pours as he awaited the parting of the doors. The car lurched and Paul clenched his fists. Then he realized the elevator was going down.

Up on his knees, Paul frantically searched the panel for a button to stop the car before it reached the third floor. It was the lower right corner and shaped like a stop sign. He pushed it in and the elevator came to a jarring halt, accompanied by an alarm bell ringing loudly.

Paul stood to think. The bruiser had said that the door was locked. What if it wasn't? What if they were waiting for him on the third floor. He couldn't go up. He had pushed all of the buttons and now the elevator would open on every floor. The alarm bell droned on, an oppressive reminder of the danger he was facing. He felt cornered, panicked. He could stay between the floors and they would eventually drop through the top of the car and he would have accomplished nothing.

The alarm was driving him to distraction. The only other choice he had was to get to the first floor as fast as possible. If he was met anywhere in between by the gun club, well, he was going to die anyway. He took a moment to prepare himself and then pulled out the red octagon. The bell ceased and the car lurched back into motion.

Paul searched out the "door closed" button. He would lay on it as soon as the door opened. The car stopped on the third floor. A bell tinged and the doors slid open. The foyer was empty. Paul was leaning on the button and the door was beginning to close when he smelled the gas.

"Jesus," slipped from his mouth. He shot his hand out between the rubber bumpers and the door jerked back open. He held in one of the bumpers and stepped out of the car. The odor was not strong but was easily discernible. Obviously no one had discovered his bomb, and yet it hadn't gone off. If he could get back into the lab and fix whatever had gone wrong, he might be able to make his escape as he had originally intended.

He stepped back inside and pushed the stop button. The din of the bell tempted him to pull it out again, but he wasn't going to be more than a minute. Paul ran down the hall toward the lab, the odor of gas getting stronger. When he reached the door and looked through the window he could see the slab of sodium metal on the edge of the sink and the water still running.

He tried the door: it was locked. Paul tried to roll up his sleeve and winced at the pain that shot up his arm; the elbow he had given the kid had taken its own toll on him. He rolled up his other sleeve so that the bulk was over his good elbow and placed it against the lower corner of the window. The sound of breaking glass was accompanied by the thick, greasy odor of propane and made him cough.

Paul pulled out a few stray shards of glass from the frame and stuck his hand through the door to open it. The coughing was making him lightheaded as his lungs continued to suck up more of the gas. Paul ran back down the hall a little way and took a few breaths of the rapidly worsening air. Then he took a big breath and held it. Back inside the lab he immediately took the sodium out of the clamp and placed it on another table. One drop of water on it now would touch the whole place off.

Looking in the sink he could see that the wad of paper he had stuffed in the drain had not held the water out; the sink was only about half full. Paul took some more paper towel and stuffed it in the drain. Then he turned up the flow and reached back for the sodium metal.

His lungs were beginning to ache, but he wanted to do this one pass and get the hell out of there. He picked up the sodium. It had mostly oxidized over, except the part that had been in contact with the table where it was clamped down. He was cautiously placing that section above the rapidly rising water in the sink when something caught his attention.

The alarm bell in the elevator had stopped.

Heart pounding, lungs burning, Paul was forced to exhale and take a breath. But there was nothing to breathe; the oxygen was so diluted with gas that he nearly passed out. He dropped to the floor, where the air was only slightly better, took a few fast and shallow breaths and then a big one.

He could barely stand, pulling himself up and taking the brick of sodium in his bare hand. He wouldn't be able to talk without losing the meager amount of oxygen he had left in his lungs. He doubted whether they would know what the sodium metal's presence meant and he was right; as soon as the kid appeared at the door, he opened fire.

Paul could only watch in horror as the bullets that erupted from the gun and pocked his body were trailed by a plume of flame that instantaneously engulfed the room. His clothes were on fire, he was bleeding to death, he could no longer breathe, and just as Paul began his final descent to the floor he plunged the sodium metal into the sink.

7. 12:15 p.m.

Brandt wheeled his Jeep though the deluge as fast as he could without losing control. The rag top was up. Somewhere a snap that hadn't been fastened clattered and water sloshed on the floor where it had leaked. He laid on the horn as he approached the gatehouse on the road and the cross arm bobbed up. He sped over the bridge and pressed his foot to the floorboard all the way to the Institute. At one point he felt the vehicle hydroplaning, calmly steered to the side until the tires caught pavement, and increased the pressure on the gas pedal.

When the Jeep bounced out of the woods, gusts of wind slammed against the side. Brandt overcorrected, and for a second he thought he was going to roll. Wind whistled through the cracks in the vinyl shell, and though the wipers were going full he could barely see out the front windshield.

He pulled into the back parking lot and opened his door to get out. Wind ripped it from his hand and pinned it against the side mirror. He left it there and stepped up onto the loading dock. After unlocking the door and stepping inside he shook the rain off of him and pushed the button to the elevator.

Zindell was going to have a fit when he found out. Brandt cursed himself for having been so careless. Most of the men had only guarded the camp prisoners; they weren't used to having anyone put up a fight. And when someone did, Brandt found his guards pitifully inept at adapting. He had to take the blame on himself for not preparing them adequately and it churned in his gut.

Assuming that Raymond had followed through with the old man, Zindell wouldn't be a problem. If he hadn't, Zindell would be extremely pissed about the kids and most likely expect Brandt himself to go about covering their tracks so that they couldn't be traced back to the Institute. Either way, Raymond was headed for the pit.

He looked at his watch. If they were running late, the operation might not have even started yet. The button he'd pushed was lit but the elevator had not come yet. He glanced at the numbers above the door. It was still on the third floor. Brandt rubbed his chin and watched. The light glowed immutably. Still watching the light, he unhoslstered his pistol, loaded the chamber and slipped it back into place.

Brandt walked around to the stairs. The door on every floor locked from the outside. Only people with any business in the building had keys, which excluded all but him, Zindell, and Zindell's two assistants. Brandt unlocked the door and stepped into the cement and steel shaft.

His footsteps echoed warily. At the second-floor he drew his weapon and pulled open the solid metal door. The hallway was well lit but empty and he closed the door and continued upward. At the third-floor landing he heard voices beyond the door. Slowly, he turned the knob and the latch bolt silently slid open.

The door was only open a crack when he smelled the gas. It startled him; Brandt wasn't usually caught off guard. The voices were now accompanied by footsteps that were heading away from him. He stuck his head out into the hall just in time to see two of his soldiers, accompanied by a white-coated assistant, open fire into one of the rooms.

8. 12:22 p.m.

Eli had nearly reached the exhaustion point several times along the way. The first time was after he had managed to get across the river. When no one else had come to the aid of the four he had killed, he had tossed the gun and spare clips over to the opposite bank. Then he had grabbed hold of a strand of barbed wire and, hand over hand, pulled himself across. His body had dragged in the current so heavily that he feared the wire might pull loose even before his arms gave out, but it held.

Another time, while Eli was running, he'd caught his foot on an exposed tree root and nearly broken his ankle. Twice he'd fallen and thought he might never get up, but he always did. His body was running on its own and he felt like a helpless hostage being dragged along against his will.

When Eli heard the screams he ran faster, as fast as his old legs would go. He made it just in time to see the doctor reach under his poncho and bring out his gun. But one of the soldiers caught him from behind and slit his throat from ear to ear. Eli winced. After what had happened to Danny, he almost lost it. His hands started shaking and he felt his resolve ebbing away. Killing was not something that came easily to him.

Two of the soldiers were kicking the shit out of Steve. The other two had dropped Phillips and were heading for Janet, who was on the ground next to Steve trying to scramble to her feet.

Before she could succeed, Eli began his assault. The ones who weren't hit right away brought up their weapons but they couldn't see him amid the swirling wind. As he trained a steady, even spray on them they did their dance of death and went down.

Afterward he waited. Had to. If anyone else came along he would have to take care of them, too. He ejected the spent clip and rammed home a fresh one. Janet was sobbing her guts out over Steve and trying hopelessly to make some sense of the carnage around her. The look on her face was so desperate that he finally had to step out into view.

"Eli!" She ran to him and fell into his arms. "Help me get him out of here," she said in between sobs. "He's hurt, please—"

"Okay, okay, honey. Let's see what we got here."

Janet helped Eli roll Steve onto his back. He was moaning; a good sign. His face was flushed beneath the mud and he had a bloody lip. It would be a little harder to ascertain what condition the rest of him was in until he came around. Eli looked up into Janet's eyes.

"He's gonna be fine, a little worse for the wear, but fine. Just stay here until he comes out of it. I'm gonna check on the doctor."

"They killed him."

She said it in such a flat, matter-of-fact voice that it was frightening. Eli had killed, Jesus, what was it, eight people now? But the way she said "They killed him," like she was telling him what time it was nearly scared the shit out of him.

"I'll be right over, hon'."

She nodded and Eli walked over to where Phillips was lying. They'd made him a new mouth right below his chin. His head was back and the red gash gaped wide open as rain washed the blood away.

Eli turned away but the only other thing to look at were the bloody corpses of the soldiers. They reminded him of Danny. Suddenly the gun felt like dog shit in his hand and he threw it to the ground. He wiped his hands on his pants legs to get the unseen blood off.

"You saved our lives." Janet was suddenly next to him. She put a hand on his arm. She looked better now.

"It won't bring Danny back." The look of surprise and pain that registered across Janet's face made Eli regret having spoken so bitterly.

"Oh, God, I'm sorry, Eli." She reached out to him and embraced him as if she understood, and Eli found himself needing her in a way he hadn't needed anyone since Katherine had died. He held her tightly and when she eventually pulled back he felt better. He could see in her eyes that she needed him too, and right now that seemed the most important thing in the world to Eli.

"Will you help me?" she said. "We have to move him in case someone comes back this way."

"Too late," came a voice from nowhere, and five gunmen oozed from the woods to surround them.

9. 12:25 p.m.

Janet could only watch, helpless, as one of the soldiers picked up Steve and began to drag him by the collar of his vest. Another took Phillips by the hood of his poncho. Eli's gun had been on the ground when the soldiers surprised them, leaving them helpless.

"Let's go," said one of the gunmen, indicating with his weapon for Eli and Janet to step in line behind the two inanimate bodies.

"Where are you taking us?" she demanded.

"Nothin's gonna happen to you—"

"Shut up," said the gunman, silencing the voice that had come from one of the two men behind her.

As they began walking the gunman ran up and took his place at the head of the procession. Janet slipped her arm through Eli's and he looked at her. He was worried—that was obvious—but he smiled anyway. The rain continued to beat down on them and Janet's body was fatigued from trembling against the cold. Her leather loafers had stained her socks and her wet jeans chafed her thighs. She prayed that Steve was all right.

"Where are we going, Eli?"

He shook his head. "Don't know for sure." But she thought he did.

The soldiers had brought them out onto a wide path, two thin straps of mud sandwiching a thick strip of weeds. It was clear that it was accessed by vehicles fairly often, but she couldn't imagine why anyone would have to drive into the woods toward the fence, where they were headed now.

When they reached the clearing she had her first clue. A large slab of cement the size of a motel swimming pool was set into the grass next to the fence. She squeezed Eli's arm but he was stone faced.

"Eli," she whispered, "what is this place?"

He wouldn't answer.

The two men in front of them dropped the bodies they were hauling, walked up to a three-foot square in the cement and began to pull up on recessed handles. The small slab scraped and clanged above the noise of the wind as the two men lifted it up and set it back out of the way. The hole was black inside.

"Eli, what the hell is this?" But his eyes were closed and he wouldn't respond.

"Dump those two in first," said the leader.

When one of them took hold of Steve, she screamed. She couldn't help it. She bolted from Eli's side but one of the men behind her grabbed her hair and twisted her head until she went down face-first in the grass.

"Easy on her, goddamn it."

Eli was down on his knees beside her, restraining her, but she kept on screaming. Her fists were balled up and she wanted to lash out against these animals. She didn't have to know what was going on to know it was bad. One of the men had backed up to the hole with Phillips' body when her screams were choked off.

Janet's eyes were riveted on a puffy white hand with long curling fingernails as it reached up out of the hole. She felt Eli's grip go lax and she assumed that he was watching it, too. The hand wrapped around the ankle of the man standing on the edge and pulled downward.

The man's other foot slipped out from under him and he fell backward into the hole, his body connecting with the far edge of concrete. Then his body twisted sideways and he disappeared. The weather muted the man's grunts as he fell, but once inside his ululations of fright cut through rather easily.

It was clear that the rest of the gunmen were scared. The one who had been hauling Steve let go while the two behind Janet and Eli ran up to the others, leaving them unguarded. It didn't matter; she was staying here with Steve. Janet wanted to run to him but with the security of Eli's arm around her she couldn't make herself move.

The shrieks from the hole continued until one of the men fired his weapon into it.

"What the hell are you doin'?" another one asked, with little conviction. The screaming had stopped.

The men were silent as they stood over the hole, their bodies tensed and their guns pointing downward. This time two hands swiped at their legs and it sent them scattering.

"Jesus! Put the fucking cover back on!"

"Fuck you! I ain't goin' near that thing."

"I'm giving you an order—"

"Fuck your orders. I ain't doin' it."

While the gunmen argued, Janet and Eli stood and one of the men ran back to them. For some reason he had his gun pointed threateningly at her, as if guarding them was his ticket out of this. He seemed confused and looked at Janet like he needed her help but she could only offer contempt, and wished that the mysterious hands would have taken the rest of the men.

10. 12:30 p.m.

Steve's consciousness returned in an even and orderly fashion. First up to bat was the pain, soft and dull in his legs and back, knifing in his stomach and arms, bright and throbbing in his head. On deck were the sounds of people talking over the wind and rain, and in the hole was the smell and taste of blood and dirt on his face.

As of yet no one was administering to him and that was fine. He lay for a minute letting the nausea pass before finally opening his eyes. His vision was blurred at first but he could make out the soldiers as well as Janet and Phillips. Then someone had him by the arms and hauled him to his feet. His eyes slammed shut.

Technicolor pain lit up his body. He wanted to scream but a previous kick to his throat had made even that impossible. Instead, a series of low moans spilled out of his slack mouth.

When he opened his eyes the next time it was as though he were in a different place. Phillips was lying beside an open hole in a cement slab. Two soldiers were taking him over to where Janet was but he could hardly stay on his feet. He was just about to let his eyes slip shut again when the Institute exploded.

The concussion was deafening. A flash of blinding light was followed by a hammer blow to his chest and Steve was knocked to the ground, fresh pain blooming inside of him. With all his strength he pushed himself up in time to see a column of black smoke rising into the air. Fragments of cement and glass were already filtering through the trees along with the rain.

The steaming ruin of the Institute, barely visible through the trees, exuded heat that even Steve could feel a hundred yards away. He looked to Janet and Eli and they came to him at the same time that the soldiers ran away. Janet wiped the wet hair from his forehead while Eli stared dumfounded at the flaming building.

All three of them turned away and covered their heads when several minor blasts rippled through the air over them. The Institute lay burning, gutted open, but the only thing Steve could think about was his father.

"We have to get Dad," he croaked, but they ignored him.

Janet was stroking his face and crying while Eli stood, seemingly mesmerized by the flames. Steve pushed Janet away and bit back the pain as he stood up. Then she took his arm and helped him as he walked over to Eli.

Eli? He wasn't even supposed to be here. Steve turned and looked at Phillips, the wound on his throat evidence of what had happened.

"Eli, where's Danny?" But the old man didn't respond.

"He didn't make it," Janet said softly.

Steve wanted Eli to know how sorry he was, but there wasn't time. Finally, Steve shook his shoulder. "Eli, we have to go get my dad."

The look on Eli's face was childlike in its simplistic terror. Then he seemed to come back to reality as he acknowledged Steve.

"But . . . what if he was in . . ."

"He was in the front of the building yesterday. He might still be there. We have to try. Please."

It hurt Steve's throat terribly to talk, but the strength in his legs was coming back and the three of them walked out of the woods and onto the Institute's manicured grounds.

11. 12:31 p.m.

Brandt threw his body down the stairwell just as the fire door blew off its hinges, and flames shot down after him. He lay on the landing, stunned, as dust floated around him. He covered his head and curled up as a series of secondary explosions rocked the building. Following each blast he felt debris raining down on top of him anew.

Several minutes after the last explosion Brandt looked up. The wreckage of the door lay askew over the edge of the stairs and the stairwell was getting hot. Brandt stood and stared in amazement and disbelief. Finally, he brushed himself off and began walking down the stairs.

12. 12:31 p.m.

Officer Dick Pollock was filling up a paper cone at the water cooler when a peal of thunder rocked the station house.

"Jesus H.," said a voice in the squad room, "would ya listen to that."

But Dick Pollock wasn't listening to anything. His eyes were riveted to the plume of smoke that was rising above the treetops south of town.

13. 12:35 p.m.

As they neared the building, Steve found he was able to jog. Janet had her arm around his waist, which hindered him more than it helped, but right now the one thing he needed more than anything else was to be touching her. The ringing of the fire alarms greeted them loudly as they rounded the front of the Institute. When they reached the front door it was locked.

Before they had left the woods, Steve had persuaded Eli to go back for one of the guns and now he hurriedly shot out the lock. Steve led the way down the hall to the last door on the right. He pushed it open and suddenly felt very tired. His father was not there.

The three of them made their way back toward the reception desk looking in each of the rooms, but each was just as empty.

"We need to call the police—" Steve stopped cold when he saw the receptionist, still sitting dutifully at her desk.

"I'll do it," said Eli. "You two go on and try and find him."

Steve and Janet ran down the connecting corridor. When they pushed open the doors at the end they were sprayed with water. The sprinklers were working. Most of the damage had been contained in the right wing of the building where the explosion had originated. But the damage there was extensive. The entire three floors above had been blasted away and Steve could see right through to the sky.

The combination of wind, rain and sprinklers had doused most of the fire, but purposeful-looking flames still shot from the exposed gas lines. The place was sturdy; it didn't look like it was going to collapse in on itself. What they hadn't expected to find were the bodies.

A dozen men and women, some in charred hospital gowns and some naked, were lying in various states of dismemberment around the outer edges of the ripped-open building. Steve put his hand to his mouth and looked away. He could feel the rumbling of grief beginning in his stomach and radiating outward until he didn't know if he could go on anymore.

Above them he could hear screams and moans; there were people on the upper floors. His father might be there.

"Steve? Are you going to be all right?"

He took a deep breath and squeezed Janet's hand. "Yeah." He took another breath; it helped. "We have to look through them."

"Eli's calling for an ambulance—"

"That might be too late!" He hadn't wanted to yell, but he had almost completely lost the power to control his emotions. He walked over to the closest body and turned it over. One side of its face was gone, a bloody pulp covering half the exposed skull. He continued examining bodies while Janet began with one a few feet away.

He looked at three more before deciding he would have to get upstairs and let Janet finish down here by herself. She could wait for Eli and then join him. But before he could open his mouth she screamed.

Steve whipped around in time to see one of the bodies holding on to Janet's arm and pulling her to the ground. She stayed down and wasn't moving. The body, on the other hand, was up on its feet. When Steve ran to Janet he found himself face to face with Zindell.

His blood shot eyes were sunk back deep into his head and his body was stooped and shaking. His lips looked as if they had been burned back from a rictus of yellow teeth. The sight froze Steve, and in that instant, a pair of skeletal hands snaked out and grabbed him by the throat.

Steve stumbled backward and Zindell fell on top of him. Either the grip around his neck was incredibly strong or Steve had just become too weak, because he felt powerless to break away.

Saliva streamed over Zindell's blackened and shriveled lips onto Steve face, and his tongue lolled out exposing the bright-red inside of his mouth. Steve thought he was hearing a siren at first and then realized it was a high-pitched squeal that was emanating from a place where Zindell's throat had been punctured.

Then without warning Zindell's eyes glazed over. Steve felt the grip on his neck slacken, and Zindell fell heavily on top of him. A small round hole on the side of Zindell's head dripped fresh blood. Steve looked up to see a man in fatigues standing about twenty yards away, just beyond the doors to the connecting corridor, holstering his pistol and walking away.

Seconds later Eli appeared and helped push Zindell's body off of Steve. Exhaustion had completely taken over his mind and he sobbed, unable to help Janet and unable to find his dad.

"Ambulance is on the way," said Eli.

"Go see if Janet's all right."

Eli turned from him and Steve tried to stay awake but his body was enveloped in sleep.

Canada, 1990

Walther Brandt stepped out into the rubble caused by the explosion. Luckily, he had parked at the other end of the building and his jeep was unscathed.

He tried not to think about what he had lost but it was no use. The police would be here in a few minutes and everything would be over. They would find the camp, the prisoners. Phillips would fill them in on everything else. At least Zindell was dead, and that was probably the best that could come of all this.

Brandt climbed into the Jeep and turned the engine over. He would have to begin again, reestablish his contacts in Germany and Egypt. But most important of all, he would have to tie up lose ends. Too many people knew of his existence; they would have to be eliminated. Hunting them down would be difficult, as they were probably jumping the fence at this minute, but not impossible.

Brandt backed out carefully, avoiding the debris strewn across the parking lot, and then drove across the grass to the access road. There might be a few men left at camp who didn't realize what had happened and he would be able to take care of them before he left.

Rain was still coming down in torrents, and the wipers would only clear the windshield for a moment before it was mottled again with water. Brandt had been down this road every day for the past ten years and he felt like he could drive it blind.

He was only a hundred feet into the woods when something fell out onto the road in front of him. It was startlingly white and he was too close to stop in time. Instinctively he twisted the wheel to swerve out of the way and realized that he had made a mistake. Water on the road sent him into a spin and when he hit the object sideways, the Jeep began to roll.

Brandt wasn't wearing a seatbelt. He pulled his hands from the steering wheel and gripped the seat below him. If he was sent flying out of the vehicle, he could be crushed to death. Better to hang on and take his chances inside.

The first roll whipped Brandt into the passenger seat and his hand slipped from his own seat. He frantically reached out for anything as his body lost control. His hand latched on to the roll bar and his head knocked open the passenger door. Then his arm twisted and he was forced to let go. His body was flailing around, his head smashing into the steering column and the gearshift jabbing into his back, but he didn't fall out.

When the Jeep finally came to rest, Brandt's body was wedged impossibly between the steering wheel and the driver's-side door. His head pounded but he could not let himself pass out. The police would be here soon; he had to get away. He shook off the pain and looked around. The Jeep was lying on the driver's side in a pool of muddy water.

Brandt tried to unfold himself but his foot was jammed underneath the brake pedal; he would have to go out through the roof. He hoisted up his pant leg and retrieved his knife, then cut a large slash in the vinyl top. When he looked out he saw what he had hit: a body.

It was a woman, naked and white, her corpse smeared onto the wet asphalt by the impact. There were more bodies coming out of the woods, and Brandt turned his attention quickly to his foot. He struggled, but it was no use; he would have to try and get his boot off. He peeked back out through the roof to see that they were even closer. The white bodies were crawling on all fours, all of them naked, their eyes closed and heads swaying.

The rear end of the Jeep was off of the road and Brandt couldn't reach his laces, so he took his knife and cut them. He poked his head back outside and counted four of them, only a few yards away and closing in fast. There was no time to free himself and he reached for his pistol, but the holster was empty.

Oh, Christ, he thought. It must have fallen out. Frantically he searched around him. The passenger door was gone and rain showered in. No. It couldn't have been thrown outside. It had to be here. He had just glimpsed the barrel of his P-38 in the rear corner of the tipped-over canopy when the first bone-white arm shot through the roof.

Chapter Nine

1. Monday, 16 December, 5:38 p.m., Seattle, Washington.

Steve unlocked the back door and walked into the house. Under one arm was the mail, under the other the newspaper, and in his hand, the papers he had just received that settled his father's estate. He tossed his keys, along with everything else, on the table and put his jacket over the end of one of the chairs.

Steve hadn't been asked to identify what was left of the body. They had used dental records he supposed. His father had requested in his will that there be no funeral and Steve had concurred. The will had also specified that all his father's assets were to be divided equally between the three children, but Steve had other ideas.

After meeting with his two sisters they agreed to let him keep the house, and enough money to finish school. The rest of the insurance money, three times the value of what Steve was taking, was to be divided between Kristy and Tina. He had signed the finalizing papers today.

He unfolded the newspaper and glanced over the front page. The story of what had transpired at "Dachau West," as the news media referred to it, had gained international recognition and was still making news. The revelation that Zindell hadn't died in South America drew mixed reactions. Some claimed that they had known all along while others began calling for renewed investigations into the "deaths" of Menegle, Bormann and the rest.

Steve set the paper back down and went into the kitchen. There was food everywhere. People he didn't even know were not only bringing casseroles and cold cuts to the door, but sending cookies and cakes through the mail. He picked at a quiche that had been left on the counter after lunch, poured himself a glass of milk that he didn't drink, and then wandered back out to watch some TV.

The living room was littered with sprays of dead and dying flowers. Too lazy to throw them away, or maybe too soon to stop grieving; he didn't really know. He picked up the remote and turned on the tube, instantly muted it, and then closed his eyes and leaned back against the couch.

He and Janet had spent a couple of days in a Vancouver hospital before coming into Seattle. Amazingly, Eli didn't have a scratch on him. They had thanked him profusely and urged him to come back to the States with them, but Eli had politely declined. He was going to help the police sort out the mess and give them a guided tour of what the tabloids called "Zindell's House of Horrors." He was also going to help by giving detailed descriptions of many of the soldiers who had vanished afterward.

From what Steve had read in the newspapers over the last two months, it seemed more than likely that it was the man Brandt who had shot Zindell. Why, nobody knew. Brandt was evidently in charge of the camp security and many of the atrocities committed there were attributed to him. The police located his overturned Jeep, covered with blood inside and surrounded with dead bodies, but he had disappeared along with the rest.

In Canada and the U.S., thousands of people were opening their homes to take in Zindell's victims. Many of them had regained partial memory while at the camp and simply kept quiet. Others had no hope of recapturing their former lives, but people seemed eager to adopt them into their families.

As for Steve's own family, he and his sisters were devastated but they were going to be okay. Steve had talked to the dean of the medical school and arranged for a year's leave of absence. He would start his first year over the next fall. Until then he would try and get his life back to some semblance of order.

The nightmares he had been having during his first month back were finally over. He attributed that to the fact that he a Janet were living together now. He had cried with her so many nights that the joy of being with her, mixed with his sorrow, was a bit overwhelming. Steve needed her now more than ever. Though they hadn't talked about it, he thought she should apply to law school. She had helped him so much with all of the paperwork he had to wade through during the past month, and she seemed to like it.

The doorbell rang and his heart revved up, even though he wasn't expecting Janet until much later. But when Steve opened the door he was caught off guard. A large man was standing in front of him, nearly blocking out the carport light.

"Are you Steve Raymond?"

Steve hesitated but didn't really know why. "Sure. Do I know you?"

"No," said the man, "but I knew your father. Would you mind if I came in for a minute?"

"No, come on in."

Once he stepped inside Steve felt vindicated for his previous unease. The man was husky and a good four or five inches taller than Steve. He was wearing a loose-fitting but elegant suit, his shirt collar worn open. He had medium-length brown hair, but what was so striking was his face. It was covered with scars and over his left eye he wore a black eye patch.

Steve suddenly realized he was staring at the man and quickly shook himself out of it. "Uh . . . here. Why don't we go sit down," he said, leading the man into the living room. Steve rushed over and turned off the TV while the man sat down on the couch.

"Anything I can get for you?" The man was already shaking his head before Steve had finished asking.

"No. I just wanted to meet you and tell you how sorry I am about what happened to your father."

Steve sat down in a chair facing him. The man had eased himself back, legs apart, arms spanning nearly the entire back of the couch. The guy was scary looking, but very friendly. Steve noticed something funny about his left hand and when the man saw him looking he held it up for Steve to see: his first three fingers were missing, only the thumb and pinky remaining.

The man shrugged. "Car accident," he said and lay his arm back on the couch.

Steve didn't know how the man knew his dad, but he also didn't want to ask him. So he just listened.

"I liked your father the first time I met him. It's funny. I wasn't really expecting to. I'm not sure now what I expected. I knew he was a famous doctor, but most of them are arrogant sons of bitches. Your father wasn't like that.

"I was mad at him for a while—it doesn't really matter why. But the more I thought about—read about what happened in the papers, the more I came to understand that he was probably one of the only men in the world I could ever have been friends with."

Steve was flattered by the things the man was saying but it also brought back the pain of his loss. They were silent for a moment and then the man continued.

"He was a hell of a guy. A little indecisive, maybe, but he came through when the chips were down and I admire him for it."

Suddenly Steve thought the man looked familiar after all, but he couldn't place him. Then the man was up off the couch.

"Well, that's really all I came to say. I'd better be going."

Steve stood and followed him to the door. "Thank you," he said weakly, still positive he knew this man. It wasn't from the hospital, he was sure of that. The man opened the door, stepped outside and then turned back to Steve.

"Oh, I almost forgot something."

The man reached inside his jacket and Steve's breath stopped when he saw the shoulder holster. Canada. The first night they were there. In the headlights of the van.

Spread out.

And again when they had been captured in the barn.

I don't want any more mistakes. You read me?

But there was nothing Steve could do. He had no place to go. He was trapped.

"Here." The man was holding out a thick leather square. A wallet. Steve took it and opened it to see his father smiling back at him from his driver's license. He looked up at the man full of questions but his mouth would not speak.

"I thought you should have it. Please believe me that I'm very sorry. I meant every word I said."

With that the man was off into the night. Steve closed the door and locked it, then looked again in disbelief at his dad's wallet in his hand.

2. 10:57 p.m.

The muted strains of "Parker's Mood" pressed against the glass front of the Owl Café, but when Janet opened the door the music washed over her in a wave. The woman taking the cover charge recognized her and smiled, then she leaned in to speak to Janet over the music.

"He's really good," she said.

"Thanks," Janet said in return. When the woman waved off the three one-dollar bills in Janet's hand, she walked in. There were no empty tables so she grabbed a vacant stool at the bar.

Steve had his eyes closed in the bright lights and sweat glistened on his cheeks and forehead. Except for the players on stage, the place was silent and she marveled at the stillness. Everyone's eyes were turned forward and no one spoke. Not many of the people who frequented the Owl, she thought, must get a chance to hear pure, unadulterated jazz.

She had gone back to work the day after they had returned from Canada; the diversion kept her mind off of the horrors she had witnessed. Steve, however, had chosen a different method of dealing with the loss of his father.

He had dug out his old alto sax—the one his father had bought him when Steve was in the sixth grade—and spent every day with one hand on a tape deck and the other on that old horn, learning "Parker's Mood" note for note. She didn't know whether Steve was that much better now, or whether she'd heard the tune so much that it would sound the same if Boots Randolph were playing it. But the music that was coming from Steve's horn sounded *exactly* like Charlie Parker's recording.

His only accompaniment was a bass player, who was a little unsure of the chord progression, and a rock-solid drummer who was keeping the whole thing together. The tune was slow but soulful, and Steve attacked Parker's runs with a vicious efficiency that made Janet smile. She would be surprised if he went back to medical school now.

She knew he was scheduled to start again next fall, but a lot could happen in a year. In fact, a lot had already happened within the past six weeks. With emotion running high and the two living under the same roof, they had seemingly spent more time in bed than out of it. People might find it morbid; Janet didn't. It only confirmed what she already knew, namely, that she wanted to spend the rest of her life with a certain saxophonist named Steve Raymond.

When the song came to a close the audience clapped loudly and attentively, Janet among them. A few people came up to shake his hand as he put away his horn, and then, as other musicians took the stage and launched into another number, she caught his eye and he walked up to her. He wrapped his free arm around her while she was still on the stool and kissed her long and deep.

"Let's get out of here," he said, after pulling away.

"Aren't you going to play any more?"

"Nope. I was just waiting for you."

"I didn't think you'd seen me."

He just smiled and she realized that she knew better. Somehow Steve always knew when she was in the room. "Okay" she said, and they walked out together into the crisp December air.

Steve didn't start the truck right away and looked deep in thought as he stared out the windshield at the streetlights. In the aftermath of the last October, the Telsen police had recovered both Steve's truck as well as his father's Porsche. Steve didn't drive the Porsche.

"Are you all right?" she asked.

"I just got the final papers today."

"So, the house is yours?"

He nodded. She hugged him and then pulled back, a little self-conscious about the cast on her left hand against the back of his neck. She had fractured her arm on an exposed jag of concrete when Zindell pulled her down. The cast was thickly covered with get-well wishes and autographs.

"I'm so sorry." Neither of them said anything else and sat silently as the windows in the cab of the truck began to fog up.

"Janet," Steve finally said. "I don't know if this is bad timing, and I really don't care. I mean, we've been living together for the past few weeks and I just . . ."

She nodded her head.

"What?"

"Yes," she said. "I'll marry you."

Steve wrapped his arms around her and pulled Janet on top of him, smothering her in kisses.

"Be careful," she said. "You're going to have to be a lot more gentle with me for a while."

Steve eased her back on the seat, the intrigue evident in his face. "Why?"

"Because, you don't want to hurt the baby, do you?"

This time Steve's mouth dropped open. "When?"

"Up there." She motioned with her head, meaning, of course, the Institute. She hadn't had her pills, and at the time she didn't have the luxury of caring. Now she was glad she hadn't.

His body seemed to tremble as he sighed deeply.

"Are you sure you're all right?" she asked, but he was smiling.

Steve laughed. "Better than I've been for a long time. Let's go out for dinner tonight. I'm tired of eating funeral food."

Janet smiled back and hugged him. It was late and she had work in the morning, but none of that mattered. At last they had something to celebrate.

E.B.O. / October 21, 1989, Bellevue, WA
/ January 13, 1991, Issaquah, WA

The only short stories I ever wrote when I started out were horror stories, all of which are collected in the previous volume in this series, If I Should Wake Before I Die. *But there was one exception. Back in the days before computer dating there were things called personal ads. Someone would pay money to put an ad in the* Seattle Weekly—The Stranger *was a little too alternative for me—and if you thought they were interesting you sent them a letter . . . in the mail, the actual mail with a stamp and an envelope. Most of the people doing this had post office boxes and so you usually didn't give them your phone number in the first letter and instead waited for a reply. If they were willing to take the time to write you back they usually included a phone number and then you set up a blind date. Unlike the detailed computer profiles of today, the whole thing was a lot more intuitive. As a result, I went on a lot of first dates. Usually you could tell within the first couple of minutes if there was ever going to be a second, and there weren't many of those. For the most part, they were coffee dates and fairly disappointing. On one of those dates, however—it was at a local bakery that served coffee, not Starbucks—I met a woman with the most incredibly ice-blue eyes I had ever seen. She clearly had no interest in me—and she wasn't my type either—but I couldn't take my eyes off of hers. They were absolutely riveting. Instead of leaving the date feeling that a lot of time had been wasted on both our parts, I couldn't get her eyes out of my mind. It wasn't long before I felt compelled to put the encounter on paper in a story. The reason for its inclusion in this volume will be clear by the end of the story. I don't believe that her name was Stella, but I have no idea after all these years.*

$tella

"Okay," she said. "I'll meet you there in a few minutes."

The receiver clicked off in my ear and I looked at it suspiciously for a few seconds before I hung up myself. I had just finished shaving and was still in my shorts and T-shirt. After hurrying back to the bedroom, I dressed and put on my heaviest coat. The coffee shop was only a few blocks away, but it was the middle of January and a bitter cold had been moving in from the East all night.

With my hat pulled down above my eyes and my collar turned up, I started out. The city looked gray and lifeless, covered by a shroud of nearly black clouds. I wasn't used to seeing it like this. Most of my waking hours were spent at night in the comforting cloak of neon and cigarette smoke. I felt vulnerable in the daylight.

It was early Saturday morning and the rain had slowed up what little traffic there was. Shops were just beginning to open their doors and shopkeepers were sweeping what dry spots remained on the sidewalks beneath their dripping awnings. By staying close to the buildings I was able to keep fairly dry.

The coffee shop was squeezed in between a grocer and a florist, and as I walked inside I marveled at how any of the three of them could remain in business these days. There were perhaps a dozen tables in the unheated room, each crowded with talkative customers. The place smelled of damp wool and cigarettes and I could hear the faint strains of Wagner in the background. Instantly I wished that I had agreed to meet her someplace else.

I was to identify her by a white bow in her hair, and while I shook the rain off my hat I looked at every woman in the room. I saw no bow. Eventually a middle-aged woman led me to the only free table left and I sat down.

I was seated with my back to the window. The table was tiny, with no cloth, and only a miniature pitcher of cream on its polished wooden surface. I smelled the cream; it was on the verge of going bad. The woman frowned when I ordered only coffee, but she went away and brought it to me a few seconds later.

I warmed my hands on the stained porcelain cup. The liquid inside was brown and steaming but, from the smell, it was unlikely there was any real coffee in it. I picked up the pitcher and dumped in cream until the cup was brimming. But when I reached for the cup my hand was shaking so badly I had to set it back on the table and close my eyes for a moment. Then I leaned down and took a sip before I was able to lift the cup safely to my lips. After another sip I set it down again and sighed. I could see my breath when I exhaled and I pulled my coat tighter.

It couldn't have been more than a minute later, though it seemed much longer, before she walked in. I had been taking small sips of coffee, to avoid having to buy another cup, and I almost spilled the whole thing when I first saw her.

She took her time looking about the room, and when she didn't recognize me I stood. Her eyes narrowed and she nodded slightly, a hint of smile playing across her lips. When the woman came up to seat her, Stella pointed toward me and the woman brought her over.

Stella. That was all I knew: her first name. From across the room I could see she was about five-six, and as she made her way between the tables her overcoat fell open. I felt helplessly captivated as I watched her hips swaying beneath the black skirt she was wearing, and the curves of her figure, accentuated by her heavy ivory sweater. In a word, Stella was breathtaking.

"Hello," she said, taking the seat across from me. "I didn't see you alone here when I first came in." She ordered coffee after that, and I said hello as she set her black handbag on the floor next to her chair.

Stella had short blonde hair that hung straight down to her neck. The white ribbon was pulled up from behind and tied on top of her head. Her face was scrubbed clean and her cheeks were high and flushed. Her brows and lashes had enough brown in them to stand out against her smooth and lightly-tanned skin. But it was her eyes that demanded the attention of all who gazed upon that face.

Browns and greens seemed to radiate a hazel fire in her irises, and as they looked back at me I thought I saw in them a compassion I had not seen in a very long time. She also had a small scar just beneath her chin. Fascinating. Far from marring her beauty, it only magnified it for me. Had I known her in another life, I would have been in love.

After the woman had brought her a cup of coffee, Stella leaned over and looked into mine. Then she picked up the half-empty pitcher and smelled it. She wrinkled her nose "This is awful."

"I know," I said, nodding, and I promptly lifted my cup to take another sip. "It's to drown out the taste of the coffee."

She laughed at that, her perfect white teeth flashing at me behind her full, rose colored lips. Confidently, she poured the cream into her own cup and took a sip. "Thank you," she said.

God, was I nervous. Could she tell how much I needed her? Could she see what a wreck I was? Could she sense my desperation? Finally, I asked her, "Do you work around here?"

"Yes," she said. "Government office. We do accounting."

"You're an accountant?"

"No," she said, and smiled at me again. "Just a secretary. What about you?"

"Musician," I said.

"Oh, what instrument?"

"Saxophone. I play in a jazz band."

"Sounds like interesting work."

"It has its moments."

I guess it boils down to loneliness. After all, there's only so much isolation a man can take. That was why I was here. The though of dying alone in some dirty basement, starving, with no lights and nothing left of my dignity was beginning to haunt me on the nights when I could actually sleep. She was my only hope.

"Do you like to read?" she asked.

Her question surprised me, and I thought about lying, but what was the point? I nodded my head and lowered my voice. "Hemmingway, Fitzgerald…"

To her credit, she didn't look around to see who might be listening. But a small crease formed between her eyebrows and she said, "How?"

"I have friends, artist, writers, actors . . . We share. It's not difficult, really."

She looked at me with different eyes now, studying, exploring, calculating. What was she seeing? Was my nose too big, or my ears? Was I too dark, or too ugly? I wanted to panic, to bolt up and run away, to say I'd made a mistake and vow to never do this again. But I knew I couldn't. The loneliness would drive me back. And if not Stella, who? There was no one else. There was no other way.

As she drank the rest of her coffee in silence, I realized that we probably shouldn't have met here, that there were too many people around. She couldn't tell me what I needed to know.

"Do you come here often?" I said, breaking the silence.

"Before work most days."

"Are you working today?"

"Yes."

"But it's Saturday."

She shrugged. "It's the beginning of the year. We work a lot of overtime."

"You must do well."

"Oh?"

"Money-wise."

"Well enough. It gives me a chance to go skiing. I like to get away during the winter. Escape. Do you?"

My eyes widened.

"Like to ski," she said, and I relaxed again.

That was something I hadn't thought of in years. The wind in my face, the cold air, the sun, the snow, the mountains. It was like something from a dream, a long forgotten memory, something read once in a book. "Not for many years," I said.

For the first time that morning she frowned, briefly, but compassionately, and our meeting was over. She wiped her mouth with a napkin and then leaned down to retrieve her handbag. "Well," she said, "I have to get to work."

She stood abruptly and I followed her so quickly I almost knocked over the table. I tossed some coins down between our empty cups and walked behind her toward the door.

As we were leaving, three people came in together: two men in black coats and hats, and a woman. I probably wouldn't even have noticed them but for two things. First, I had long ago ridded myself of the habit of averting my eyes from men wearing black, and second, the woman was wearing a white bow in her hair.

She was taller the Stella by a few inches. Her blue eyes had an almost milky dullness to them, and her face, though pretty, was etched with determination. Her blonde hair was long and curly, and tied back with a white ribbon. Our eyes met briefly as we passed each other and then, just as quickly, I was alone on the street with Stella.

"Should I walk with you?" I asked, so unsure of myself that I was perspiring, despite the chill and rain.

"Please do."

We had walked only a short ways in silence when she said, "Thank you for sharing a table with me, Mister . . ."

I was stunned. We were alone, of course, but I had no idea why she would have asked in that way. The only thing I could imagine was that she needed my real name for some reason. I had been Bernhard Koenig for so long, I almost didn't remember who I really was. But it came out anyway.

"Kohler," I said. "Benjamin Kohler."

She stopped dead in her tracks, and by the time I had managed to do the same I was two steps in front of her and had to turn back to face her. We were standing beneath the awning of a tailor's shop with rain pelting down all around us. There is no way to describe the look on Stella's face, but it was there. I couldn't read it so I did nothing until she spoke.

"You don't look like a—" I put my finger to her lips. She didn't move to stop me.

"Isn't that how *you* get away with it?" I took my finger away and she nodded.

"That's why I have to go," I said. "Get out of here. I can't eat. I can't sleep. I can't work. I'm so alone, sometimes I think it's going to kill me."

Then she took my hand in hers and looked at me with those deeply expressive eyes and said, "Take me with you."

I didn't even have time to think about what her words meant when a noise a block away caused me to look over Stella's shoulder. Then I knew. I knew everything.

I knew what that look on Stella's face had been: puzzlement. From the door of the coffee shop burst forth the woman I had seen earlier, along with the two Gestapo agents. They were running down the street toward us and I turned back to Stella.

We were the same, she and I. I knew that now, too. In a city of millions we had met by accident, and my loneliness, if only for the briefest moment, was over. "What's your name?" I said, as though the lethal threat beyond us were a million miles away.

"Kirsten—"

My finger once again touched her lips and met no resistance. "Go to work, Kirsten. Stay hidden—stay alive. And remember me always."

The look of puzzlement had once again been allowed to possess that perfect face, but I could stay no longer. They had almost reached us. A streetcar was passing by and I ran for it. The other woman in the white bow, the one I had talked to on the phone, had made arrangements with and planned to meet— the real Stella—was screaming for me to stop.

I had just managed to reach for the car when I was knocked aside and fell to the wet pavement. The sound of gunfire had been followed instantly by a searing pain in my leg. And as I lay there in the burgeoning Saturday traffic, horns blaring and people shouting, I wept for companionship I would never know. I wept because I had not escaped. And I wept because I had not died.

About the Author

Eric B. Olsen is the author of six works of fiction in three different genres. He has written a medical thriller entitled *Death's Head*, as well as the horror novel *Dark Imaginings*. He is also the author of three mystery novels, *Proximal to Murder* and *Death in the Dentist's Chair* featuring amateur sleuth Steve Raymond, D.D.S., and *The Seattle Changes* featuring private detective Ray Neslowe. In addition, he is the author of *If I Should Wake Before I Die*, a book of short horror fiction.

Today Mr. Olsen writes primarily non-fiction, including *The Death of Education,* an exposé of the public school system in America.

Mr. Olsen currently lives in the Pacific Northwest with his wife.

Please visit the author's web site at https://sites.google.com/site/ericbolsenauthor/, or contact by email at ericbolsen@juno.com.

Printed in the United States
By Bookmasters